Heather Barnett grew up i[...] English and French from [...] from writing, her interests are classic literature, cats and comedy. She is head of marketing at an agency near Oxford and lives by the river Kennet in Berkshire. *Acts of Kindness* is her debut novel.

For more information on Heather and her books, please visit her website – www.heatherbarnettauthor.com or join the discussion on Twitter @WritesHeather.

Acts of Kindness

Heather Barnett

SERPENTINE

BOOKS

First published in Great Britain by Serpentine Books
This edition published in 2021 by
Serpentine Books Limited

www.serpentinebooks.com
info@serpentinebooks.com

A CIP catalogue record for this book is available from the British Library.

ISBN 978 1 9138 7405 6

Printed and bound in Great Britain by Clays Ltd,
Elcograf S.p.A.

For my parents,
two of the kindest people I know.

'Life is mostly froth and bubble,
Two things stand like stone.
Kindness in another's trouble,
Courage in your own.'

Adam Lindsay Gordon

Chapter One

'Help. Help, please? I'm having a panic attack!'

At the other end of the Tube carriage, a ginger-haired girl in her early twenties was sitting forward in her seat, one hand pressed to her chest, the other gripping the pole beside her.

'Please, help me.'

Her eyes darted around the carriage from face to face as she panted, the colour draining from her cheeks. Opposite her, a pair of Japanese tourists exchanged uncertain glances. The man on her right was leaning back, eyes closed, arms crossed high on his chest.

Bella took a deep breath and made her way down the carriage towards the stricken girl, moving Tarzan-like from handhold to handhold in case the Tube surged back to life. On the way, her brain consulted its knowledge of panic attacks and came up with... nothing. She crouched down next to the girl, who was watching her, wide-eyed and pale.

'What's wrong?'

'I can't breathe, I need to get out!'

'They're probably waiting for a platform; it'll go again in a minute.'

'I know! But I'm having an attack!'

Right. So, a logical explanation wasn't going to relieve the symptoms. Bella resorted to comforting noises.

'Okay, don't worry. Shh. It'll be fine. Try to breathe slowly.'

Try to breathe slowly? During a panic attack? Was that the best she could do? Perhaps she should hold a paper bag over the girl's face. A quick mental stock-check revealed she didn't have a paper bag. She suspected a plastic one wouldn't be well received. She was running out of ideas and variety in her comforting noises when there was a judder and the train lurched back into life. The girl seemed to be calming down: she sat back a little in her seat. Bella crouched awkwardly beside her; unsure if she was still needed or not. Eventually, she was forced to stand to ease her cramped muscles but she remained at her post, one arm around the pole next to the girl. The train pulled into the station and the girl got to her feet. As she passed Bella on her way out, she squeezed her arm.

'Thank you, so much.'

The doors slid open, the girl got out, and Bella found, for no reason that she could explain, tears had sprung into her eyes.

❦ ❦

Bella's mobile rang as she sat down at her large, minimalist office desk, sunlight streaming in through the plate glass windows and revealing the dust on her collection of miniature cacti.

'Bella Black speaking.'

'Good morning, Ms Black.' The voice was confident, professional. 'My name's Catherine Knight, I'm calling from Acorn Consulting about a role that's come up here at the company. We believe you'd be an ideal fit; do you have a moment to talk it through?'

Bella got up and shut the door that opened onto a larger, open-plan office. She'd heard of Acorn Consulting, of course, it was up there with the world's biggest advisory firms. 'I'm not looking for anything new, but—'

Catherine cut her off. 'Of course not, but we have an opening here for a digital marketing director that may interest you. A brand-new position. You'd be responsible for running inbound campaigns in EMEA across our suite of consultancy propositions. The role sits one rung below board level and the salary is commensurate...'

Bella fought hard to stop herself accepting on the spot what was, almost, her dream job. Double the salary she was currently on – double! – as well as more responsibility and an employee benefits package that sounded like Mariah Carey's dressing-room rider. The only downside was that it was based in the countryside, two and a half hours out of London.

'Come for an interview and then decide,' urged Catherine.

An interview. Just an interview. Why not? By the time she put the phone down, she had agreed to be at Acorn Consulting at eleven thirty the following Tuesday. It was only later, as she gazed out through the window at visions of the five-star spa days her new salary could fund, that she remembered being called 'Ms' Black. That was odd, as the decree absolute hadn't come through yet and officially, she was still a 'Mrs'. Perhaps it was a slip of the tongue, or Catherine hadn't wanted to guess at Miss or Mrs and get it wrong.

🍂 🍂

At eleven fifteen on the appointed day, having arrived ridiculously early and parked in a layby for a while to kill time, Bella turned in to the main gates of Acorn Consulting. They were imposing, each topped with a carved stone acorn. She drove down the long, straight drive, noting with surprise a herd of deer by a lake over to the right. Catherine had forgotten to include working in a nature reserve in the list of benefits. Rolling down the window she breathed in the sweetness of the country air. The road was on a gentle incline and when she reached the top, she got her first view of the Acorn Consulting building. It was a vast stately home. Nothing was missing, from the sweeping stone staircase at the bottom, to the ornamental battlements at the top and the cedars throwing stark shadows across luminous lawns on either side.

A discreet sign directed her around the back to the car park, which was shielded from the house by extravagant topiary. Starting to wish that she hadn't killed so much time, Bella parked up and hurried back towards the main entrance, heels sinking into the gravel path. Another discreet sign, this time on the front door, invited her to ring the bell. She couldn't hear it ringing inside but almost instantly the door opened and she was blinded by unnaturally white teeth. The teeth sat between lipsticked lips, which in turn fitted into place under a neat, lightly tanned set of all the other features one would expect to find on the average face. The voice that greeted her was American. *That explains the teeth*, she thought.

The woman beckoned Bella in with a great, generous sweep of her arm.

'Come in. You must be Bella. I'm thrilled to meet you. My name's Kelly.'

The woman's demeanour suggested her whole life had been spent preparing for this, her chance to assist Bella Black. It seemed almost churlish not to think of something more momentous in response than 'Thanks.'

Bella walked in, feeling more and more disoriented. Had she come for a job interview or a dinner party? Her surroundings didn't make things any clearer. The spotless tiled floor stretched away towards a grand staircase. A couple of uncomfortable-looking chairs and – sofas didn't feel like the right word, but she couldn't think of a better one – were grouped to one side, flanked by plants on marble pedestals. Four or five doors, all closed, led off the hall. The desk was bare. Nothing suggested this was an office; Bella looked around in vain for a water cooler, a telephone – even a bin, for God's sake.

Kelly was still displaying her teeth.

'If you'd like to take a seat, I'll let Catherine know you're here.'

How? thought Bella. *Telepathy?* She felt a little silly when Kelly went around the back of a walnut desk and slid out a flat drawer containing a laptop and a phone. Of course. They clearly went to great lengths to maintain the authenticity of the place. If you flipped up a sofa cushion, you'd probably find a wireless charging station. Her bottom had barely touched down on the immaculate upholstery when a door opened and a smartly-dressed woman appeared, one hand extended for shaking. Bella leapt up.

'Ms Black. I'm Catherine Knight. Good to meet you. Did you find us okay?'

'Yes, no problems at all. Such a beautiful place.'

'Shall we go ahead then? It's a bit of a walk I'm afraid.'

They made their way down corridors, up steps and through ante-rooms, Bella praying all the while that she wouldn't be asked to orienteer herself back to the entrance hall as part of the interview. Finally, they reached a comfortable room, all buttercup yellows and golds, with full-length windows overlooking a walled garden.

However, Bella noticed little of this because of the man who stepped forward to greet her.

A flirtatious male acquaintance had once told Bella that whenever he met a woman for the first time, he made a point of seeing how long it took her to touch her hair. Touching your hair was, apparently, an unmistakable sign that you had registered a man's interest and were open to it. Bella remembered this as her hand crept up towards her head. She yanked it back down, cheeks flushing red.

'Let me introduce Ben Elliott,' said Catherine, as Bella and Ben shook hands. 'Our chief marketing officer. You'll be reporting to him.'

Another thing you left off the list of benefits, Bella found herself thinking. They sat down around a low table which was set out with tea and coffee.

'You'll have noticed that Catherine said *will* report to,' Ben said, with a smile that had Bella accidentally fiddling with her hair again. 'From our point of view, we already know that we want you for the job. What we're here to find out is if you want to work for us.'

Bella tried to look surprised, pleased and modest at the same time. She started to open her mouth, feeling she should ask an intelligent question, or at least prove that she was able to string a sentence together, which she hadn't done so far in this room.

Ben held up a hand. 'Don't say anything yet. I want to show you something that should make things a little clearer.'

He picked up a remote. The oil painting across the room from her dissolved into pixels and was replaced with the Acorn Consulting logo. God, they were good at the authenticity thing!

The logo, in turn, faded into white and was replaced by a shot of a woman, sitting in a room very like theirs. There was

6

something about her that suggested royalty: she wouldn't be out of place as the queen of a small European country.

'Hello. My name is Isadora Faye and I'm CEO of Acorn Consulting. I review the reports prepared on every potential candidate for our vacancies, and using the detailed evidence they contain, I handpick those I know will complement our ideals.'

The detailed evidence? Bella shifted a little in her gilt chair. This didn't sound like the usual LinkedIn trawl.

'I know you're probably wondering what this is all about. This isn't a typical interview. But then Acorn Consulting isn't a typical company.'

Isadora Faye disappeared, to be replaced with an aerial shot of the sprawling house and estate buildings. She continued in voice-over as the camera panned down to the front of the building.

'Acorn Consulting was established by my ancestors over two hundred years ago. Back then it was known as Acorns & Company. This house was our family seat and we have operated from these lovely surroundings ever since. Acorn Consulting, AC for short, is a successful business, turning over forty-six billion pounds and making a net profit of four point three billion in the last financial year. No doubt you'll have done your homework on us, and know that we are a multinational organisation, headquartered in the UK but with offices all over the world. We offer management consultancy services to businesses in sectors including financial services, IT, utilities, aviation and health.'

Okay. This was sounding a bit more like what she had been anticipating, even if she hadn't been expecting it via pre-recorded video. Bella took a sip of her tea and relaxed back into her chair.

'Should you decide to join us here at AC, you'll also play your part in delivering those services. For part of the time.'

The camera stopped showing off the house and the long line of blue-chip client logos which had been trooping across the screen, and returned to Isadora in her chair.

'That's right. Only *part* of your time will be spent working for Acorn Consulting.' The camera shot tightened on her face. 'The rest will be spent working for our charitable concern, the OAK Institute. This is where I have to ask you to take a leap of faith.'

Bella risked a curious glance at Ben and Catherine. They were both watching her. She looked back at the screen.

'I can't tell you what the OAK Institute does.' Isadora paused and looked down the lens, unblinking. 'I can promise you that its aims are for the good of humanity all over the world and there is nothing illegal or immoral involved. However, its work must remain strictly confidential. If you accept the job here at AC, you will go through a three-month induction, after which, if we feel certain you can maintain confidentiality, you will begin working for OAK.'

Isadora's face broke into a smile and the tinkly background music became positively jolly.

'Now, I know that's a lot to take in and you'll have plenty of questions so I'll pass you back to the team there on the ground.' Which made it sound as if Isadora was speaking to them from a cloud. 'I hope I'll get to meet you in person very soon.'

The image faded into the Acorn logo then back to the oil painting. Catherine and Ben were looking at her. The room seemed very quiet all of a sudden.

'Erm.' Oh God. What to say. Think of something sensible. 'Erm, I…' Nope. She couldn't get any further than 'Erm, I…'

Ben stood up. 'We've all been through this. We know exactly what you're thinking. If only you could work out where the hell the front door is, you'd be heading straight for it. I suggest we go and get some lunch. That'll give you a chance to start getting your head around it all.'

Will lunch be al fresco, she wondered. *A circle of Druid-like figures ripping lumps of flesh off an unidentifiable barbecued sacrifice?* As it turned out, although the dining hall was more ornate than your typical staff canteen, it was reassuringly normal. Ordinary-looking office workers sat around tables eating and doubtless complaining about how busy they were, just like in a million other offices across the globe. They served themselves from the buffet and took their food over to a table at which a man was already seated. Ben took charge of the introductions.

'Bella, I thought you might like to meet one of my team. This is Oscar.'

Oscar shook her hand with a shy smile. He was tall and wiry, and stooped a little as if he was uncomfortable with his height. From the side, when he stood up, he looked like a question mark.

When they were settled at the table, Bella turned to say something to Oscar but stopped dead when she saw the look on his face. He was staring at her and when he saw he had her attention he widened his eyes to their fullest extent. Then he lifted his napkin by two corners, until a couple of inches of it were visible above the tabletop. The other two were sorting out glasses of water and his subtle movements hadn't caught their attention. At the top of the napkin, he had written in capital letters: 'SAVE ME'. He made certain she had seen the message before lowering the napkin. Her heart thumped in her chest and her cheeks glowed. *Save him from what? What's he scared of?*

Before her shocked brain could rally enough to frame a question, Ben grabbed a corner of Oscar's napkin, snatched it off his lap and read it. Oscar's spooked expression was wiped clean off his face and he let out one enormous laugh before shrugging his shoulders at Bella. 'Sorry. Couldn't help it.'

Ben glared at him. 'Every time. Every single time.'

'That's not true! Last time I wrote "Help" in the palm of my right hand before I offered it to shake.'

'Oh yes,' said Catherine, a hint of disapproval in her tone. 'I remember that. You were disappointed because Ajay didn't notice and his hand was so sweaty it rubbed the ink off.' She shifted round in her seat, eyes scanning the room. 'There he is.' She pointed out a man in a checked shirt on a nearby table to Bella. 'Ajay joined a couple of months ago.'

Oscar pulled a semi-contrite face. 'Sorry. Can't resist. I remember what it was like when I came for my interview. You hear all that stuff about a secret society and you're convinced you're going to be brainwashed by Hare Krishnas. Then you have a bit of lunch and find out everyone's totally normal. Complete anticlimax. So, I like to spice things up a bit. And I've never actually put someone off. Have I?' He frowned and looked over at Ben.

'You'd know if you had.'

❦ ❦

After lunch came a short tour of the beautifully preserved offices before a formal presentation. Ben took her through her role and the organisational structure. Catherine detailed the jaw-dropping package and benefits. Nothing more was said about the OAK Institute. About three o'clock they were wrapping up.

'I think that about sums things up for us,' said Catherine, disconnecting her laptop from the screen. 'Obviously, we hope you like what you've seen today and that you'll be joining us as soon as your notice period allows. But you'll want to think it all over, so I'll catch up with you on, say, Thursday? Would that be okay?'

It sounded to Bella – as did a lot of what came out of Catherine's mouth – like a well-honed spiel. 'Yes, Thursday should be fine.'

'Good. Do you have any questions for us before we finish for the day?'

What a ridiculous thing to ask, thought Bella. *Who on earth wouldn't have questions?*

'Are you able to tell me anything more about the OAK Institute?' she asked. 'I understand that it's confidential, but…'

They both smiled. Catherine was about to answer in what Bella could tell would be the negative when Ben cut in.

'Look, think of it this way. Yes, it's frustrating that there's this big secret no one's willing to let you in on. We get that.

But all we're asking you to do is give the place a try for three months. We're offering a great role on a highly competitive salary. After three months you get to find out what OAK does – and, by the way, what it does is incredible, you won't be disappointed. But if you decide before the three months are up this place isn't for you then you walk away. Simple.'

When he put it like that, it did seem simple.

Chapter Two

Bella bombed down the M4, car crammed with all the belongings that wouldn't fit in the removal van, singing along to her music at full volume. As tower blocks and terraced houses gave way to trees and fields, her best friend's words echoed in her head. 'But, Bella, how can you live out of London?' Zoe had asked, her tone expressing astonishment that any right-thinking person would choose to live anywhere else. Zoe was a born-and-bred Londoner who thought the area around the edge of the Tube map should be marked 'here be dragons'. 'You'll be lonely. Isolated. Sad!' she'd gone on to insist.

'It'll be fine, Zoe. I'm going to rent for a bit and see how it goes. I can always come back.'

She didn't point out that she was already lonely, isolated and sad. And that had nothing to do with geography. The truth was she desperately needed a change and the job would be the perfect catalyst. It was a time of snap decisions. Her old life was over but the future was fuzzy. If she left herself too much time to think she might stagnate; life would swirl on past her.

The change made her feel euphoric. It would be transient, she knew, but while it lasted, she revelled in it. She was free and life was full of the unexpected. She gave herself licence to hope. Right up until the moment Ella Fitzgerald came on, singing, 'Every Time We Say Goodbye'.

With a sudden intake of breath, she was back in the kitchen on Hartley Road with Mark. After an hour's strangely calm discussion sitting side by side on the living room sofa, they'd got up to make a cup of tea. Something about the normality of turning the kettle on and putting teabags in their usual mugs, contrasted to the life-changing conversation

13

they'd just had, hit them both. She'd felt the tears welling up and his eyes reflected hers. He'd squeezed her hard against his chest but there was no comfort in it, now the gesture wasn't a promise of love as it always had been. It was like being held by a stranger.

She took her hand from the steering wheel to grab a tissue, her shoulders shaking with sobs. A sign loomed up for motorway services and she took the exit, pulled up in the car park, and let her emotion wear itself out. When would she be safe from these emotional ambushes? She could go two or three weeks without getting upset. Then she'd stumble into an unseen trap and the pain would shoot straight through her, raw and devastating.

The sight of her new home brought a smile to her face. She had rented a house in a group of converted barns by a river: an idyllic spot with Waitrose and a cosy gastropub five minutes away. Before she'd even located the teabags, neighbours – Angela; an elegant, bohemian-looking woman in her early fifties and married couple David and Pauline; early sixties, both rather red-faced and scruffy – had popped round with wine and welcoming words. Ha! That'd show her friends back in London. Most of them wouldn't recognise a neighbour if they bashed them over the head with a cup of sugar.

A couple of nights settling in with the help of her parents, some revitalising walks in the countryside and her spirits remained high. On the Sunday evening, after her parents had left, she began to feel nervous at the prospect of her first day at work. Pouring herself a glass of red wine, she reheated the casserole her mum had left and settled down to eat it off a tray. The room was cosy with the glow of the wood-burner and candles on the mantelpiece. *Midsomer Murders* was on the telly. All was peaceful.

Someone rapped on the door.

Bella considered ignoring it for a split second before What Others Might Think of Her raised his shaggy head. What Others Might Think of Her was her constant companion, and the impetus behind many of her actions. She put the tray aside.

A woman holding a brown paper bag stood on the doorstep, the porch light picking out a halo of wild blonde hairs. She looked at Bella through smeary glasses and said nothing.

'Hello,' Bella said. 'You must be from…?' Number 3? Number 7? A secure mental health unit?

'Knickers!' said the woman.

Bella froze.

'Knickers!' the woman repeated, thrusting the bag at her. 'When you move into a new house you can never find a pair of clean knickers on the first morning. That's why I give them as a gift.'

What, even to the men? thought Bella. Out loud she said, 'Oh! What a clever idea. Thank you. It's not actually my first night, but…'

The woman pushed past her without waiting to be invited in. Bella followed her down the hall and into the living room.

'Lovely,' declared the woman. 'Cosy.' She looked at the tray of food and waved Bella towards it. 'Carry on! Nothing worse than letting your tea go cold.' She sat down on an armchair, rested her chin in her hand and prepared to enjoy the spectacle of Bella eating casserole.

Half the enjoyment of eating the casserole came from doing it alone, off a tray, in front of the telly. Bella had no desire to put on a performance. 'Don't worry, I can warm it up later. Sorry, I didn't catch which house is yours? I've met

Angela from next door and the couple from number five so far.'

'Oh, I don't live here, dear.'

It dawned on Bella, with a feeling akin to cold porridge sliding down her back, that she had let a complete stranger into her house who carried bags of knickers around as gifts. Her glance fell on the poker by the fireplace.

'No,' the woman continued, 'I live over the other side of the village. But I like to welcome all newcomers, you see.'

Bella was still weighing up blunt objects. 'You must get through a lot of knickers,' she said, mechanically.

'Small sacrifice to·make new neighbours welcome. Where have you come from, dear?'

'Acton, West London.'

'Well. London's a nice place as long as you like noise and foreigners. That's what I always say. Do you like noise and foreigners?' Before Bella could answer the woman gave a chirruping laugh. 'Of course you don't, dear, seeing as you've moved out. Quite right. And do you work?'

Bella admitted that yes, she did work; half expecting to be told that work was nice if you liked taking jobs off men.

'Lovely, dear. Got a job here in the area? All lined up?'

'I don't know if you'll have heard of it. It's a place called Acorn Consulting, over near Halfway.'

The smile dropped like a shutter.

'Acorns? You're going to work at Acorns?' The woman regarded Bella through narrowed eyes. 'You do *know* about Acorns, don't you?'

Bella raised her eyebrows.

'I don't want to worry you, sweetheart,' the woman continued, 'but something's not right there.'

'Something – what do you mean, something's not right?'

The woman jumped up, as if a buzzer had gone off in her pocket.

16

'Well it's been lovely chatting, dear, but I have to go now. Goodnight. I'll see myself out.'

And she was gone, so abruptly that it took Bella a moment to realise that she'd plucked the paper bag out of her hands on the way past. Which she was rather put out about, as she'd been curious about those knickers. Her bet would have been size sixteen with polka dots, but equally, she wouldn't have been surprised to find a pair of lacy crotchless numbers.

Now she wasn't sure if there had been knickers in the bag at all.

Bella had been found wandering in increasing desperation around entirely the wrong part of the building on her second morning, suffering flashbacks to the time she'd been trapped in Hampton Court maze for the best part of three hours. Monday had been fine because Kelly had escorted her to her office, but left to her own devices on Tuesday, she'd gone astray. At the sight of Catherine rounding a corner ahead, Bella had hailed her in the manner of a stranded Londoner spotting a taxi with its light on.

'Catherine! Hi! I can't find my office, am I going in the right direction?'

Catherine had blinked once, Bella wasn't sure whether in disdain or disbelief, before pasting a good impression of a sympathetic smile on her face and striding down the corridor towards her.

'You're miles out, Bella. Directions not your strong point?'

When they reached the marketing department, Catherine handed her over to Oscar with instructions to show Bella the way in future.

17

'Perhaps you two could meet in the lobby in the mornings?'

Bella wanted the ground to swallow her up. 'Please, there's no need, I'm sure I'll work it out.'

'No, no!' Oscar insisted, waggling a finger at her. 'I couldn't have it on my conscience, the thought of poor old you going round and round in circles, scratching your last message to the world on the wall in biro. Surviving off scraps donated by passers-by. Doesn't bear thinking about.'

The next morning, he was waiting for her as promised, tapping away on his phone in one of the gilt chairs in the entrance hall. Another colleague from the marketing team, Lauren, a shy woman in her late twenties, arrived at the same time and as she chatted to Oscar, Bella hung back and surreptitiously snapped pictures of landmarks along the route. By Friday she was confident enough to declare that she could find her way alone and, barring one wrong turn, she did.

There had been several meetings during the week: inductions with other departments, team meetings and one office-wide briefing. So, when everyone started to get up at ten o'clock that Friday morning, Bella did the same, even though she hadn't seen a meeting request in her calendar.

'You're not on the attendee list for this, Bella,' Ben said. 'It's an OAK meeting. It'll be a couple of hours; we'll see you at lunch. Sit tight.'

They all filed out and the room was silent. Right. This felt a little odd. A couple of other things had happened during the week to remind her of OAK's existence. Oscar turning on his screensaver when she propelled herself across the office in her chair to ask him a question. Folders on the network she couldn't access. But this was the first time anyone had mentioned it by name. After a few minutes, Bella realised she'd read the same paragraph several times without taking it in. She might as well go and get a cup of coffee. Ben had said 'sit tight' but she could pop out of their room for a drink, surely? The corridor was quiet. She went to the vending machine which was hidden in a large oak cabinet between two windows. Then paused. There was no law against her going to another vending machine. She turned right and headed down the long corridor that ran all the way along that wing of the building. Still no noise, no people. As she continued through the building, meeting no one, her confidence grew. She listened at the door of the main conference room where they'd had the office briefing earlier in the week. Empty. She went up a couple of floors and peeped into rooms. Nothing. Then right up to the attic floor. Some of the doors up here were locked, but there was silence behind them. Back downstairs she peered into the main entrance hall: even Kelly wasn't at her desk. Where on earth did OAK business happen, then – and more to the point, what the hell was it?

Bella had had many dreams about the OAK Institute. A particularly vivid one involved the discovery that Isadora Faye was actually her mum. She still looked like Isadora, but she was definitely Mum. Mum lived on the roof of the Acorn Consulting building and they had played chess with a giant chess set until Bella remembered she didn't know how to play chess, and became very anxious. She'd woken up with a niggling feeling of disquiet which had lasted into the morning. In another dream, she'd opened an Alice-in-Wonderland-style tiny door behind Oscar's desk and found herself on the stage of an empty theatre. She was back at university, about to play Juliet in the end of term production, but they'd forgotten to turn the stage lights on and she was wearing nothing from the waist down. That time she found she'd been dreaming with her eyes open, sitting bolt upright in the dark.

She stood, undecided, in the corridor. Her eye rested on a small round hole in the cornice. That wasn't like them, they kept everything in such good repair. She looked more closely.

Her heart in her mouth she turned and almost ran back to her office. What an idiot. Of course there would be security cameras, hidden like everything else modern in this building. For the next hour and a half, she worked without a break, one-half of her mind wondering what would happen when they came back. Would Ben give her a bollocking for trying to spy on OAK before her probation was up?

At midday, no one had returned and she went to the dining hall. She was the first one in but after a couple of minutes, people started arriving in dribs and drabs. Lauren joined her at her table, where she was trying to force a salad down her dry throat.

'Hiya. You all right?'

Bella nodded. 'Mmm. Fine. Fine, thanks.'

'We have that meeting every month. You'll come too, once your three months are up.'

All through lunch everything seemed normal. The same the rest of the afternoon: it seemed she'd got away with it. As she set off home that evening, she vowed to restrain her curiosity in future.

Chapter Three

That weekend her friend Zoe came to stay. As they were finishing up a takeaway curry, Zoe wanted to hear more about Oscar and Ben.

'These work colleagues of yours sound interesting, Bel. Ben and... Ollie was it?'

'Honestly, Zoe, there's no romantic potential there. Oscar is hilarious but I don't fancy him, and Ben is slightly scary because he's so... competent.' She faltered.

'...but you do fancy him,' Zoe finished for her.

'No! No, I don't.' She was firm. 'Anyway, I don't think I'm ready to be looking around for prospective boyfriends. At the moment my main criteria for a man would be that he has to be the exact opposite of Mark. Which can't be a sensible approach.'

Zoe took a swig of her beer. 'Jesus, I'm not saying go looking for a second husband. Have some fun. Sleep with some unsuitable people. Make the most of being free to flirt again.'

Bella started clearing away the plates. 'Not sure that's a good idea to put into practice with work colleagues. Which just leaves the neighbours. I mean – I suppose, to be fair, Mr Price would fit under your heading of unsuitable people.'

'I'm guessing, from your strangely smug tone, that Mr Price is the guy on the Zimmer frame we passed on the way to the Indian?'

Bella smiled her confirmation and disappeared with the plates into the kitchen. Zoe was about to follow her in with the empty takeaway pots when there was a knock at the door.

'I'll get it,' she yelled. 'It could be Mr Price!' She was still giggling as she opened the door and found herself swept aside by a blonde, middle-aged woman who dripped all down the corridor and into the living room.

'Bella! You've got a visitor.'

Bella hurried into the living room, wiping her hands on a tea towel.

'Hello, dear.' The woman was drenched, hair plastered to her head. 'I thought I'd pop by. You forgot to take your knickers.' She pushed the sopping wet paper bag into Bella's hands. 'I won't sit down. I'm a little damp. It's raining.'

'Yes,' Bella agreed. She glanced at Zoe long enough to establish that her friend had identified this woman as being the same nutter that Bella had already told her about.

'Well,' said Bella. 'Er... thanks for the knickers, but...'

'And I wanted to check how you were getting on at Acorns.' The woman sat down absent-mindedly and helped herself to a banana from the fruit bowl.

'I don't want to seem rude,' Bella said, 'but I don't even know your name.'

'Maggie. Maggie Thatcher.'

Zoe and Bella looked at each other.

'Well... Maggie, it's lovely of you to bring the knickers and everything, but—'

'The thing is, you see, with Acorns, they can't be trusted. They take people and tell them lies to suck them in. And if you don't like it...' She used the banana to mimic a knife cutting her throat. 'That's what happened to my Teddy.'

Maggie's silent buzzer went off again and she sprang out of her chair. Stuffing the remaining half of the banana in her mouth, she gave the skin to Bella with one hand and grabbed the paper bag with the other.

'I've got to go now,' she mumbled through the banana. 'Be careful, dear. Very careful.'

The front door slammed behind her.

'Bloody hell.' Zoe shook her head. 'Bloody hell! And people say London's dangerous.'

※ ※

The next afternoon, after dropping Zoe off at the station, Bella rang the doorbell of the house next door.

'Sorry to disturb you, Angela, is this a bad time?'

The woman paused for a moment, one hand resting on the door jamb, the other holding a very fine paintbrush tipped with pink. The penny dropped as she associated the young woman on the doorstep with the new arrival she'd welcomed with the gift of a peace lily some days previously.

'No, no, come in!'

She led Bella through to the kitchen where an easel was set up, a rough outline of the garden beyond beginning to take shape on the canvas. Curled up on the bare wooden table was a silver tabby cat. Angela put the kettle on and gestured to one of the comfy-looking armchairs pulled up next to the open fire which made Bella's cheeks glow after the cold air outside.

'Make yourself at home. Tea? Coffee?'

'Coffee would be lovely.'

'Settling in okay?' Angela asked, reaching for the mugs.

'Yeah, really well thanks. Everyone's friendly, unlike back in London. When I was in Acton, we lived in a converted Victorian house and I probably said five words to the people in the other flat the whole time we were living there. In the week I've been here, I've met nearly all the neighbours. David and Pauline in number five even invited me to their drinks party next month! Are you going?'

'Absolutely. If it's anything like the last one it'll be a hoot. Arthur Price got trolleyed and gave us a demonstration of Irish dancing. Not easy on a Zimmer frame.' Angela's eyes twinkled. 'It's a shame there's no one nearer your age here. I'm sure they wouldn't mind if you brought some friends along.'

'Yes, they said I could bring someone. My friend Zoe was here from London this weekend actually. She loved the house, all the nooks and crannies. Including the fact that the eaves cupboards have a gap that goes right the way through to your house! Did you know that? I found out when I was putting boxes away.'

'I do remember something about that now you mention it,' Angela put the mugs down on the table with a smile. 'I won't sneak through in the night, promise!'

'Ha! Well, speaking of unexpected visitors... do you know a Maggie Th—'

Before she could get any further Angela's hand flew to her mouth.

'Oh... bugger! Sorry! I knew there was something I meant to do when I came to see you that first night. I was going to warn you about Maggie.'

'That's really her name then? Maggie Thatcher?'

Angela nodded. 'Unbelievable as it sounds, yes. So, she came round to see you?'

'This was her second visit. She wanted to know how I was getting on at work. I've just started at Acorn Consulting.'

Comprehension swept across Angela's face.

'Oh, dear. You poor thing. That's a double whammy then; you've stumbled on her two obsessions. Strangers in the village and Acorn Consulting.'

She pushed a plate of biscuits in Bella's direction.

'It's a very sad story. Maggie's husband, Teddy, worked at Acorn Consulting. Had done for twenty years. They don't have children and Maggie's never worked, she stayed at home and looked after Teddy. Anyway, one day in the run-up to Christmas he disappeared. Went off to work in the morning and never came home. The police were called but according to his colleagues, he never arrived at the office. Maggie was distraught, as you might imagine. It was all over the local news. They had search parties out in the woods; they even dredged the lake. But he's not turned up and they haven't found his car. They were hopeful about that as it was quite distinctive, a little yellow kit car.'

'Poor Mrs Thatcher.'

'Yes. Maggie was already… idiosyncratic, but she's got worse since he disappeared. In the first few days, she'd go out walking for hours on end, looking for Teddy. She's still out looking for clues and calling the police to tell them about suspicious characters. I think coming to check out any new arrivals is her way of keeping tabs on the community.'

Bella sipped her coffee. She was ashamed that she had mentally ridiculed the poor woman.

'There was no indication that Acorn Consulting was involved though, right?'

'No,' Angela replied. 'I mean, not that I know of.'

The first month went by and Bella started to feel like less of an outsider in the office. People weren't standing on ceremony as much and she relaxed enough to respond in kind to Oscar's deadpan delivery, often earning herself one of his characteristic single 'Ha!'s of appreciative amusement. Lauren was starting to come out of her shell, chatting over lunch about her gruelling triathlon training and even suggesting an after-work drink one evening when they were both in the office late. By six o'clock on the Friday of her fourth week, only she and Lauren were left in the office. It was Valentine's Day. Unusually, Ben had left on time, perhaps for a date, or an evening with his girlfriend – or boyfriend – if such a person existed. Bella had so far gleaned nothing about his personal life. Oscar was driving down to Devon for the weekend to visit friends.

Bella had been caught up in what she was doing, but her eyes were starting to feel dry against her contact lenses. Time to call it a night and head home to a planned evening of indulgence – fish and chips from the chip shop in the village, gin and tonic and something from her Hitchcock collection. She started shutting down her laptop, then, on the spur of the moment turned to Lauren.

'Hey, I've been invited to drinks with the neighbours tomorrow night and they said I could bring a friend. Do you fancy it? If you're free, that is.'

Lauren blinked uncertainly. Bella charged on.

'I mean, they're all our parents' kind of age so I'm not saying it'll be very exciting. I just...'

She could see Lauren was trying hard to make eye contact and stopped to let her speak.

'I'd like to come. Thanks. I'm not doing anything on Saturday.'

Bella smiled. 'Great! I'll text you the address. Do you want to meet at mine at seven thirty-ish?'

❦ ❦

She looks gorgeous, Bella thought as she opened the door on Saturday evening. Lauren was wearing skinny jeans with heels and her normally severely coiffed hair was loose in a very cool-looking afro. The rather middle-aged trouser suits and polo necks she wore at work hadn't prepared Bella for such a glamorous weekend look.

As they crunched across the gravel between the houses, Bella said in a low voice, 'If it's too dull we can always make our excuses. Give me a nudge or something if you're desperate to leave.'

'I'm sure I won't be.'

The door opened and Bella was sure she wouldn't be desperate to leave either. Looking down at her was the face of an Adonis. Very possibly joined to the body of an Adonis but it seemed rude to do a full top-to-toe pat-down before being introduced.

Bella hesitated. 'This is number five, isn't it? David and Pauline's?'

'It is.' The voice matched the face. Bella wound a strand of hair around her forefinger so tightly it started to cut off the blood supply. 'I'm James, their son.'

Untangling the finger, Bella introduced herself and Lauren, then followed him through to the large open-plan living area. She glanced at Lauren, wondering if she felt equally dazed, but Lauren smiled back at her as if it was an everyday occurrence to meet the human incarnation of a Greek god in the house next door. Pauline tottered over to greet them, her pink face looking shiny with the effort of entertaining – and perhaps a few glasses of wine. Bella went through the introductions again.

'And I see you've met James! I was so chuffed when he called this morning and said he was coming for the weekend. I thought, thank goodness there'll be someone for our new neighbour and her friend to talk to instead of a load of old fogeys! It's such a shame Anna couldn't make it too, isn't it, James?'

James agreed it was a shame, but she was on call this weekend. *Oh*, thought Bella. *Anna*. Dr Anna, by the sound of it. Who couldn't make it down today with James. Then she saw the wedding ring. Typical. She should have known better than to think she would stumble across an outrageously attractive single man at a middle-aged drinks party in the wilds of Wiltshire. Zoe's advice to sleep with unsuitable men was all very well, but she had her moral code, enforced by the invisible eyes of What Others Might Think of Her. She wouldn't go for a married man, ever.

The three of them − she, Lauren and James − naturally gravitated together during the evening, occupying a corner of the kitchen near the drinks. Lauren became as animated as Bella had ever seen her. She and James discovered a shared love of mountain biking, much to Bella's chagrin as she found herself excluded from discussions of suspension forks and disc brakes. At one point they were so engrossed in a comparison of the same endurance bike ride they'd both done in New Zealand that Bella sidled off to say hello to Angela.

Angela jerked her head in James's direction. 'Bet you weren't expecting that?'

Bella feigned ignorance. 'What?'

'Oh, come on. *Him*. James! Shame he's married. I hope your friend's picked up on that?'

Bella shook her head. 'Don't worry, I'm sure she has. I'm sure it's all perfectly...' She waved a hand towards them and then realised she was indicating empty space. James and Lauren were nowhere to be seen.

An hour or so later, as she and Angela were drunkenly debating the various merits of mojitos versus Singapore slings, with much material evidence to draw upon, she got a text from Lauren.

Sorry to disappear. James wanted to show me his bike and I lost track of time. Thx for a lovely evening, going home now. See you Mon x

Bella snorted to herself. Show you his bike indeed. Showing you his something no doubt... It seemed that some people didn't share Bella's strict moral code when it came to married men.

In the office on Monday, Lauren looked like butter wouldn't melt in her mouth. Bella had misjudged her. She'd assumed that shyness was a sign of timidity, but perhaps not. She was a dark horse, that was for sure. She tried a couple of broad hints, but Lauren wouldn't take the bait – James's name never passed her lips, and in the end, Bella was forced to resign herself to silent speculation.

Chapter Four

The weeks flew past and almost before Bella knew it the end of her probation period was upon her. On that Friday she dressed with particular care. She knew that whenever possible Isadora Faye herself would conduct a new employee's induction to the OAK Institute. Bella hadn't met Isadora, who by all accounts was something of a recluse.

Her mouth was dry as she entered the building. She hadn't been told what to expect, just that if she passed her probation she would be inducted to OAK. Crossing the hall, she said good morning to Kelly, who leapt up and sprinted over with a smile.

'Bella! So. The big day.' The teeth were as dazzling as ever. 'If you wanna go up to the top floor, room 157, they're waiting for you there. Good luck.'

Kelly threw her arms around her and Bella's Britishness shot up to eleven on the scale as she reciprocated with a couple of feeble pats on the other woman's back. Released, she headed for the stairs, her stomach turning over. She was dying for a cup of tea but it seemed inappropriate to arrive at such a portentous meeting holding a mug.

Room 157 was long and narrow, with a gleaming mahogany boardroom table down the middle. On one wall a tapestry had been raised in gathered loops to reveal a big screen. Catherine and Ben sat side by side at the table, unsmiling. Ben indicated that she should take the chair at the end nearest the door.

'Morning, Bella. Tea? Coffee?'

His tone was more formal than usual. Neither he nor Catherine had a drink, but they each had a printed report laid in front of them on the glossy tabletop. Taking the chair indicated, Bella shook her head. Ben picked up the report and glanced through a couple of paragraphs before proceeding.

'We're here today to discuss your probation period. Catherine has pulled together this report based on input from myself and the team, and other sources.'

Other sources? Like what – or whom? wondered Bella.

'I'm delighted to say that on the whole, you've performed extremely well,' Ben said.

When Bella was twelve, she'd had a school report including a summary section from her form teacher. The teacher had propounded at great length Bella's achievements through the year, her excellent qualities and the fact she was a pleasure to teach. If he had to pick out one area for improvement, he said, it would be that she should raise her hand more often in maths lessons. Bella had taken in nothing from that report other than that she hadn't done well in maths. She had continued, throughout her life, to root out the tiny negatives in a field of positives, like a pig hunting truffles. Ben's use of the phrase 'on the whole' struck fear into her soul. 'On the whole', meant there were some areas she hadn't performed well in.

He put down the report and picked up a remote control.

'In fact,' he continued, 'I would be offering you a permanent contract right now if it weren't for one thing.'

Something cold dropped into the pit of her stomach. She knew what he was going to show her. Security footage of when she went nosing around the building during the OAK meeting. Oh God. The screen came alive and sure enough, there was a shot of her walking down one of the corridors.

Something was odd though – she was holding her phone up in front of her. She hadn't had her phone with her when she'd done her reconnoitre that day.

'Why,' asked Ben, scrutinising her, 'were you taking pictures of the building in your first few days here?'

'Oh!' Was it worth trying to make something up that would make her seem less of a moron? No, best to be honest. 'Oh, that! I've... sorry, this is ridiculous. I've got a terrible sense of direction. As Catherine knows, in fact – she had to rescue me one morning, didn't you, Catherine? I thought if I took pictures of landmarks on the route to the office, I'd be able to get there without people having to shepherd me all the way from the entrance hall.'

Comprehension swept across Catherine's face and she said, in deprecating tones, 'I can certainly confirm that Bella got lost on her second day. She was over in Human Resources, with no idea how she'd got there.'

Ben's shoulders relaxed. 'In that case, Bella, I'm delighted to offer you a contract as a permanent employee of Acorn Consulting. Congratulations. Would you like to accept?'

Bella grabbed the outstretched hand and shook it so hard Ben flinched. 'I'd love to. Thank you.'

'Excellent. Cup of tea to celebrate?' While he went over to the cabinet in the corner and poured out the drinks, Catherine pulled a bell-rope that dangled against the wall.

Ben handed round cups and saucers and they sipped in silence, waiting.

A muffled bell chimed at the other end of the room and Ben strode to the door. Catherine stood up and Bella hastened to do the same. In the doorway, a small, immaculately coiffured woman appeared. Bella resisted the urge to curtsey. Isadora Faye crossed the room and paused at the opposite end of the table before sitting, and gesturing for the others to do the same.

'Good morning, Bella,' she said. 'It is my great pleasure to introduce you to the Organised Acts of Kindness Institute.'

※ ※

Until Isadora had spelt out OAK's name in full, it had never occurred to Bella that it was an acronym; she'd never seen it written down. The Organised Acts of Kindness Institute. It sounded as unlikely as the Monster Raving Looney Party. But at least, unlike at her interview, she had the benefit of having got to know these people for three months. She was excited to find out more, rather than unsettled and anxious. Even the obscure warnings of Maggie Thatcher had faded into the background in the face of the day-to-day normality of her job and colleagues.

Isadora nodded to Ben, who pressed a button on the remote. A portrait of a woman appeared on the screen. She could have been straight out of a Jane Austen novel with her empire-line dress, understated string of pearls and pink and white complexion.

'My ancestor, Emma Faye, established the Organised Acts of Kindness Institute over two hundred years ago. She also incorporated Acorns & Company, both to conceal and financially support the work of the Institute. She was an heiress. One of the wealthiest women in England. Like many of her female contemporaries, she was frustrated by the limited role society afforded her.' Isadora paused to take a couple of sips from the glass of water in front of her. 'After the early death of her husband she began to look for a philanthropic outlet. She took seats on the boards of several charities, but her ambition was to do more.'

Ben and Catherine must have heard this story a hundred times but they showed no sign of it. Catherine leaned forward, chin in hand, eyes gazing at Isadora in what looked very much like adoration.

'Emma had three children: John, Edward and Beatrice. When John, the eldest, was seven years old, he was playing with the local farmer's son in the farmyard. The two were leaping from a hayrick onto the ground. On one particular jump, John landed on a nail sticking out of a piece of wood, which had been hidden under loose hay. He screamed. His playmate screamed also. The men were out in the fields and the farmer's wife at the market. A stranger, passing by the farm on his way to the nearby market town, came to their aid. He removed the nail from John's foot, which bled profusely, bathed it and bandaged it with his handkerchief. John, by then, had calmed enough to tell the man where he lived. Despite it being quite out of his way, the man put John on his pony's back and led him home.'

Isadora took more mouse-like sips of the water. It seemed incongruous to hear words relating to children's feet, blood and nails coming out of that neatly-lipsticked mouth.

'Emma was grateful, as any mother would be. She tried to offer the man a meal, money even, but he would accept nothing. He said it was no more than anyone would do. She thought about that. It was no more than anyone like he, or she, would do, but not everyone in the world is alike. This was her epiphany. Small acts of kindness were random. One never knew if or when they might occur. What if one could introduce method into kindnesses and increase their frequency? How imperceptibly and yet how materially humankind would benefit from the cumulative effects of unlooked-for kindness. Emma, at that moment, conceived the basis of the OAK Institute.'

One more tiny sip and Isadora stood up, looking at Bella as if they were co-conspirators, as if she were Willy Wonka about to show Charlie his factory. 'Come and see what it has become.'

Catherine stayed where she was while the others filed out through the far door which led into a small, windowless hall. Ben opened the wooden door in the opposite wall, revealing a tiny old-fashioned lift.

He swung the grille open and waved Bella inside. 'I'll leave you in Isadora's capable hands.'

Bella pressed herself against the back of the lift, trying to leave as much room as possible for Isadora who stood in front, with her back to her. There were buttons marked 3, 2, 1 and G. Ignoring these, Ben reached in and pressed a button marked 'Assistance' before slamming the grille back into place. The lift whirred into life and began to descend. Bella had an excellent view of the top of Isadora's head. Her grey hair was stiff with the dull sheen of hairspray and a faint smell of roses emanated from her when she moved.

The lift came to rest with a jolt.

After a moment in which nothing happened, Isadora moved her head an infinitesimal amount in Bella's direction. 'Could you, dear?'

It dawned on Bella that Isadora was waiting for her to open the door. She shuffled to the front and grappled with the stiff handle. Once she'd unclasped the fastening, it swung open without effort and they emerged into a part of the building Bella hadn't seen before. If the main house was perfectly preserved, with all hints of modernity tucked behind curtains and under rugs, this was the polar opposite. The atrium in which they stood had a flat glass roof through which flooded natural light. Along the stark white corridor ahead of them a row of solid steel doors punctuated the right-hand wall. There wasn't so much as a stray ceiling rose in sight. Disoriented, Bella turned to find her companion watching her like a gleeful child.

Isadora beckoned her with a finger upon which glittered an enormous amethyst. 'Come.'

Bella took a deep breath. Whatever was behind those steel doors couldn't be as bad as her anxiety dreams. Particularly if it happened to be her mum, who would be a welcome, if unexpected, addition to the scene.

They approached the first door and it became apparent that Isadora could operate doors by herself when absolutely obliged to, as long as she didn't have to touch anything. She stood close to a small panel beside the door and commanded, 'Open.'

Sesame, Bella was thinking to herself as the door slid aside.

'This,' announced Isadora, 'is one of our observatories.'

For a moment, Bella thought she had stepped into one of her dreams. Everything was movement, colour – her eyes were telling her brain impossible things about the depth of field. Gradually, as if she was staring into one of the 'Magic Eye' posters that had covered her walls when she was a child, she forced the pieces of the puzzle to make sense. There were perhaps a hundred people in the room, wearing headsets and carrying tablet computers. Every millimetre of each concave wall was covered in television screens.

She followed Isadora over to stand behind a man in a green T-shirt and glasses who was absorbed by the action on one of the screens. It showed a young woman, hesitating at the bottom of a flight of steps in what looked like a train station. She grasped a large suitcase and started to heave it up the stairs. On the first step, she nearly overbalanced and had to grab for the handrail, struggling to hold on to the case with her other hand as commuters shoved past her and streamed up the stairs.

The man in the green T-shirt was speaking into his headset and typing on his tablet while he watched the girl on the screen. From the left side of the shot, an unremarkable middle-aged man in a suit appeared. Without a word, he took hold of the suitcase, flashed a brief smile at the young woman, and carried it to the top of the stairs. She sprang up the stairs after him and seemed to be thanking him before he strode off out of sight.

The man's attention then switched to a different screen, and as Bella looked around she realised this process was being repeated over and over, thousands of times, all day long. Unsuspecting members of the public were being helped via the medium of millions of cameras and microphones which acted as the eyes and ears of this covert team.

When she was a little girl, Bella's grandmother had told her that Jesus was watching her all the time. *All* the time. That had made her stop and think. And for a while Jesus's eyes would pop into her head at inopportune moments, halting the progress of an index finger towards a nostril or making her close the door to the biscuit cupboard and climb back down off the stool. As she got older, she formed her own opinion about Jesus and his eyes, an opinion which she didn't share with her grandmother for fear of upsetting her feelings. Nonetheless, despite being certain that nothing godly was peering over her shoulder, Bella found herself almost always behaving as if she were observed. Her constant question to herself was what would people think of this or that act that she was about to perform.

Here in the observatory, Jesus's eyes popped into her head again without warning. All those times when she'd imagined she was being watched – she *was being watched*. As she and Isadora weaved their way through headset-wearing hordes in the observatory and Isadora explained some of the technology in use, she realised the full extent of OAK's eyes and ears. They hacked into CCTV, webcams, security cameras and spy planes. They installed hidden cameras in vehicles and appliances. Their agents wore tiny cameras in their clothing. It struck Bella that she herself had probably been helped by the OAK Institute in the past.

Isadora indicated a screen in the centre of the far wall which displayed a number that was changing from 11,348 to 11,349. 'The kindness tally for today.' She seemed lost in thought for a moment, then gave a slight shrug and added, 'Well, it's still early I suppose.'

'Will I... Will that be part of my job?' asked Bella.

Isadora shook her head. 'The observe and deploy teams are specially trained. They are recruited for that work.'

Something in her tone gave Bella the impression that she wouldn't fulfil the criteria for the observe and deploy teams; not by a long shot.

They left the room and were passing down the corridor as Isadora continued. 'You'll find there are a lot of specialisms at OAK. Different jobs require very specific skillsets. But all our people are integral to the correct operation of this organisation, from the elite teams you've seen in action here right down to the smallest, greenest leaf on the OAK tree,' she said, crinkling her eyes at Bella.

Bella wasn't terribly flattered by the implication that she was the smallest, greenest leaf but made no comment.

They passed by more observatories down the long corridor, Isadora's deportment and the way she held her head perfectly balanced atop her shoulders bringing to mind a ballet dancer – or perhaps a rather strict ex-ballet dancer who now taught novices.

'The scale of this…' Bella trailed off, indicating the numbers of rooms packed with people. 'Where does all the money come from to fund it? There must be thousands of people employed by OAK.'

She saw Isadora shoot a glance at her and wondered if she'd overstepped the mark. Before answering, she led Bella through a door and up a short spiral staircase to a mezzanine overlooking one of the observatories.

'It's a very astute question, my dear,' she replied, as they stood by the glass barrier and looked down on the milling mass of observe and deploy staff, each wrapped up in his or her own on-screen drama. 'AC is the front company and does provide some financial support, but not enough to run an operation like this. It's vast, as you suggest, although only operational in the UK and parts of the US to date. We plan further expansion into the US this year, and Europe the year after. We *did* try a pilot expansion into Paris.' She sniffed and plucked an invisible thread from her sleeve. 'Sadly, the levels of hostility we encountered from the average Parisian demanded a much greater level of kindness intervention than we're able to finance at this point.

'We generate income for OAK from various sources. I mentioned my ancestors were wealthy – the Fayes are one of the largest landowners in England. We invest our income from our property holdings, and we also own a portfolio of companies whose affiliation to OAK is not public, but whose income helps to support us.'

As she finished, she gave Bella a tight smile which seemed to indicate the topic was now closed.

Looking at her standing there, in her classic Chanel suit, against the backdrop of glass, steel and screens, Bella felt a question rising to her lips that not even the warning growls of What Others Might Think of Her could repress.

'Why do you do it?' she asked. 'All the money and effort that it takes, why not just run AC as a normal business?'

Isadora laughed and turned to face Bella, one manicured hand resting lightly on the glass barrier.

'You might as well ask why…' her eyes darted around the space above Bella's head as she searched for the right analogy, '…why Shakespeare wrote plays or why Mozart composed music. OAK is my life, it's why I'm here on this earth. And besides, if we weren't here, you'd know about it, my dear.' Unexpectedly, she took one of Bella's hands in both her own. Isadora's hands were soft and dry, the grip firm. 'Imagine if those little positive interactions with strangers that brighten your day stopped happening. How would you feel? If your car broke down and no one stopped to help. If you forgot your money and no one would lend you your bus fare home. If you were choking on something in a restaurant and no one stepped forward to save your life.'

The grip tightened on her hand. 'I can tell you exactly how you would feel. You would feel abandoned, neglected, hurt, alone. You would resent those around you. You would come to expect no fellow-feeling from others and in return, you would show none. The world would be a colder, crueller place. That is life without the OAK Institute, my dear, and don't you forget it.'

Chapter Five

Back downstairs, Isadora commanded another door to let her in. It obeyed and her face lit up as the room inside was revealed. 'This is my favourite place in the whole complex.'

It looked like a library designed by a sufferer of obsessive-compulsive disorder. Row upon row of books, as far as the eye could see, all bound in the same fawn shade of leather, all the same height and thickness. The fact that this was Isadora's favourite place said something about the woman, it was as neat and immaculate as she was. Bella had an urge to pull a book out of line or add a mismatching one, anything to break the monotony, like wanting to yell 'Who gives a fuck!' in the middle of a boring meeting. The only point of contrast was a large oil painting on the back wall, which depicted a woman who bore a striking resemblance to Isadora. The woman looked to be in her early forties and the style of her satin shift dress, multiple strings of pearls and elbow-length gloves suggested it had been painted in the 1960s.

'A relative?' Bella enquired, as they paused in front of it.

'My late mother, Elizabeth Faye. She died not long after this was painted.'

They stood in silence for a moment and then Isadora beckoned her on through the room, which had been decorated in the style of the original house, with elaborate cornicing and chandeliers. They passed shelf after shelf of the beige books. At the far end, Isadora turned to the left.

'This,' she said, in a tone of triumph, 'is The Librarian.'

The man woke up with a start. He had been sitting with one hand resting on his chin, his elbow on a large wooden desk, dozing. Rousing himself, he rose to his feet with quiet dignity. Marred slightly by tripping over the chair leg as he manoeuvred himself around the desk.

'Charmed,' he murmured as he clasped Bella's hand in both of his own. The strength of the alcohol fumes suggested he'd been steeped in spirits overnight. He was a compact, stocky man. Broken veins snaked, purple, across his nose and cheeks. He wore a three-piece suit which appeared encrusted to his body. Nothing about him marked him out as an ideal candidate for the guardianship of a valuable collection of books. He returned to his seat behind the desk, while Bella and Isadora sat in creaky leather armchairs opposite. Opening a deep drawer, he produced a decanter and three glasses.

'It is tradition,' Isadora explained, 'that new members of the OAK Institute toast their arrival with The Librarian.'

Bella knew she was the only new arrival for a couple of months. The Librarian must have been keeping his toasting arm in good practice in between. He sloshed a generous measure of golden liquid into each glass. Whisky. She hated whisky, it made her feel sick. Ever since she was seventeen and it had been produced at a house party late on in the evening, leading to a marathon vomiting session.

They raised glasses and clinked them. As they held them there, elevated, there was a moment of complete silence. The steel door shut out any external noise, and the thick carpet and millions of pages were like blotting paper for sound.

'A single act of kindness may change a day, a life, the world. Kindness is powerful. OAK is mighty,' The Librarian said, as if he were reciting a spell, with Isadora murmuring along with him.

His unfocused gaze met Isadora's and held it before he knocked back his drink. Isadora sipped at hers, as she had done her water. Bella raised the glass, let the liquid touch her lips, felt queasy and put it back down.

The Librarian refilled his glass. 'This room contains the history of the Organised Acts of Kindness Institute, from the very day it began. Your name will now be added to its annals.'

He looked at her as if she had won the lottery.

'Gosh,' she said. It seemed inadequate.

Tossing back his drink, he staggered over to a row of glass cases that were fixed to the wall. He put his hand in his trouser pocket. Bella saw the hand hunt around beneath the greasy tweed, before coming out empty. He held it palm up and frowned. His other hand entered boldly into his other pocket. The investigation was repeated. He swayed, grabbed on to one of the cases and righted himself with a business-like cough. Bella sneaked a glance at Isadora and found she was looking unconcerned. The Librarian was now patting himself down in the most unlikely places before trying his waistcoat pocket, his face lighting up as he extracted a key.

'This,' he declared, 'is the key to our most valuable case. I always keep it here, close to my heart.'

He seemed satisfied that he had conducted himself with aplomb and proceeded to open the cabinet. A very old book, bound in fawn leather like all the rest, was produced. It was dropped on the floor, recuperated, polished against The Librarian's trouser leg and placed with a reverential flourish on the green leather of the desk.

'This is the First Record.'

He smoothed the binding with one trembling hand before opening the book at the first page. Having cleared his throat, he read aloud.

'Thursday, October 21st, 1814. Mary Cutler gave an apple and a penny to a vagrant who was sheltering under White Horse Bridge. This is the second kindness of the Organised Acts of Kindness Institute.'

Out of the corner of her eye, Bella could see that Isadora was mouthing the words as he spoke. When The Librarian finished, he closed the book and regarded Bella from underneath his unruly eyebrows, waiting.

'The second kindness?' She turned to Isadora. 'Because the first one was the man helping Emma Faye's son?'

Isadora looked pleased. 'Well done.' She took the book from The Librarian and turned over the pages, rings flashing in the light of the reading lamp. 'The Institute was modest to begin with. Just Emma and two of her servants, Mary Cutler and George Jennings. Emma recorded every kindness in this book and subsequent books. Over time, as she grew more confident and more ambitious, the Institute expanded. She recruited more staff to the position which would come to be known as agent. Slowly, with extreme secrecy, she built an organisation which would bring help and happiness to people all across the country.'

'Why in secret?' Bella asked. 'Why can't OAK be open about its activities?'

The Librarian snorted.

'Think about it, my dear,' said Isadora. 'If people knew the kind stranger who helped them was being paid, the sense of gratitude and fellow-feeling they experience would diminish. It follows that the recipient of the kindness would then be less motivated to carry out their own act of compassion when the occasion arose. OAK isn't purely about helping someone in the moment, it's about encouraging the spread of benevolence. That's why we carry out small, individual acts of kindness instead of funding the type of large-scale community projects that we feel are better managed by charities and government departments.'

'And speaking of government departments...' added The Librarian, with a knowing look at Isadora over the rim of his near-empty glass.

'Well yes, quite.' She smiled. 'As The Librarian suggests, if our operations were public we would be subject to regulation. We would have to defend the use of every piece of monitoring equipment and every iota of data. It would be impractical. The amount of data we gather is enormous, and growing all the time. You can see some of that for yourself here in the library. Every kindness perpetrated by OAK is recorded on the page of a book somewhere in this room. Up until 2003, that is, when we became 100 per cent digital.'

The Librarian's shoulders slumped and he snatched the book out of her hands, dropped it on the floor and manhandled it back into its case.

'Some things are still done the proper way though,' he announced as he resumed his seat and opened a drawer. Yet another beige book was produced and opened. 'Everyone who has ever worked for the Institute gets entered into the Register of Names.' He stabbed the page with a thick, yellow-tipped finger. 'Including you.'

He reached across the desk to where a fountain pen stood upright in a silver holder. As he drew his hand back it caught Bella's glass and knocked it over. Isadora flinched backwards and Bella whisked the book out of the path of the liquid. The Librarian swore, pulled a filthy-looking handkerchief out of his pocket and started mopping up.

Bella had accidentally closed the book as she grabbed it, and now began to leaf through to find the right page. The pages were full of uniform columns of handwritten names and dates. Near the middle of the book, her eye was caught by a crossed-out name.

Teddy Thatcher.

The Librarian stuffed the damp handkerchief back in his pocket and held his hand out for the book. Putting it back down on the desk he refreshed himself with another measure and added a splash to Bella's glass before performing the ceremony of inscribing her name underneath that of the last member to join OAK.

Bella was biting down on the inside of her lip where the skin was rough from being gripped between her teeth when she was anxious. One part of her brain was just about following what was going on in the room. The Librarian was producing more artefacts such as the first photographic record of an act of kindness. Isadora was providing the commentary in the form of more potted history of OAK.

Why is Teddy's name crossed out? Bella thought. According to Angela, he disappeared without a trace. Which meant that no one knew if he would be coming back or not. *But maybe someone does know?*

She shook herself. *This is ridiculous*, she thought. She knew AC now – even if she'd only recently been introduced to OAK. It was staffed by normal people – perhaps unusually bright and capable people, but normal nonetheless. Their work was above board. OAK's whole ethos was about helping people. It wouldn't go around knocking off its employees. For a split second, she considered asking Isadora about the crossing-out. There would doubtless be a straightforward explanation and she could stop her imagination going into overdrive. Perhaps that was the best approach.

Then everything went silent. The core of her brain had relied on the superficial part to monitor what was going on – and it had let her down. Isadora and The Librarian were watching her. Someone had asked her a question, but she had no idea what it was.

Putting a limp hand to her head, Bella murmured, 'I'm feeling a little faint. Perhaps it was the whisky, so early in the day, I'm not used to it.'

She saw Isadora flick a puzzled glance at her undrunk glass. The Librarian picked up the decanter.

'Or 'praps you need a drop more to settle your nerves?' When she shook her head, he set about settling his own instead.

Isadora stood up. 'It's time for the OAK debrief.' She performed something between a nod and a bow as she thanked The Librarian, who returned the gesture before slumping back into the position they had discovered him in.

As they passed through the shelves towards the door Bella glanced back in time to see his eyelids droop and close.

The 'debrief' was the ten o'clock gathering that had piqued Bella's curiosity in her first week. It was held in an enormous underground conference hall which had a square stage jutting out from the back wall and banks of seating on the other three sides. A vast screen covered the wall above the stage, onto which as they entered a video was being projected, showing the interior of a packed Tube train pulling into a station. A young man, wearing jeans which threatened to drop to the floor at any second, got up from a seat and began to push his way through the crush. As he neared the exit there was an exclamation and a woman tried to grab his arm. She missed but called out and a man further down the carriage stepped in front of the boy, blocking his exit. The woman squeezed her way through and handed the boy a wallet. He looked shocked, felt his back pocket and said a hurried thanks before jumping off as the warning signal sounded and the doors began to close.

Ben stepped onto the stage. 'As you can see, the fashion for wearing jeans slung low is continuing to cause young men to lose phones and wallets from their back pockets. Observe and Deploy teams, please remain vigilant.'

Over the past three months, Bella had become less intimidated by Ben. Now, seeing him give a presentation in front of what looked like several thousand people, she was reminded of her first impression of him, the aura of authority. There was no sign of nerves, he could have been having a chat with an old friend rather than addressing what looked like the entire population of a small town. He was someone you would want on your side in a crisis; but also someone you wouldn't want working against you. She'd seen a ruthless streak in him at times when he was working on projects that he was passionate about. Maybe that was what made him so flipping attractive. He was an unknown quantity. Plus, he was incredibly good at what he did. Bella had always found that appealing.

At university, she'd developed an embarrassing crush on a middle-aged tutor with a paunch because of his startling intelligence and the way he communicated his passion for the Romantic poets. If excellence in one's field could outweigh age and paunches, what might it do for someone as attractive as Ben?

Bella preferred not to think about it, because whenever she did, the annoying, sensible part of her piped up that a) he was her boss; b) he seemed to be a stranger to self-doubt, whereas she was in thrall to it; c) she didn't even know if he was single, married, gay, straight or what; d) he'd never shown the slightest romantic interest in her; e) her emotions were still fragile from the breakdown of her marriage... This went on through the whole alphabet.

Ben left the stage and Oscar took his place. Now there was someone who was on her wavelength. They had the same sense of humour. He was reassuringly human, with foibles and lapses in confidence. Oscar was talking the audience through some figures. She recognised the software they used to monitor social media, but not the figures he was sharing. There were millions of Twitter accounts being crunched, sliced and diced before her eyes.

'This month, OAK-backed Twitter accounts have followed six million new Twitter users,' Oscar was saying. 'We've retweeted over seventeen million tweets. We've been responsible for thirty per cent of trending topics.' As the list of topics streamed downward from the ceiling, she realised OAK had been pushing positive search terms up the trending list at the expense of anything vicious or abusive. There was a spontaneous burst of applause. Oscar looked pleased in spite of himself as he acknowledged the audience's appreciation and returned to his seat at the edge of the stage.

A further hour of presentations elapsed as different departments shared the month's successes and failures (or 'opportunities for improvement' as they were labelled). Bella only realised Isadora was no longer beside her an instant before she stepped onto the stage. She was greeted with rapturous applause.

Holding up her hand for quiet, she waited until the noise had died down. 'Thank you. And thank you to everyone who has presented today. Before we reveal the Kindness of the Month Award, I have two matters to share with you.' Under the bright lights, she looked like a pristine, silver-haired doll. Bella felt one of her urges coming over her to do something to break up the symmetry, maybe muss up the helmet-like hair or smudge the perfect bow of coral lipstick. She screwed her face up as she mentally defaced the unsuspecting woman.

'The first matter,' Isadora was continuing, 'is to welcome a new member of the OAK family.' The world around Bella went white as she was picked out in a beam of light and her image was transmitted to the room via the big screen. A thousand people were hushed into silence as a giant image of her gurning face hovered above the stage. The gurn was replaced by a look of blank horror, which in turn was replaced by an unconvincing smile of gratification.

Isadora appeared to have noticed nothing as she pressed on. 'Many of you will know Bella Black from her work at Acorn Consulting. From next week she will also be operating as part of OAK.' She paused to allow polite applause to ripple around the vast space. 'The second matter refers to our expansion plans. I understand there have been rumours that the short hiatus in new office openings a few months ago indicated a change in strategy. I am delighted to tell you that these rumours are false. We are forging ahead and will have completed our initial wave of US office openings by the end of this year, several months ahead of schedule!'

There was applause and cheers from around the auditorium. She allowed it play out for a few moments and then raised a hand for silence, nodding and smiling.

'Thank you. I'd now like to invite our chief people officer, Catherine Knight, to join me on stage to announce the winner of the Kindness of the Month.'

Seeing them standing side by side, Bella was struck by the similarity between the two women. Not in looks, so much, but Catherine's sleek chignon was her generation's version of Isadora's over-styled coiffure and, like Isadora, everything she wore was neat and tasteful. They had the same air of professionalism and reserve. Bella had a vision of them rolling off the conveyor belt at Businesswomen R Us Inc, Marks One and Two, with a million identikit models trooping off the production line in their wake.

'Thank you, Isadora.' Catherine smiled at the other woman and then turned to address the audience. 'This month's award goes to a very special team. Let's take a look at the footage. This was filmed in Southampton earlier this month.'

The big screen showed a busy road, with a couple of pedestrians walking along the pavement. One of the women was eating what looked like crisps or nuts from a packet as she chatted to her friend – or perhaps her daughter, mused

Bella, there was a resemblance between the two. Something was wrong, Bella realised as the older woman stopped walking. The packet had fallen to the floor, the woman who had been eating was leaning forward coughing, the other woman slapping her on the back. Even though she was convinced this story must have a happy ending Bella found herself holding her breath, nails digging into her palms as her fists clenched. In between slaps the younger woman was trying to flag down passing cars but the traffic continued to stream past. And then an angel appeared, borne not on clouds but in a blue Fiat Panda. The little car pulled up at the side of the road, disgorging a middle-aged woman in denim who strode across to the choking woman, performed the Heimlich manoeuvre, watched the obstruction fly from throat to pavement, returned to her car and drove away. The two women watched her go, open-mouthed.

'What makes this kindness of particular note,' Catherine told the crowd as the image of the two pedestrians froze on the screen behind her, 'is that the agent you saw was off-duty. Guy Bredon from the Observe & Deploy team saw the incident and realised that Shannon Clarke, who a few minutes earlier had come off a long shift, was the nearest agent to the scene. He sent her an urgent alert and we've all seen what happened next. Moments like this remind us how powerful kindness can be and the impact OAK has on the world.' She gazed out into the room for a moment or two, not at the audience, it seemed to Bella, but through them and beyond to where years' worth of kindness-related memories unfurled across her line of sight. 'Don't forget, all winners of the Kindness of the Month will be eligible for the annual Elizabeth Faye Memorial prize. The prize recognises the year's most impactful kindness and will be announced at our Christmas party.' A polite smattering of applause greeted this announcement, while Isadora and Catherine smiled at each other. 'Guy and Shannon,' Catherine called out, 'please come and up and accept your award.'

When the award had been handed over, Isadora picked up the reins again.

'Thank you. And now, I am delighted to be able to unveil the kindness total for the month.' The projection displayed a number with so many noughts it struggled to fit on the screen. 'That's a point three per cent increase from this time last year.' She raised her hands and clapped towards the audience, turning to acknowledge each sector of the room like a singles champion at Wimbledon. The audience clapped enthusiastically back.

Isadora allowed them a few moments of self-congratulation before announcing, 'Time for the US reports.'

She stepped off the stage and attention turned to the screen, on which appeared a woman with very short caramel-coloured hair who introduced herself as Theresa Loomier. She proceeded to report activities in North America, where kindness figures were lower as the operation was still in its infancy compared with the UK. But to Bella, who was still getting used to the idea of OAK, the thought of all those agents out there, undercover, both in the UK and across the pond was proving to be hard to take in. One day, she presumed, she'd be as blasé about this as everyone around her. But for now, her brain felt under attack and as the meeting wrapped up, she stumbled out towards the oasis of normality which was the staff canteen with a feeling of relief.

Chapter Six

In the dining room, Bella grabbed a salad and a roll from the buffet and headed to their usual table. The marketing team and Catherine were waiting for her with a large cake, 'Congratulations!' piped across the middle. They gave her a round of applause as she approached and her cheeks reddened.

'Thanks, everyone, that's really kind of you,' she said, pressing her hands to her burning cheeks. 'You shouldn't have got a cake, gosh, I wasn't expecting that.'

'It's a tradition in the team,' said Ben. He'd reverted to his usual self after the formal tone of her end-of-probation meeting. 'Lauren makes them.'

'Wow.' Bella was impressed. The cake was piped with tiny perfect roses along the edges and intricate latticework on the sides. Lauren looked pleased but waved a dismissive hand.

'It's also tradition to take the newcomer for a celebratory after-work drink,' Ben said as they resumed their seats. 'If you're free tonight?'

Bella mentally checked her social calendar and mentally confirmed that it was a desert. 'I'd love to,' she said.

'There are so many things to celebrate, after all,' Oscar added. 'You must be the first-ever new employee to do a passable impression of the Incredible Hulk while being introduced to a large contingent of the UK staff.'

'Oh my god,' she sputtered as they all burst out laughing. 'Don't! What an absolute nightmare! Someone could have warned me that was going to happen, I would have made sure I was looking suitably bland.'

'I don't think anyone realised your default expression when watching presentations was quite so terrifying,' Oscar drawled. 'Otherwise we would have done.'

She started to attempt an explanation, realised it wouldn't go well and changed the subject. 'There were so many people there today. How many are there on the UK payroll?'

'There are around 200,000 UK members of OAK,' Catherine told her. 'Five thousand of them are based here at HQ. Nearly everyone else is in the field.'

Bella shoved a stray piece of rocket back in her mouth before responding. 'In the field?'

Catherine nodded as she peeled a clementine. Bella rarely saw her eat anything but salad or fruit. 'Field agents. They work for OAK but hold down full-time jobs in areas where the potential for kindness is maximised. You'll find a lot of nurses are OAK agents. They get a lot of opportunities to do small kindnesses for people. Teachers, too.'

'Mmm,' agreed Oscar, 'but you'll also find them in places where kindness might be in short supply. They make up the shortfall. Or places where you might be in more need of kindness than usual.'

'Such as?' Bella was regretting having the seeded roll. She was trying to speak without opening her mouth too much in case she had poppy seeds stuck between her teeth. She probed her mouth with her tongue, located one wedged in a gap and tried to subtly dislodge it.

'Such as DIY stores,' Oscar replied. 'If you've ever stood looking at the rows of things that claim to do what they say on the tin and you're desperately trying to work out if you need eggshell, satin, gloss or whatever, it's probably an agent that's saved you. IKEA, too,' he added. 'People are always in need of kindness in there. As well as the field agents there are also branch agents. They don't know they're working for

OAK. We plant HR professionals like Catherine here in large organisations to hire and train people to be kinder than your average Joe.'

'Public transport is another key location for us,' said Ben, 'as you'll have seen in the briefing today. We have a large concentration of agents working in London on the Tube. It's a technique known as "PH neutral". Where there are high levels of unfriendliness and aggression, we introduce more than average numbers of agents to try to bring the atmosphere back into balance.'

Bella had stuffed the last bit of roll in her mouth and couldn't reply other than to pull an enquiring face.

Oscar said, 'As an ex-Londoner, you'll know you don't get much more aggressive and unfriendly than your average London commuter.'

She swallowed her mouthful in a hurry. 'That's a bit harsh!'

Oscar shrugged. 'The stats don't lie. Now. More importantly, we're all gagging for some cake. What are you waiting for?' He shoved the cake a little closer to her and passed her the knife.

As she positioned the point on the surface, Ben said, 'Don't forget to make a wish.'

His tone was jokey, but when she glanced up, he was looking into her eyes and there was something intimate about it, as if they were alone. Her stomach flipped over.

She plunged the knife into the cake, all the way to the silver board, then brought the handle down and began cutting out the slices.

'What did you wish for?' Lauren asked.

'If I told you it wouldn't come true,' she replied with a smile as she passed a piece of cake across on a paper napkin. And the truth was she wouldn't have been able to put it into words. She'd wished with her heart, not her brain – a yearning prayer for the world to turn itself right-side up and for her to find her place in it.

❦ ❦

Bella had many, many more questions about what she'd seen at the OAK meeting but as soon as the cake had been eaten it was time to get back to work. Back in their office the rest of the afternoon was taken up with Oscar showing her what their team did for OAK, and how her role would fit into it. Her temporary laptop was replaced with a shiny high spec one, and she was issued with a top-of-the-range phone which made her personal one look like it was from the 1980s. There was no point carrying two phones around, she thought, as she swapped her contacts over and slipped the old one into her drawer. And there was something quite appealing about having a new number that Mark didn't have access to, it underlined her fresh start.

Ben had been elsewhere for most of the afternoon, but at four thirty he came back into the office. 'Come on then, that's enough for today. Let's go and get a drink.'

Bella looked up from her screen. 'Are we sharing cars or...'

'You won't need a car.'

They shut down their laptops. *Where the hell can we get a drink around here without a car?* Bella wondered. The AC house was surrounded by acres of parkland on all sides. She looked down at her new green suede heels.

'Won't need a car?' she muttered, throwing a questioning look at Lauren.

'We won't be walking far either.' Lauren gestured down at Bella's feet. 'You'll be fine, don't worry.'

They trooped out of the office but to Bella's surprise turned right, rather than left towards the main exit.

Ben led the way, calling over his shoulder, 'Oh and Bella, if you get the urge to start taking pictures of landmarks again,' – his sudden smile disarmed her – 'repress it.'

'I'll do my best.'

They came to a halt by one of the hidden vending machines.

Good Lord, she thought. *I know I'm not in London anymore, but tell me this isn't their idea of 'going for a drink'?*

Ben tapped a code into the vending machine and stepped back. The machine slid forward and to one side, revealing a lift. The doors opened and they all piled in, Bella fighting hard to keep her jaw from sagging open. When they'd descended and the doors slid aside, they were back in the ultra-modern underground surroundings of OAK. They passed through a lobby into one of the austere white corridors, Bella examining the panels of glass above her head through which the last rays of afternoon sun streamed.

'But how—' she began.

'How come you can't see the glass from above ground?' Ben finished for her.

She nodded.

'Technology. A lot of what you see in the gardens isn't real. You remember the room where you had your interview?' he asked.

She nodded again, transported back there with the help of a sudden waft of his citrusy aftershave as he walked beside her – the same one he'd been wearing that day.

'It overlooks a walled garden,' he said. 'The plants and the soil look like the real thing, but they're artificial. They've been engineered so that from above and side-on they appear solid, but from underneath they're transparent. When you took the lift down to OAK with Isadora this morning you arrived in the main atrium. The glass ceiling of the atrium is beneath the walled garden.'

Bella's brain tried to grapple with this, on top of everything else she'd learnt that day and then she gave a slight shake of the head. The only way to cope, she decided, was to go with the flow. Trying to make sense of it logically wasn't an option.

They turned a corner and found themselves face to face with a red brick wall. In the centre of the wall was a sturdy wooden door with a stone surround and above it, a cream, painted square set into the bricks, upon which was painted 'The Royal Oak' in elegant script. Under the writing was a picture of an oak tree harbouring a ginger cat on one of its lower branches. A girl was depicted climbing up a ladder propped against the trunk, one hand held out towards the cat.

'Kindnesses to animals too?' queried Bella as Catherine stepped aside to let her go first.

'Of course,' the other woman replied, seeming surprised at the question.

Inside was what real ale aficionados would call a 'proper' pub. Horse-shoe shaped bar in the centre of the large room. High-backed wooden booths along one wall. Roaring fire. Brass fittings, low ceilings, flagstone floors.

The place was packed. People turned and smiled as they entered, one or two raising their glasses to Bella in congratulation. Other than the cosy authenticity of the place, the main thing that hit Bella as she entered was a great wave of goodwill. The pub was overflowing with it, it oozed out of the walls, gushed out of the pumps and hung like smoke in the air. She found she was smiling. It was hard not to. When she looked at the others, they were smiling too.

Oscar got the drinks in as the others found themselves a table by the fire. They all toasted Bella and then, after everyone had taken a sip, she asked, 'What is this place?'

Ben raised an eyebrow at Catherine. 'Catherine's always the person to ask when it comes to OAK history.'

The firelight glinted off her hair as she spoke, sparking silver tones among the blonde. 'This is a replica of a pub in the next village,' Catherine explained. 'Isadora told you this morning about Emma Faye. She was succeeded as head of OAK by her daughter, Beatrice, who expanded the remit of the Institute considerably. When she was preparing to step down, in favour of her daughter, she wanted to show her gratitude to the agents who had worked for her. The story goes that one day she had thanked an agent who had performed a difficult and demanding set of kindnesses. She tried to give him some money to buy himself a drink but he refused. When she asked why, he explained he would like nothing more than to go to the local inn for a drink or two but couldn't. He was afraid he might get drunk and let something slip about OAK. The other agents felt the same, so she arranged for a replica of the pub to be built down here, where agents could drink together and share their experiences without fear of being overheard.'

Ben nodded and took a sip of his pint. 'Now the Institute is much larger and there are people working in all kinds of job, it's not just agents who come here. Any member of OAK is welcome.'

Bella scanned the room and spotted some familiar faces at nearby tables. She also saw a lot of highly-forgettable faces – an attribute which she was coming to recognise as the hallmark of an agent. If no one recognised you, you could keep on carrying out acts of kindness in the same area without being remarked upon.

'We've got Royal Oaks all over the country.' Oscar added. 'All identical. They've got them in the US too now. Although they probably call them Ye Olde Royal Oak over there.'

'And,' Bella twiddled the cocktail stirrer in her gin and tonic, 'the memorial prize that you mentioned earlier, Catherine. That's in honour of Isadora's mum, right?'

'Yes. Elizabeth Faye is a very important person in the history of OAK,' Catherine said. 'Taken from us far too young.'

The atmosphere became serious, people sat up straighter in their chairs. She waited for Catherine to expand but she was looking down at the table, running a finger around the rim of her glass.

'It's an important part of OAK history and worth knowing,' Ben said, picking up the thread. 'OAK is a hereditary organisation, as you probably know, Bella. As soon as Isadora Faye was old enough to understand what OAK was, she also realised that when she was older, she would take on the running of it. Which, if you think about it must be pretty tough. Whatever your hopes and dreams might be for your life, you have to set them to one side because your path has already been mapped out. Isadora struggled with that as she was growing up. There were times when she felt proud to be following in her mother's footsteps. But in her teenage years, she began to feel stifled. Her father died when she was fourteen and according to Isadora that had a huge impact on her outlook. It brought home to her how valuable and short life is. And when she was eighteen years old, she rebelled and ran away from home.'

Bella tried to imagine a rebellious Isadora. Short skirts, tattoos, hanging out with ne'er-do-wells from the wrong side of the track. Her brain underwent a rebellion of its own in trying to picture it.

'How do you know all this?' she asked Ben.

'She told me the story herself, a long time ago,' Ben replied. 'She ran away from home and went to Paris. She wanted to disappear, get away from her mother and OAK, be someone else for a while. A normal teenager, not the preordained head of a very unusual family business. She stayed in Paris for a few months – only her younger brother knew where she was. They were close, she trusted him to keep her secret.'

Oscar picked up his pint and the beer mat clattered from the bottom onto the table. Everyone jumped.

'Sorry!' he exclaimed.

'One day,' Ben said, ignoring the interruption, 'she came home to her apartment in Paris to find the phone ringing. It was her brother calling to tell her that her mother had died of a heart attack. Isadora rushed home. Her mother was forty-five, no one had suspected she had heart problems. The doctors said it could have been brought on by stress. Imagine how you'd feel in that situation.' He raised his eyebrows at Bella, who shook her head in sympathy. 'Your father's dead,' he continued, 'your mother's been left to run the family as well as a huge organisation on her own. And then you – her grown-up daughter who should have been helping her –

make things worse. All your mother's worries build up to such a point that they kill her. That was Isadora's thought process, anyway. Isadora blamed herself for her mother's death.

'After the initial shock, in the days following the funeral, she began to pull herself together. OAK had been temporarily without a leader but Isadora stepped into the breach. She took up the reins, promising herself that she would make up for everything in the way she ran OAK. Every waking hour would be dedicated not only to maintaining the status quo, but to carrying out her mother's dearest wish – expansion. OAK at that time was operational in most of England but her mother had shared with Isadora her plans to recruit agents right across Britain and abroad. Of course, at forty-five, her mother had believed she would oversee these plans herself.'

'So, in a way,' Bella said, 'Elizabeth's death has made OAK what it is today? We wouldn't be expanding into the US if Isadora hadn't made that promise?'

'We can't know,' Catherine cut in. 'Perhaps Elizabeth would have achieved the same level of progress if she'd lived. But what we do know is that no one could have put more effort and love into this organisation than Isadora has.'

Ben excused himself, saying he'd seen someone he needed to speak to and Lauren got up to go to the loo.

'Another drink, Bella?' asked Catherine.

Bella looked down and realised she'd finished her first one already. 'Better not – driving and everything.'

'You don't need to worry about that when you're drinking at The Royal Oak,' Catherine said matter-of-factly before squeezing her way to the bar.

Bella looked at Oscar. 'Because... the local police are branch agents? Trained to turn a blind eye to a first offence?'

Oscar pulled a face. 'You've just had the one, yeah?'

'Well for God's sake, I don't bloody know anymore! If you'd told me about the kind of stuff that happens here a few months ago I'd have thought you were mental. Whereas now, if you told me there was a helicopter waiting to fly me home tonight, I wouldn't bat an eyelid.'

Oscar shook his head in amazement. 'How did you guess...?'

'What?'

'No, okay, no that's not true. I'm messing with you.'

Her hands crept up towards his neck and he feigned defending himself.

'Christ! Fine,' he said. 'I'll tell you. Anyone who drinks at The Oak gets delivered home afterwards, free of charge, along with their car. We've got a team with those foldaway scooters that go in your boot.'

'Oh. Fair enough. I don't suppose they also deliver you to the loo and back by any chance?'

Squeezing through the scrum she found the Ladies down a little passageway at the back. She caught herself humming a happy little tune as she pushed open the cubicle door and broke off mid-note. Here she was, hanging out with work colleagues in a secret underground faux pub, at the end of her first day's indoctrination into a top-secret organisation which monitored and infiltrated the lives of ordinary people in two continents. Surely it was abnormal to be experiencing happiness? The correct emotion would be terror. Or panic. A bit of both maybe.

She flushed the authentic-looking chain and tried hard to feel a bit of either, but they weren't forthcoming. Perhaps when she woke up tomorrow morning the complete unreality of this situation would hit her but until then she wasn't going to worry about it. Humans as a species excelled at adapting, she'd read that somewhere. And if she did say so herself, she was adapting to this situation with remarkable grace and style. And indeed panache. Did she mean panache?

She leant on the large porcelain sink and stared at herself in the mirror. She might be tiddly.

'Tiddly'? Where had that word come from? It was the kind of thing her gran would have said. She was still shaking her head at the marvels and mysteries of memory as she made her way back to the bar. She may have grace, style and – debatably – panache but what she didn't possess, she remembered as she reached the end of the passage and pushed open the door, was a sense of direction. Instead of finding herself back in the crowded main part of the pub, she was in another, smaller room. She should have turned left out of the toilets, not right.

The three occupants of the room were Ben, Lauren and another man who had his back to the door. They were huddled around a small table, looking more serious than anyone else she'd seen that evening. When he heard the door open Ben's head flew up and he looked around, hostile.

'Oh! Sorry,' Bella said. 'I came the wrong way out of the toilets.' It sounded lame, even to her ears.

Ben's look hadn't softened and there was nothing jovial in his tone as he said, 'Forgot to take pictures of the landmarks this time?'

Lauren attempted a reassuring smile but Bella could see she was flustered. Bella glanced at the stranger – or what she could see of him from the back. He had short dark hair and wore a blue shirt that was pulled taut against the muscles of his arms and shoulders. A bomber jacket hung over the back of his chair. He was massaging his right shoulder, as if it were stiff, with his face turned a little to the left. Something about him was familiar. She apologised again and backed out of the room. As soon as the door closed, she heard Ben say something that sounded like 'Thought you'd locked that?'

Back at the table, she found it hard to join in the conversation, her mind still whirring on the little tête-á-tête-á-tête she'd stumbled across. A few minutes later Ben and Lauren rejoined them.

Ben made a point of sitting next to her and murmuring, 'Sorry about before. Bit of work that couldn't wait until Monday.'

She nodded and made an understanding face. But she remembered the hostile look in his eyes and the anxious feeling lingered.

The party broke up soon after that. Everyone seemed to have caught Bella's subdued mood and soon they were all in their respective cars with their Royal Oak chauffeurs.

Bella was thinking about Lauren and whether she could be caught up in something sinister. It seemed unlikely; she was such a well-meaning person. And what kind of 'sinister' thing could it be, anyway? Ben and Lauren had needed to discuss a work issue with a colleague and they wanted somewhere quieter than the main bar to do it. But why had Ben seemed so angry at being discovered?

Something the driver said penetrated her thoughts and she started paying attention.

'Been down this way plenty of times I 'ave. Fella named Teddy Thatcher used to live over your way.'

'Oh, really? What happened to him?'

She saw the driver glance shiftily at her in the rear-view mirror.

'Well, he... er...' He put the indicators on as he prepared to turn off the main road. 'This is the way I go, over the common and round that way, you know. Been in the village long, have you?'

He kept up a determined flow of chit-chat until he'd pulled up in front of her house and retrieved his scooter and helmet from the boot.

'Night then. See you soon I 'spect.'

Bella jumped at a dog's bark and saw David and Pauline taking their unmanageable whippet-cross out for his late evening walk.

David and Pauline who had hosted the drinks party. She gawped at them as she realised where she'd seen the unknown man in the pub before. He was no other than their son, demi-sex-god-and-bicycle-lover James.

Chapter Seven

'A single act of kindness may change a day, a life, the world. Kindness is powerful. OAK is mighty.'

Bella found the Institute's motto popping into her head as she turned into the drive and pulled up by her front wall, gravel crunching under her tyres. 'A single act of kindness.'

What about a single act of *un*kindness, did that have the same power?

She delved into her memory for an example of either and it was an unkindness which surfaced first. Was that significant? Did unkindness leave more of a mark? Or was it a random quirk of the brain that spat that particular memory out? The incident that had popped out of the archives was from when she'd been at school, years before. She'd been going through what her mother would tell her was a phase; falling in and out of friendships. She must have been about fourteen, girls could be so bitchy at that age. At that point in her school career, there was a certain girls' toilets on the second floor of the school that was the favoured place for their group to hang out. One break time, she'd headed up to the loos and found two 'friends' there. They were sitting side by side on the floor, backs against the tiled wall, knees drawn up under their grey A-line skirts, whispering. She'd hesitated, then gone over. They'd stopped talking and looked at her with cold, cruel stares.

'Can I sit here?' she'd asked, as she lowered herself to the floor beside them. *Why did I ask?* her older self wanted to know. *What right had they to decide?*

'No, sorry,' one of the girls had replied, continuing to stare. 'This is a private conversation.'

Bella had shuffled to her feet again and walked what seemed like miles across the speckled grey floor, aware of their eyes on her back in the silence. As soon as the door closed behind her she'd heard them laughing, loud and shrill. Not a major incident in anyone's life. So why had it stayed in her memory all these years?

She slid the key out of the ignition and gazed, unseeing, through the windscreen at the unruly rose bush which smothered her garden wall. When she forced herself to think about why that particular moment at school had remained with her, she realised it was the sense of rejection. One of her own personal demons. No one likes to feel rejected, of course, but to someone who drew on others' opinions to validate their view of themselves, it was devastating. Perhaps it was a moment such as that which had first endowed What Others Might Think of Her with its vicious teeth and claws.

Locking the car, she let herself into her house, going through the motions like an automaton. At least she was aware of her insecurity, that was a good first step. Like an alcoholic admitting that a vodka chaser with their morning orange juice might not fall into the category of 'a cheeky drink'.

She dumped her handbag on the table in the hall and glanced at the clock. Plenty of time for a cup of tea. She needed to snap out of this mood as well, it was time to be positive. Yes, she had insecurities. Everyone did. But at least she knew her enemy. She'd recognised her enslavement by What Others Might Think of Her and she was determined to loosen the chains.

Bella made the tea in her favourite mug – bone china with small turquoise dots on a white background – and carried it through to her bedroom to pack. She had a couple of hours before the OAK car was due to collect her and take her to the airport. As she was pondering a favourite dress in green cotton which had a tendency to crease, her phone buzzed. A text from Zoe, asking how Lauren had been at work that past week.

After her moment of epiphany, when she had realised the stranger in The Royal Oak with Ben and Lauren was Adonis aka James, Bella had been itching to find out more. If Lauren already knew him, why hadn't they shown any signs of recognition at his parents' drinks party? And if she didn't know him, what was he doing deep in conversation with her at the OAK Institute a few weeks later?

She started to feel like a conspiracy theorist. Everywhere she looked she uncovered something suspicious. Teddy Thatcher's name crossed out in the Register of Names. The shiftiness of her Royal Oak chauffeur. Lauren and James disappearing together at the drinks party without warning; then reappearing in a private conflab at The Royal Oak. What with moving to a new place, starting a new job, and the overwhelming weirdness of OAK, she felt like she'd walked into a hall of mirrors. Everything around her was so confusing that she couldn't distinguish between reality and paranoia.

She'd settled in her mind that she would somehow try to tease the information out of Lauren. There was no point trying to do it at work, she would invite her round to the house. Remembering that Zoe was due to come over the following weekend, she'd invited Lauren to join them for dinner.

Zoe had arrived mid-afternoon on the Saturday and they'd gone to the supermarket to pick up ingredients for dinner. Back at the house, Bella started chopping lamb for the tagine while Zoe made hummus under her direction.

'Whack a dessert spoon of tahini in with those chickpeas, Zoe. Then a good glug of the extra virgin olive oil, a squeeze of lemon juice, garlic, salt and pepper and blend it all up. I can't believe you don't know how to make hummus.'

Zoe waved a tahini-covered spoon at her as she mock-yelled back: 'I've got a one-year-old, mate! I barely have time to open a tin of beans let alone whip up Middle-Eastern dips from scratch. Who do you think I am, Nigella Bloody Lawson?'

Bella reached past her for a clean chopping board to cut the vegetables on. 'You've not always had a one-year-old, though, have you? And you also have a husband who works from home. And an au pair.'

Zoe tentatively licked the tahini spoon, pulled a face and dropped it in the sink. 'Au pair shmo pair. Mathilde is about as much use to me as a chocolate teapot most of the time. Less – at least I could eat a chocolate teapot. I only keep her on because she's so bloody *nice*. Every time I think I'm going to send her packing I look at that angelic little face and cave in.'

'Not like you.'

'What, to be nice to someone? Thanks a lot. Where's the garlic crusher then?'

Bella opened the drawer under the hob and fished it out. 'You know what I mean. You're not known for keeping your opinions to yourself.'

Zoe crushed the garlic into the bowl and swirled the mixture around with a clean spoon. 'Oh, I don't know. I think they injected me with some kind of pathetic-ness drug along with the epidural when I had Amelia. I never used to be this emotional.' She was waving the spoon again. 'Like today, for instance. I've still got my baby-brain and managed to leave fifty quid in the cash machine at Paddington. Fuck knows what I was thinking, it even beeps at you, doesn't it? But I took my card and was like, right then, that's me done, and wandered off. Then I hear this guy shouting at me, so I turn round and he's running after me with this wad of cash in his hand!'

Bella paused in her chopping. 'What did he look like?'

'What did he *look* like? That's your first question? You did get it was my cash he was giving me, didn't you? If you're thinking there's a gorgeous millionaire prowling around Paddington throwing money at lone women you're out of luck.'

Bella repressed a smile. 'No! I don't know, I wondered if he was young, old, a tourist, or…' She tailed off.

Zoe shrugged and thought for a moment. 'I can't remember what he looked like.' She went on to describe how she'd thanked him and, overwhelmed with unexpected emotion, found herself welling up.

Agent, Bella thought.

❦ ❧

Once the tagine was in the oven, Zoe went to the spare room to call home while Bella laid the table.

Bella had grown attached to the house in the few months she'd been there. The living room was her favourite place. It was the right size to feel cosy but not cramped, with a dining

73

table at one end and the sofas at the other, grouped around the wood burner. That evening she'd set candles out on the table and along the mantelpiece and lit the fire. The artificial light was kept to a minimum, one lamp on the small table by the sofa and a floor lamp at the other end of the room.

Zoe reappeared as Bella stood in the doorway admiring the candlelight glinting off the wine glasses and the contrast of the white linen napkins against the bare sanded wood of the tabletop.

Peering over her friend's shoulder, Zoe enquired, 'Erm... You did say it was your friend Lauren coming round from work? Not the very-capable-boss-who-you-don't-fancy-only-in-fact-you-blatantly-do?'

'Yes, that is what I said.' She turned and stood with her hands on her hips, waiting with eyebrows raised for the next jibe.

'Right. You didn't forget to mention that you also fancy Lauren, did you? Because this looks like you're planning to seduce her. I'll make myself scarce.'

'Well if you did it would ruin all my plans,' Bella purred, indicating the place settings, 'when you can see that I'm planning a threesome.'

The doorbell rang before Zoe could answer. Bella picked up the bottle of red wine from the sideboard and thrust it into her hands as she passed her. She went to open the door, calling over her shoulder, 'I like candles and firelight. Is that a crime?'

Her words of welcome stuttered and ground to a halt as she found Maggie Thatcher on her doorstep, swiftly followed by Maggie Thatcher trundling down the hall. Bella followed her into the living room, looking for the bag of knickers but it seemed to be missing this time.

'Oh, you again, is it?' Maggie said, on seeing Zoe sitting on the arm of the sofa pouring herself a large glass of red wine. She seemed to take Zoe's presence personally.

Zoe gave a smile that showed all her teeth. 'Yep, me again. Can't seem to keep away.'

Maggie pushed a couple of magazines off the armchair and sat down, taking in the candlelit table as she did so. Her nose wrinkled. 'Friends of Dorothy's, are you?'

Zoe looked puzzled. 'Nope, don't know any Dorothys.' She slid a sly look Bella's way. 'One or two dotties, though.'

Bella made an odd noise as she tried to smother a giggle. She was annoyed that it had sneaked out. She was determined to treat Maggie with more respect now she knew her history.

'Can I get you a glass of wine, Mrs Thatcher?'

'Can't drink red wine, dear, gives me wind.'

Bella could see from the look on Zoe's face that she thought they'd had a lucky escape. 'We've got white.' Bella offered. 'Or I could make you a cup of tea?'

'I'll have a Dubonnet on the rocks.'

'Erm…'

'Or a pale ale.'

'I don't think I…'

'Or a stout.' She said this as if it was her best and final offer.

'I think I've got some Guinness in the kitchen that I had in for making steak and ale pie,' Bella said.

Zoe leapt up. 'I'll go, Bel! Don't want to keep you from your guest.'

Bella perched on the arm that Zoe had vacated.

'What brings you round this evening, Mrs Thatcher?'

'Call me Maggie.' All thoughts of friends of Dorothy seemed to have slipped away. 'I wanted to show you this.'

Maggie pulled something out of her coat pocket and pressed it into Bella's hand. It was a photograph, creased in a couple of places from having been stuffed in her pocket. Maggie, looking more well-kempt than she did now, but with the same unfocused stare, stood against a low wall, one arm flung out as if to indicate the beauties of the hills behind her. Beside her was a man; a full foot shorter than her, made up of spheres. His bald head was a sphere, on top of a spherical body, with two protruding eyes on either side of a little round nose. Even his mouth was an O.

'He looks very nice,' Bella said, as she handed it back. It wasn't the most ringing endorsement in the world, but it was true.

Maggie put the photograph away. Bella clocked that she was wearing the same clothes as on the two previous visits. A long beige mac, mid-calf pleated tartan skirt with sensible shoes and a pale green sweater. Underneath the sweater, she wore a cream blouse: one collar tucked in and the other out. Her hair was wild and her glasses skew-whiff. What must her life be like? Her husband was missing. It was doubtful that she had many friends, her – Bella sought for a tactful word – 'difficult' personality would see to that.

'Help me find him,' Maggie said, her urgent tones snapping Bella back to the here and now. 'Help me find him, dear, please. They're keeping him in there somewhere. A prisoner. You could look for him.'

'I…' Bella shook her head, unsure how to respond, 'I wouldn't know where to start, Maggie. I've only been there a couple of months. Wouldn't you be better off asking someone who's been there a while? Someone who knows their way around?'

'I don't trust *anyone* at Acorns,' Maggie hissed. 'The longer you're there, the more they suck you in. Brainwashing, that's what it is.'

Before Bella could reply the doorbell rang.

'I'll get it!' said Zoe, who had reappeared with a pint of Guinness for Maggie.

As soon as Zoe had left the room, Maggie stood up and grabbed Bella's arm with her free hand.

'Please. Please help me. I can't trust anyone else!'

They heard the front door opening and closing then voices coming down the hall.

Bella placed her hand on top of Maggie's. 'Okay, I'll try. I don't know what I can do, but I promise I'll try.'

The look of relief which had lifted Maggie's expression vanished the instant she caught a glimpse of the person entering the room. She took a step away from Bella and very deliberately hurled the contents of her glass at Lauren, who sprang backwards out of the path of the liquid.

Bella watched her, stunned. 'What on earth…'

Handing Bella the empty glass she said, 'Won't drink under the same roof as *her*.' Maggie stalked out past Zoe and Lauren, who were standing like statues by the living room door. Zoe looked bemused but Lauren was aghast. They heard Maggie open the front door and slam it behind her. There was a moment of awkward silence. Then Zoe pointed down at the carpet where the Guinness had drenched an area into a brown teardrop shape surrounded by petal-like spatters, stark against the cream. 'Quick, that'll stain.' With tangible relief, they all bustled about getting cloths and tea towels.

'It's salt or white wine for a red wine stain, isn't it? Anyone know what it is for Guinness?' asked Bella.

Lauren offered to Google it, sitting herself on the very edge of one of the dining chairs. The sense of shock started to ease.

Zoe sat back on her heels; one palm pressed to a tea towel that she'd placed over the stain. 'I mean what the hell – what the *hell* – was that all about? That woman is a complete psycho, Bella, you've got to stop inviting her in.'

'I don't invite her in, she just comes.'

'It's my fault.' Lauren's soft voice from the other end of the room surprised them both. She'd put down her phone and was sitting with her legs crossed, one foot flicking nervously from side to side. 'She hates me.'

'Well,' Zoe stood up and stretched each stiff leg in turn, 'I don't want to be rude but that's stating the bleeding obvious.' Her frank smile took the edge off her words.

'Something awful happened not long ago,' Lauren said, her voice so low that the others had to strain to hear. 'Her husband went missing. He worked for AC.'

Bella picked up the bottle of red that Zoe had left by the sofa, went over to the table and poured a glass. Taking the seat next to Lauren she pushed the glass wordlessly towards her.

'Thanks.' Lauren took a good glug. 'I needed that. I haven't seen Maggie since it happened. And that time was awful.' She shook her head, hands cradling the bowl of the wine glass. 'When Teddy — that's her husband — went missing, Ben and I went to see Maggie to... well, to see if there was anything we could do to help.'

Bella examined Lauren's face as she spoke. Something didn't ring true, why would Ben and Lauren be the ones to go and offer help? Wouldn't AC send someone like Catherine from the HR team or even Isadora herself?

'It didn't go well,' Lauren continued. 'As soon as she realised we were from AC she lost it. She threw a mug of tea at me.'

She got that angry at being offered help? thought Bella. Even for Maggie that seemed far-fetched.

'Doesn't like drinking with you, that's for sure,' remarked Zoe.

'No,' Lauren agreed with a short laugh. She was starting to look more like her usual self. 'She definitely took against me more than Ben, for some reason.'

'Maybe she fancied him?' suggested Zoe. 'Good-looking, is he?'

Bella could have killed her. Lauren flushed and tried to laugh again before carrying on.

'You joke, but... it was all very strange and sad. It really shook me up but I don't hold it against her. I feel sorry for Maggie. She's been under a lot of emotional strain; it must be awful, your husband going missing like that.'

'What happened to him then?' asked Zoe.

Lauren shrugged. 'No one knows. He vanished into thin air.'

'Had he been acting strangely beforehand?' asked Bella, spotting a chance to do her first bit of investigation on Maggie's behalf. 'Did anyone notice anything odd?'

Zoe threw her a look. 'Steady on, Marple.'

'I didn't work with him,' Lauren replied, 'but according to his team, there'd been nothing out of the ordinary. And the police haven't managed to turn anything up so far.'

'Poor Maggie,' Bella said. She knelt and peeled back the tea towel. A large beige stain remained on the carpet. 'That's my deposit gone then. What did Google have to say about Guinness stains?'

'Google says professional cleaners, I'm afraid,' Lauren said. 'Or a rug.'

It was lucky tagines didn't suffer from being left in a warm oven, because it was late when they sat down to eat. Bella was feeling a bit tipsy from having necked several glasses of red wine on an empty stomach. She was hoping, judging by the others' red-wine-lips, that she wasn't the only one. Her tongue felt thick in her mouth and she ate more than she wanted, hoping to soak up the alcohol. *Must stay clear-headed*, she reminded herself. This wasn't an occasion to relax, she was supposed to be getting Lauren to lower her guard. If this had been a spy film with Bella in the lead role, the other two would now be verging on catatonic while she retained her rapier-clear brain. Something had gone awry in her planning.

'Delicious tagine,' Zoe said, gesturing vigorously with her fork. 'Best yet.' She didn't notice a piece of butternut squash flying over her shoulder. Raising the fork to her mouth she was puzzled to find it empty.

'Mmm,' Lauren agreed. 'Thank you, Bella. It's lovely. The hummus too.'

'I'm glad to hear you say that.' Zoe flopped back in her chair with a self-satisfied air. 'I made it. It's bloody good, isn't it? Surprisingly simple to make. Just a bit of brown paste and some whatsit peas.'

'I doubt Lauren would be surprised that it's simple. You've managed to pick on Acorn Consulting's star baker to give your cookery tips to, Zoe. Unlucky.'

'Ah, but savoury dishes aren't my strong suit. That's more Ben's field.'

'Ben's?' Bella's cheeks warmed from more than the red wine as a new idea trotted into her consciousness. 'He's er... he's cooked for you, has he?'

'Yes, a couple of times.'

The warm glow of the alcohol began to ebb. Why hadn't she thought of that possibility before? What an idiot. That would explain why they were so often together, in The Royal Oak for instance. Memories started flooding in now of times when Ben had called Lauren out of the office, or she'd seen them murmuring together away from the others.

Lauren was speaking again and Bella tried to concentrate. 'It's not just me he's cooked for,' she explained, 'it's the whole team. On team-building evenings.' She dolloped a spoonful of hummus onto her plate and ripped off a piece of flatbread, oblivious to the dramatic swoop of emotions she'd evoked in Bella. Bella tried not to look at Zoe, who she suspected would have been more observant, despite the wine.

'We sometimes have team cook-offs,' Lauren continued, after swallowing a mouthful, 'on our annual team trips. I expect we'll do it this time.' She turned to Zoe. 'Our team and a few others are going over to the US office for some meetings.' To Bella, she added, 'You should suggest this recipe. Ben'd love it, he's into Moroccan food. Mind you, I expect he'd love anything you did.'

The muscles in Bella's throat constricted as she tried to think of a subtle way to encourage Lauren to expand.

Zoe had no such muscular handicaps. 'D'you reckon he fancies Bella, then?'

Lauren brushed a stray crumb of flatbread off her cheek with the back of a hummusy hand. Her eyes flickered towards Bella then back to Zoe. 'I'd say he's got a soft spot for her. Mind you, so's Oscar – another guy in our team. But then she *is* stunning.' She said it matter-of-factly, as if she was saying she *is* female, or she *is* five feet nine.

Zoe reached out a hand to stroke Bella's cheek as she said to Lauren, 'Don't tell her things like that, she'll only become an even bigger pain in the arse.'

'Oh, fuck off,' was the most cutting and clever thing Bella could think of to say.

Zoe shoved her plate out of the way and leaned forward on the table, arms crossed, watching Lauren as she shovelled more food into her tiny frame. 'Come on, then. You can't stop there. What makes you think Ben's into our Bella?'

'Oh, I don't know. Nothing specific, I guess. I catch him looking at her sometimes, you know, in a way he wouldn't look at me, for example.'

'That could mean he can't stand her,' Zoe pointed out.

'Thanks, Zoe,' muttered Bella.

Lauren laughed. 'No, I'm pretty sure that's not what those looks mean. Ben's hard to read though, who knows?'

'Sounds like there are lots of mysteries in your office,' Zoe said as Bella went into the kitchen to get dessert.

Bella wanted to hear more about Ben, but was scared of betraying too much interest. Plus, the still-sober part of her brain reminded her sternly, she had a job to do. She hadn't even mentioned James's name so far.

'How about you, Lauren, anyone you like at work?' Bella asked as she returned with bowls of lemon sorbet. 'Or anywhere else for that matter?'

Lauren nodded. 'There is, but I don't get to see him much.'

Just in the back rooms of pubs and at middle-aged drinks parties, Bella thought, but she was temporarily silenced by an attack of brain freeze.

'Why don't you get to see him?' Zoe asked.

'He works in one of our other offices.'

Zoe was nodding. 'Dong listance relationship.' She paused, brows furrowed, as if replaying the sentence in her head. Seeming satisfied that it was beyond reproach, she continued. 'Bloody hard. I've done it. What's his name?'

'James.'

Bella nearly spat sorbet all over the table. She hadn't expected Lauren to be open about it. It couldn't have gone better if Bella had briefed Zoe beforehand – in all likelihood it would have gone much worse. Zoe's acting skills weren't up to much.

'Whereabouts does he live then?' Zoe's interrogation continued.

'He's based over in the US, at our North American head office. We met on a team-building event.' Her eyes sparkled as she looked over at Bella. 'He'll be there next week on our trip.'

Bella's wine-soaked brain tried to process this information. 'But... Didn't you see him last week? In the pub?'

Lauren looked nonplussed. 'No, what...' Then the penny seemed to drop and she froze. When she spoke next, she sounded stilted. 'Oh, no. Wrong James. Where's your loo, Bella?'

Bella directed her down the hall and she and Zoe started clearing the table. When Lauren came back, Zoe was clattering around in the kitchen, humming something unintelligible. Under cover of the sound of the dishwasher opening and cutlery being hurled into it, Bella asked, 'Is it something to do with OAK? Is that why you don't want to talk about James?'

Lauren looked scared as she said, in the quietest of whispers, 'Please drop it, Bella. Please, please, don't mention it again.'

Chapter Eight

Passport, money, keys. Phone charger. Books. Heating and hot water off. Bins out. Bella ticked off her list. Everything seemed to be done.

A car pulled up out front. She went over to the window and saw a pale blue Jaguar saloon. Bella had heard that this model had been chosen as the standard OAK fleet car based on research into what style and colour brought most happiness to the average person. OAK never missed an opportunity to brighten someone's day.

Downstairs the driver lifted her suitcase into the boot and Bella settled herself onto the cream leather of the back seat. It would take a couple of hours to get to the airport and she hoped the driver wasn't chatty. She wanted to sit back, watch the countryside pass by, and think. Her decree absolute had come through on Thursday, turning the page on her marriage and Mark. She hadn't heard from him in months now nor did she feel any desire to. This trip had come at just the right time. It might be for work, but it represented to her a celebration, jetting off somewhere hot and sunny to celebrate her freedom.

Of course, 'freedom' was subjective. When she breezed home of an evening and pottered around the house doing what she wanted, when she wanted – then it felt like freedom. When she turned off the TV late at night and listened to the silence in the house, before getting into bed alone – then it didn't. She missed companionship though, not Mark himself. Time and distance had sharpened the focus as far as he was concerned.

'Alright in the back there?' The voice was loud and cheerful, that of a natural extrovert. Her heart sank.

'Fine, thanks.' Perhaps if she kept her responses short, he'd get the hint.

'Off somewhere nice?'

Bella wasn't sure if her destination was supposed to be a secret. Certainly, she knew its existence wasn't marked on any map she'd seen. Google Maps showed a landmass in that area but gave it a different name to the one she'd been told, and topographically it looked different to what she'd been given to expect. The driver was an OAK employee so it shouldn't harm to say, but she opted for a non-committal answer.

'Mmm. Looking forward to it. S'going to be a long flight though, I might try and have a quick nap.'

What Others Might Think of Her shook its shaggy head disapprovingly, but the driver gave her a thumbs up in the rear-view mirror.

'You go right ahead, my love. Get your head down. Need to get your rest before a long-haul flight. Don't mind me, I'm used to driving along in the peace and quiet, nothing better...' He carried on in this vein for the next ten minutes, by which time Bella had indeed succumbed to the gentle rumble of the car as it flew along the motorway, and fallen asleep.

❦ ❦

On finding that she was sitting next to Ben on the plane, Bella wasn't sure whether to be pleased or not. On the one hand, it would give her the chance to get to know him better, but on the other hand, no one looks or feels their best on a long-haul flight. *Focus on the positives*, she reproved herself. *Here's your chance to dazzle him with your charm.*

Two hours in and her charm was still waiting for its big moment to burst onto the stage. Ben had exchanged a few pleasantries with her, then opened up his laptop and worked in silence, earphones in. She wondered for a moment if she was expected to do the same, but across the aisle she could see people reading. She pulled her paperback out of her handbag, *Thinking, Fast and Slow*, whose premise was that people have to try to balance the fast, instinctive part of their brains with slower, more reflective thought processes.

When she thought about OAK, her instinctive brain said something was wrong. It took the snippets of insubstantial information she had about Teddy Thatcher, Maggie's paranoia and Lauren's fear at the mention of James's name and added it up to equal something worrying. Whereas the more logical, reasoning part of her brain took a step back and assessed the people involved, including Isadora, Ben and Lauren, on all the interactions she'd had with them. It calculated a low likelihood of a murder or a kidnapping going on at her place of work and decided there was a straightforward explanation for everything, which would come out in the end. Her instinct then shot back that nothing about OAK was straightforward. Her reasoning told it to shut up and be quiet, it needed to think.

Smells of reheated food wafted down the aisle, making her stomach rumble. She'd been looking forward to this, she loved aeroplane food. The neat little foil-covered compartments, the clever space-saving arrangements, the array of titbits from crackers and cheese to a tiny pudding – everything seemed novel on a plane. When the attendant came to pass the trays across, Ben put his laptop away and they began to eat. *Right*, thought Bella. *Now's the time. Dazzle him with your scintillating conversation. Draw him out of himself. Shine, goddamnit.*

She couldn't think of a thing to say.

After they'd eaten for half a minute in silence, he said, 'I know I'm in the minority, but I love aeroplane food.'

She beamed. 'Me too! I don't know why people don't like it.'

'It's something about the way they fit everything together. All these well-thought-out little portions.'

Bella nodded. 'Yes. Exactly.'

They fell silent again. She sensed that he wasn't uncomfortable with the silence, but all the same, she didn't want to waste this opportunity. It was a bit of a leap of topic, but once she'd finished chewing a mouthful of macaroni cheese, she asked,

'Have you always been at AC? A lifer, like Catherine?'

A forkful of chicken halted on its way to his mouth. 'Nope. I joined eight years ago.' The chicken continued on its journey.

He didn't seem to welcome the topic but she couldn't resist pressing for more information. 'Where were you before?'

'I worked for the government.'

'Oh. Doing what?'

'Intelligence.'

Intelligence must mean spying. She concentrated on undoing her bottle of water without jabbing him in the side with her elbow. Bella imagined that most people, hearing that he worked in 'intelligence', went wide-eyed and made references to James Bond. She was determined not to betray any unusual level of interest and nodded as if he had said he used to work in retail.

'Why the change to AC?'

'I was recruited, like you. And it was at a time when I was looking for a change.'

It was hard to read his face when they were sitting close together, side by side. She paused, hoping he would go on, and when he didn't, she tried a different tack.

'Mmm. I was in need of a change myself when AC got in touch.'

He put down his knife and fork and looked at her. 'I know, Bella. When AC recruits it uses all available information to research the candidate. They take a year or two over it. You've seen the observatories, you know how far our reach spreads.' He let this sink in for a moment. 'Only Catherine, Isadora and I have seen your file. It's confidential. But we have to be sure we have the right person. And we knew we did with you. Remember the girl on the Tube having a panic attack? She was an agent. Your final test. We have to be sure the people we hire are intrinsically kind, as well as being qualified in all the other skills we need.'

She hadn't considered that the 'file' Isadora had referred to at her interview might be something huge and intrusive, filmed and written records built up over a period of years. What exactly did they know about her? What did Ben know? What private things had she done, thinking she was alone, that he had seen?

'Bella.' Ben was scrutinising her as these thoughts tumbled through her head.

She was still thinking, recalling – all those painful conversations with Mark, all the ugliness, the despair of the break-up. Had they watched that? Ticked a box, given her a score?

'Bella. We only evaluate what we feel morally justified in using. Nothing private will have been used, we assess things that any passer-by or work colleague could see. It just happens that we've got thousands of passers-by in the form of our observatories. If anything is captured by accident via in-home devices or mobile phones, it's deleted by Catherine's team before it can be included in the report.'

'Catherine's team? I thought you said—'

'You've got to remember, there are millions of pieces of data to be trawled through. It takes a team to do that. But the information is cut up and spread across the team of analysts so it can't be pieced together.'

He shifted round in his seat, forcing her to look at him. 'There are three important things you need to know, Bella. One, we're all in the same boat. Every single person on board this plane, every single person who works for OAK, was recruited the same way. They were identified from superficial information as a potential fit and then monitored for, typically, a couple of years. Which leads me on to point two. Thousands of people are monitored as potential candidates, but only a few are chosen. That means that you're exceptional. What we saw in you was better than all the others.'

That gave her pause for thought. She hadn't considered the possibility of there being other candidates for her job who'd been monitored and discarded in her favour.

'The final point is that you have to be a grown-up about it, Bella. OAK is an enormous, highly secret, highly effective organisation. It works because we pick the best people and we can be confident they won't let us down or betray our trust. It's too important to take risks on. If that means we have to make people feel uncomfortable by checking that they're trustworthy and they're the best candidates, so be it. This isn't some temping agency where we can take a punt on people.'

The remains of her main course were cooling in the aluminium tray. Ben's thigh was pressed against hers but she didn't even register it. Whatever he said, whatever assurances he gave, they'd spied on her for two years. It was like finding out someone you thought was a casual acquaintance had been living on the other side of a two-way mirror in your bathroom. This was the worst place to get a piece of disturbing news.

'Excuse me. I need to go to the toilet.' She stumbled over him in her eagerness to get out and made her way down the aisle, steadying herself on the headrests as she went. She glanced at some of the faces as she passed through the plane. Had any of these people watched intimate scenes from her life on some hacked webcam?

The toilet was empty, thank God – Bella pulled the door closed behind her, flipped down the seat and dropped onto it, head in hands. She felt sick, like she might cry, and mainly she felt like an idiot. She'd seen the puzzlement in Ben's eyes – he thought she knew. Thought she'd been intelligent enough to put two and two together. Bella had been told there was a file on her right from the start. She knew what OAK could do – she should have worked it out. If she delved into the mess of emotions she was feeling at the moment, she had to admit that she was more upset by feeling stupid even than by discovering she'd been spied on.

After she'd had time to calm down, Bella splashed some water on her face, took a deep breath and made her way back to her seat. The main body of the plane was hushed, lights dimmed. Here and there, insomniacs were picked out in individual reading lights or by the flickering blue screens in the headrests in front of them. A couple of people glanced up as she passed and she couldn't help feeling a little sick. *Did you watch me break up with Mark? Did you trawl through footage from my bathroom, my bedroom?*

Ben looked up as she approached. 'How are you feeling?'

She stepped back to allow him out of his seat, then slid past him.

'I feel... a bit stupid. And a bit creeped out. But I'll get over it.'

He clicked his seat belt back into place, frowning. 'I can understand the creeped out bit. But why you would feel stupid...' he shook his head. 'You know well enough, everything about OAK is a shock at first. A lot of data is collected – too much, maybe. No one but the most paranoid person would suspect what goes on.'

She was awoken after an hour or so's broken sleep by the sensation of the plane dipping its wing. All that was visible at first through the window was navy-blue water flecked with white. Then, as the plane wheeled round, she saw an island shaped like an oak leaf, outlined by a wide border of turquoise water and a thin strip of white beach. The stem was a long, narrow peninsula of land jutting out into the blue. Six bays, three on each side of the island, carved the land into the familiar shape, and a ridge of tree-clad mountains formed a slash of darker green along the length of the island.

'That's...' Words wouldn't come. She turned to Ben. 'That's... mental.'

'That's Le Chêne.'

Chapter Nine

Theresa Loomier stood in front of them. Bella recognised the vice-president from the videos of the weekly territory reports.

'I appreciate you all must be tired so I'll try to keep this as quick and snappy as I can.'

Theresa had the most soothing, mellow voice Bella had ever heard. It was hard to imagine how she was going to keep things snappy. If someone had yelled 'Fire!' at that moment, Bella imagined she would smile gently at them all, push her gold-rimmed glasses a little further up her nose and amble away like a turtle across the sand.

They were seated in a large, thatch-roofed, open-sided structure on the beach, like an enormous wooden bandstand. The only walls were at the back, behind the bar; the other sides of the hexagon had struts with shutters that could be pulled across if the wind was high. Bella had an unobstructed view of white sand and topaz water glittering in the setting sun. This view, along with the heat, the welcome cocktail and the mellifluous tones of the speaker, made concentration a battle.

'I hope you'll find your time here worth the journey.' Theresa clasped her hands in front of her.

'So, people. First, it's time for some relaxation. We're gonna eat some beautiful fresh fish and shellfish. We're gonna drink some rum. And later,' she paused and nodded, her gaze roaming around the faces before her, eyes shining, 'we're gonna sing!'

There were some whoops and a smattering of applause from the audience – Bella suspected that was the locals. The

93

British contingent, on the whole, was looking brave and polite; suspecting the worst but determined to keep a stiff upper lip.

'And remember, on Le Chêne,' she raised her hands and tilted her head to one side as if waiting for a catchphrase. The audience obediently chanted back at her: 'Everyone's one of us.'

'That's right, everyone's one of us. Like the Stepford Wives,' murmured Oscar in Bella's ear.

A couple of hours later and Bella was glad they were surrounded by agents, as it required superhuman levels of benevolence to find anything to applaud in the performances. So far, the sole performer with any discernible talent had been Theresa herself, who had given a soulful rendition of 'River Deep, Mountain High'. Lauren had been seen trying to drag a man – who Bella later discovered was her long-distance boyfriend, James – to the microphone but when he demurred, she grabbed Ben instead. Bella had a little moment of disappointment when Ben opened his mouth. He was off-key throughout and struggled with the higher notes. Singing wasn't one of his many talents, it seemed. But maybe that was a good thing, it helped remind her he was only human.

The song finished and she took the opportunity to slip away to the loo, dangling her sandals by the straps as she padded across the still-warm sand to the main building. When she bounced off the door frame, she reflected that she might have had too many rum cocktails. And definitely too many gin ones. The face staring back at her in the mirror seemed to be on a loop; jerking a little from side to side as she tried to focus. Most of her eye make-up had smudged in the heat but something told her that trying to reapply in this state could do more harm than good. No one likes to go back into a party and hear people ask each other who ordered the clown.

The door opened and the impressive figure of Theresa Loomier filled the frame. She took one look at Bella and put a muscular-looking hand on a sturdy hip.

'Huh.' She nodded, as if she'd always suspected this was what she would find in the ladies' toilets. 'You got a case of rum-face, sweetheart.' She opened her voluminous handbag and started retrieving pots, compacts and brushes which she laid out on the countertop. 'You give me five minutes,' she paused and looked at Bella, 'maybe ten, and I'll fix you right up. I used to be a make-up artist, among other things.'

Things were being done to her face now, to her cheeks, her lips, her lashes. It did flash through Bella's mind that she might open her eyes and discover she'd been face-painted as some kind of animal, but it felt so soothing that she could barely find it in herself to care.

'Go ahead. Take a look,' urged Theresa, head on one side as she assessed her handiwork.

The face in the mirror was expertly made up, the skin matte and clear. It still jerked from side to side but Theresa couldn't be expected to fix that. Before Bella could thank her, Theresa had disappeared into a cubicle, calling out, 'Kindnesses within OAK don't count, you know. That one was a bonus, on the house.'

❦ ❦

After breakfast the next day, the UK contingent was split into their teams to be briefed on the latest kindness innovations in North America. Lauren's boyfriend James led the first session.

'If you'd like to gather round, I'll show you an initiative we launched at the back end of last year,' he said.

The room resembled a lab – cool, white and sterile, and unexpected after the wood and thatch of the buildings she'd seen so far. Her team had been joined by seven or eight locals. James, sandy-haired and fresh-faced, was waiting for them by a large round table in the middle of the room. He tilted the tabletop up until it was almost vertical and came round to stand beside them in front of it.

'Take a look.'

The entire tabletop was a mirror. Bella realised the lighting must be incredibly flattering because her reflection looked like an Instagram filter had been applied to it. Glancing up at the ceiling she saw rows of standard LEDs, nothing special.

She glanced at the other faces in the mirror. Lauren was shooting shy glances at herself and turning pink. Oscar was tilting his head from side to side and inspecting all angles. Ben was looking at her, Bella.

'Pretty good, huh?' James was watching their reactions. 'It's got built-in filters. Come round and see.'

They all trooped around the back where a web of tiny wires was embedded in the surface.

'Our team has already started installing them in restrooms and malls across the US. We'll be infiltrating a range into the retail market in the second quarter of the year.'

'Can I ask a question, James?' Bella said.

'Sure!' He looked eager as a puppy as he swung round to face her.

'Is this kindness? Aren't we lying to people? We're not making them more attractive; we're making them *think* they are. In certain places – and not in others.'

James tapped on a tablet as he responded. 'Sure, great question. We thought about that. What we did is we set up one of these mirrors – secretly, of course – in a public restroom and surveyed people on their state of mind as they went in and again when they came out. These are the results.' He projected a graph onto the screen behind him. 'Ninety-eight per cent of those surveyed said they felt more confident after they'd used the restroom. More importantly, eighty-three per cent said they were happier. And, as we all know, happier people are kinder people.'

Oscar was looking thoughtful. 'And you had a control group, I take it? You did another sample – excuse the pun – at another public loo?'

'Absolutely. Of course.'

'Good. Because, thinking about it, I for one am always happier when I've, ahem, evacuated my bowels than beforehand.'

There were a few sniggers, but James responded straight-faced. 'You're totally right, and our research confirmed that. However – and this is crucial – the uplift in self-reported happiness and confidence having used our special filter mirror was over thirty per cent higher than in those respondents who had used the standard facilities.'

Bella glanced at Ben. His mouth twitched as he caught her eye. She suddenly felt shy and dropped her gaze.

'Oscar,' Ben said, 'if you've got any more useful insights to share about your toilet habits perhaps you could produce a one-pager rather than discuss them here?'

'I've produced many things in my time, Ben,' Oscar retorted, 'but a one-pager isn't among them.'

James was already moving on to the next example. 'Okay, team. Something else we're pretty proud of on the kindness innovation front. The video you're about to see is from CCTV in a franchise of a fast-food restaurant. We own the franchise.'

He hit play. On the screen, people were queuing to place their orders. A grossly obese man was talking to a server at the front of one of the queues. Bella was struck by the size of him, his belly slung down low over his thighs in the tracksuit bottoms. He was handed a tray with two burgers, two portions of chips and two milkshakes. He took it, turned, and shuffled off out of shot. The video ended.

James rewound the film, pausing it at the point where the obese man took the tray of food.

'Nothing jumped out at you, right? All looks like a normal restaurant. But the food that this guy' – he pointed with a red laser to the fat man – 'has been given is not the same as the food that that guy' – he pointed to a small, skinny man – 'has been served. And that's not just because one of them ordered a Mega-Burger and the other a Chick'n'Cheese.' He flicked on to a different screen and an architect's drawing of the restaurant appeared. 'You see these panels in the floor, and these points in the ceiling? These allow us to scan customers at the counter for weight, body mass, and other key indicators. A customer such as this gentleman on the right, morbidly obese, gets served a low-fat, high fibre version of the standard recipe.'

The group started calling out questions.

'Why not serve everyone the low-fat version?'

'Doesn't it taste different?'

'How fat does someone have to be before they get the "special" meal?'

James looked flustered, unsure which question to try to answer first.

Before he could address any of them, Ben, who had been silent until this point asked, 'What about the ethics?'

James opened his mouth to reply but was beaten to it by a calm voice from the back of the room which said, 'We take ethics very seriously. As you know, Ben.'

Theresa had entered the room unnoticed. 'I'll be pleased to take you through the philosophical argument later, but right now you need to head into the bunker. As a matter of urgency.'

As she finished speaking an ear-splitting alarm rang out and everyone was out of their seats in an instant, chairs clattering to the floor, belongings left scattered across the table as they hurried to the exit.

Chapter Ten

Lauren grabbed Bella's arm and shoved her into a stairwell. Ahead of them, others were already streaming down the stairs and through double doors into a huge, windowless concrete space. A woman carrying a tablet came over and asked for their names. Staff with armbands clanged the thick metal doors shut and came round handing out bottles of water.

'It's a satellite,' Lauren explained, as they found somewhere to sit. 'Most of the time we know when they're passing over and it's built into the schedule, this must be a new one. Nothing to be worried about. It'll probably be over in, what, half an hour? Forty minutes?'

'That's right,' added Oscar. 'Unless they detect us and blast us to smithereens. In which case it'll be over a lot quicker.'

Lauren glared at him. 'Will you stop it?' Turning to Bella she said, 'He's joking. There's no danger whatsoever. It suits us to keep Le Chêne a secret, that's all. We use technology to disguise the coastline, making the island seem much smaller. When there's an alert we all get out of sight to avoid them picking up movement or heat.'

'Are you saying no one knows this island is here, outside of OAK? I mean the real island, not the fake one on Google Maps,' Bella said.

'We're pretty sure they don't. Because maps show it as uninhabitable and we're so isolated we don't get many people investigating.'

'But…' Two hundred years ago she could have understood it. Today, the world was very small, how could they 'hide' a bit of it? 'When planes fly over—'

Lauren shook her head. 'They don't. We amended the neighbouring countries' systems so they each think the airspace belongs to the other one, and they keep out. And it's not on any commercial flight paths.'

Around them, people were settling down into the institutional-looking plastic chairs, chatting, reading from the stacks of magazines dotted around on tables or taking the chance to rest their eyes for a few minutes. Catherine passed their little group, looking pale and – unusually for her – dishevelled.

Bella nodded in her direction. 'Wonder what's up with her?'

'Claustrophobic, maybe?' Lauren hazarded, distracted by the sight of James approaching. 'Some people struggle being trapped underground until the alert's over.'

Bella wasn't close to Catherine but she didn't feel comfortable about letting her go without at least checking on her. Oscar was flipping through a copy of *Time* magazine, yawning. James had taken Lauren's hand and was whispering something in her ear.

'I'll go and see what's up,' Bella said to no one in particular, before setting off in pursuit.

Catherine had turned down a corridor above which hung a sign for the ladies' toilets. To Bella's surprise, as she rounded the corner, she saw Catherine had walked straight past the entrance to the loos. There was nothing up ahead other than a dead-end, inset into which was a door – to a cupboard, she assumed, as it had a keyhole but no handle. As

Catherine placed the palm of one hand against the door, she heard the footsteps behind her and span round, her face white.

Bella held up a reassuring hand. 'Sorry, I didn't mean to give you a shock, I wanted to check you're okay, you don't look too good.'

The expression in Catherine's eyes was distinctly unfriendly. She turned her back to Bella and placed both palms against the door, arms stretched, head drooping between them.

'I just need a minute,' she said. 'I'll be fine.'

'Can I get you something? Some water?'

Catherine seemed to grasp at this. 'Yes, water would be good.'

Bella hurried away and when she returned, Catherine had slumped to the ground, sitting with her back against the cupboard door, head on her knees.

After draining the glass, she forced a smile. 'Thanks. I'll be okay now. I need a bit of time on my own.'

Bella hesitated. 'If you're sure?'

Taking the empty beaker, she turned to go, and as she did something clanked behind the door. They looked at each other in surprise and then Catherine shrugged.

'Boiler cupboard, I guess.'

❧ ❧

That evening was the team cook-off. Each group had to make a dish from scratch, to be served as a part of a buffet. After eating, the diners would score each other's food.

'It's a bit like *Come Dine with Me*,' Oscar told Bella, 'but without the witty commentary. Scoring is anonymous. I tend to be firm but fair. Anything with avocado in it gets zero.

Bananas score ten. It's a good system which has served me well over the years.'

They were meandering, pleasantly lethargic in the evening warmth, along a sandy path rustling with dry leaves.

'Do people get competitive?'

'God, yes. There's an actual cup at stake, you know. It's gold – solid gold, mind – and shaped like a cupule.'

'Like a what?' Something small and quick rustled through the thicker carpet of leaves that bordered the path. It was too dark to see what it was, but her guess was one of the sleek little lizards which seemed to be everywhere. On her terrace earlier she'd counted seventeen skittering across the walls.

'A cupule. Good God, woman, how long have you worked at OAK? A cupule, you ignoramus, is the little cup that an acorn sits in. It protects the acorn. That's why Isadora's guards are called the cupuli.'

'Isadora's guards?'

Oscar stopped dead and stared at her. 'I mean. Honestly. It's like talking to a newborn monkey. Is there anything you *do* know?'

'Yes. I know you go shopping with your eyes shut.' He was wearing a luminous Hawaiian shirt.

He strode forward, wafting away the insult with a wave of his hand. 'I'll let that one pass. Your feelings were hurt. Isadora's guard – the cupuli – is a small, hand-picked team tasked with protecting her. Her safety is their sole responsibility. Some of them shadow her like your typical bodyguard. Others are more elusive. Field-based. Their role is to be her eyes and ears – to pick up useful intelligence.'

They were nearing their destination now, a long, low hut which had been assigned to them as their kitchen.

'Why would she need intelligence?' Bella wanted to know. 'On what?'

'On anything that could pose a risk to her. She's our most valuable asset, you know. OAK's heart and soul. A hereditary ruler.'

'I hadn't thought of it like that before.' Only now did the implication dawn on Bella of the fact that from OAK's inception until the present day, it had been run by Isadora's ancestors. 'But she doesn't have children, does she? What happens when she dies?'

'Good question. *Great* question.' He raised his eyebrows at her as he opened the door. 'But one for another day, we need to get cooking.'

The room was bright and clinical. Stainless steel gleamed. A knot of people, including Catherine, Lauren and Ben, stood by the counter on which sat a large cream envelope, debossed with an oak leaf.

Ben pushed the envelope in her direction as she and Oscar approached. 'I think Bella should do the honours as it's her first time.'

'What is it?' she asked, taking the proffered envelope.

'It tells us which course we have to cook and the main ingredient we need to base our recipe around,' he said. 'They're drawn at random.'

Slitting the envelope open and pulling out a thick piece of card, Bella read aloud, 'Course: main. Ingredient: lamb.'

'Damn.' Lauren's face fell.

Oscar gave her a look of sympathy. 'Hoping for dessert? Never mind, I'm sure James'll get other opportunities to nibble on your cupcakes.'

She went bright red and muttered, 'Shut up!'

Ben continued as if Oscar hadn't spoken. 'That gives us plenty of scope. Anyone got any good lamb recipes?'

'Bella does a lovely lamb tagine. Don't you, Bella?' enthused Lauren.

'We've got two and a half hours, enough time to do a quick cheat's version I guess,' Ben said. 'Could be a winner – things with a bit of heat often go down well.'

'Well...' Bella could just about remember the recipe, but all their hopes would be pinned on her, what if it went wrong?

They all looked at her.

She put the card down on the table. 'Lead me to the lamb.'

❦ ❦

Making thirty portions of tagine in competition conditions was a considerably different undertaking to knocking up a dinner party dish at home. The vast quantities of meat in the fridge struck fear into her soul but the others helped with the calculations, their previous cook-off experience coming in useful. Two hours of chopping, stirring and tasting later, they were ready. Bella was surprised at how delicious it was, better than the one she made at home although she didn't volunteer that information.

'This is a winner, mark my words,' said Ben, after the final tasting. 'We'll be flying home with the Cupule in our hand luggage.'

'I don't want to pour cold water on your enthusiasm,' Oscar remarked, 'but you say that every year.'

Ben shook his head. 'No doubt about it. This one's a winner.'

Bella finished plating up the last dish.

'I'll help you get these loaded onto the trolley, Bella, and we'll take it over to the service area,' Ben said. 'It only needs two of us, the rest of you can get changed and go and get the drinks in.'

A metal trolley had been left for them outside the entrance to the hut. As Ben finished washing up the last enormous pan, and the others trooped off towards the bar, Bella carried the cloche-covered dishes outside. On her final trip to the trolley, something crossed the edge of her vision. She strained her eyes in the direction of the movement. It was pitch black between the pools of lamplight. There – she saw it again. Someone was moving between two huts on the other side of the path. Something in the way the figure was half-crouching, as if trying to avoid observation, caught her attention. A light snapped on in one of the huts and lit up the figure of The Librarian. Bella missed her footing and dropped the metal dish with a clatter.

Tagine spattered across the ground. When she looked up, The Librarian was gone.

'Are you okay?' Ben stood in the doorway.

'Shit! Shit! Oh God, sorry.'

Taking in the scene, he touched her on the shoulder.

'Don't worry. We can sort this.'

He got another dish and a spoon from the hut. The dish had dropped the right way up, and about a third of it remained unspoiled. They set about taking the tops off the other dishes on the trolleys and pinching a bit from each to add to the reduced portion.

'Everyone will get a smaller portion – which is ideal. Always leave them wanting more,' he said with a smile.

'Thank you, I can't believe I did that. Something gave me a fright.'

'What was it?'

She hesitated. 'I thought I saw The Librarian. Over there, by that hut.'

Ben frowned. 'The Librarian? He's not here. He never comes on these trips.'

'I know he wasn't on the plane with us, but I'm sure it was him.'

She thought alarm flashed across his face for the briefest moment but then he turned away to grab the trolley. 'Better get the food to the dining room, we'll be disqualified if we don't hurry.' He looked at her again, one hand on her arm. 'It must have been someone else. Trust me, he's not here.'

It was late, or perhaps it was early by now. Everyone else had faded away. The little gold cup shone in the rays of the citronella candles on Bella's beachfront terrace. An empty bottle of champagne stood on the table in front of them, beside a half-full one which Oscar grabbed, swigged from, then passed to Bella.

As she reached for it, she noticed the cigarette in her hand. 'Shit! I'm smoking!'

Seeing that she wasn't immediately taking the bottle, Oscar swung it back towards his mouth, clashing it against his teeth as he did so. 'Ow! Fucking bottle.'

'Look, though. I'm smoking!' To illustrate the fact, Bella took a drag, eyes wide.

'Yeah, yeah. You've done that what-a-shock-I'm-smoking bit already.'

'But you don't understand. I haven't smoked...'

'…for ten years. You said that too.'

'Oh.' She took another drag, deep into her lungs, then tilted her head back and watched the smoke plume into the air. She looked tenderly at the cigarette. 'I've missed you.'

'Swap.'

'Eh?'

Oscar grabbed the cigarette from between her fingers and thrust the bottle at her.

She took a swig. 'Okay, that's enough. My fag back, please.' Reaching out to take the cigarette she found herself grabbing his fingers instead.

'That's not… Oh.'

All was silent for a moment until Oscar broke the kiss and yelped, looking down at his left hand where the cigarette had burned down to the filter. He flicked it away.

'Come on,' she said, leading him through the patio doors into the bedroom.

Chapter Eleven

When she was thirteen, Bella had gone on an 'outward-bound' trip with her school. Despite the fact that her aptitude for sports was on a par with a cat's ability to mastermind a hostile takeover, she'd embarked on this adventure full of naïve optimism. She was convinced that she would be the first to climb the mountain, the one kindly urging on fellow pupils too scared to step out over the precipice on the abseil rope.

It had been a brutal lesson in self-knowledge.

Twenty minutes into mountaineering, in horizontal wind and sleet, she had confided to the perky camp leader that she thought she had frostbite. This information had been greeted with an exhortation to keep her pecker up but no material aid of any kind. She had struggled up to the top of the mountain, last, with fellow pupils shouting back condescending encouragements at her through the, by now, swirling snow. She had hoped to redeem herself on the abseiling, but while shrieking, excited teenagers went for their second or third giddy descent ('Would you like to try it facing forward this time, Sammy?' 'Why not, Miss!'), Bella had trembled at the edge of the cliff for half an hour before being lowered, screaming, over the edge, by two coaxing instructors.

Broken down, her shining mental image of herself lying in shattered pieces, she held on to the thought of the final day's activities to pull her through that bitter week. Orienteering. An activity which required no mental toughness or physical agility. Trudging through a dripping forest with a plastic map was something even she could attempt without tears.

By this stage, her optimism had vanished and she had the good sense to acknowledge that her map-reading skills were unlikely to be stellar. The memory of losing her way in a department store a couple of weeks before and having her mother summoned over the PA system still stung. Fortunately, she had been put in a team with Ryan, the most popular, sporty boy in the class and Freya, a pretty girl who was new to the school, but, crucially, had lived in the Lake District. She was bound to know all about rambling and using a compass.

Freya may well have done, but Bella never got the chance to find out. At the first opportunity, while Bella was thrashing around in some bushes looking for a well-hidden place to go to the loo – calling out, 'Just a minute! Won't be a minute! Don't go without me!' – Ryan and Freya had slipped off together for an extended snogging session. Bella had emerged from the bushes to an ominous silence and the dawning realisation that she was going to have to try to find her way back without a map or compass, as her companions had taken these with them.

She got up on a rock and yelled. Help had not been long in coming, and when it did, she had the grim satisfaction of seeing Freya and Ryan sent back on separate minibuses with the promise of two weeks of detentions. Since that day, she had accepted her limits and never attempted any kind of outward-bound activity, particularly orienteering.

Until now.

Someone – Theresa, maybe, she wasn't sure – had decided that a fun team-building activity would be to drop them all in the middle of the island in pairs and let them race to find their way to designated locations.

Bella had been paired with an earnest US colleague called Marvin. She contemplated his stocky calves, taut and bulging beneath the flapping Bermuda shorts as they trudged down the jungle path ahead of her.

'You okay back there?' Marvin swung round with the pack on his back, his teeth gleaming in the shadow thrown by his wide-brimmed hat. The jungle was quiet, dimly green and humid; they were hemmed in by glossy leaves. When they stopped walking the only noises she could hear were small things scurrying around in the undergrowth. She didn't like to think what the small things might be.

Marvin pushed his hat back and wiped sweat from his forehead, flicking it to the ground. 'You don't look too good. You need to rest?'

God, she would love to rest. On a super-king-sized bed with cool, crisp sheets, in a darkened room. With a jug of iced water beside her.

'No, let's keep going.' She took a swig from her tepid water bottle and Marvin crashed off again through the undergrowth, having checked his map and compass. At least he seemed to know how to use both of them, meaning she wasn't required to think. She trudged on, keeping her eyes on his dusty black walking boots. The main thing was to get back so she could collapse on her bed and sleep. Sleep was what she needed, that and a time machine to go back to last night and not kiss Oscar. Or do anything else with Oscar. What the hell *had* she done? For the umpteenth time, she went over what she could remember. Hazy recollections of kissing on the terrace. Tumbling into bed. A blank. Waking up when the alarm went off at 6am and stumbling to the bathroom to be sick. Returning to the empty bed and wondering if she'd had a vivid dream. Lying on her side, head pounding, and noticing a golden gleam out of the corner of her eye: the Cupule. Starting to feel the nausea rise again as she realised it had all definitely been real.

Bella stumbled over a tree root, grabbed on to a trunk to steady herself and felt something gash her hand.

'Shit! Ow! Oh, for fuck's sake!' Could this day get any worse? She examined her palm. Bright red blood flowed out of the raggedy wound. She swayed and then Marvin was beside her, lowering her to the ground with careful hands.

'Woah, steady there. Sit back against this tree. That's a nasty cut, hold on.' He lifted his hat, unknotted the bandana he wore underneath, padded it up then pressed it into her palm. A whiff of scalp entered her nostrils as he bent over her, and her stomach churned. He took her other hand and made her hold it over the makeshift bandage while he slipped off his backpack. Rummaging around, he found a first aid kit.

'You're not having a good day, huh?' He smiled at her, concern in his eyes. She couldn't find the energy to think of anything to say and instead shook her head. Her hand hurt and she was concentrating on not being sick. Even shaking her head made it worse. Marvin peeled away the bandana. The blood pumped out again, but less vigorously. 'Okay, let's hold that on there for a little longer. Then we'll clean it.' He was kneeling in front of her on one knee, holding her injured hand up in a firm grip. She felt like he was about to propose. Closing her eyes, she knocked her hat off her head and let it flop back against the tree. She didn't care what insects might be taking advantage of her position to take up residence in her hair. She wished she knew what Oscar was thinking. At the briefing that morning he'd traipsed in looking as pale and ill as she felt. They'd caught each other's eyes and both glanced away. There hadn't been a chance to talk, even if they'd wanted to, before they all got sent in different directions for team-bonding fun.

She felt Marvin pulling the bandana away and opened her eyes. The bleeding had slowed to a bulging red line along the wound. He took an antiseptic wipe and cleaned it then applied a bandage from the first aid kit, securing it with some surgical tape. She lifted her hand and inspected his work.

'You'll make a great doctor someday, Marvin. Have you got any super-strength painkillers in that kit?'

He pulled out a blister pack and popped two ibuprofen into her left, uninjured hand. Swallowing them with more tepid water, she let her heavy eyelids close.

'Listen.' Marvin's voice was a jolt, had she been asleep? 'I'm worried about you. Could be heatstroke, could be the shock of that nasty cut. Either way you need to rest up for a bit.'

She wasn't about to disagree with that.

'There's no phone signal out here but I reckon we must be thirty minutes' tramp from home. Maybe less. I'm going to leave you here while I go and get some help, okay?'

A thrill of panic ran through her at the thought of being abandoned, faint and bleeding, among the unknown critters that rustled around her. She started to shake her head and attempt to get up, but as she moved, she felt a sensation like a giant ball bearing rolling from one side to the other of her skull and she froze.

'I know you'd rather not be left alone but I think it's our best option right now. I'll be as quick as I can. Here, I'll leave you my spare water bottle.'

Dear old Marvin, standing there with his anxious expression and his pink polo shirt with its dark V of sweat.

'You're a brick, Marvin,' she said, taking the proffered bottle.

'Oh, hush now,' he looked pleased and embarrassed. 'Sit there and take it easy. I'll be back before you know it.'

And then she was alone. Thoughts seemed to swim into view from nowhere and then disappear with a hollow pop. The Librarian swam through first, bloodshot eyes glaring. Ben and Oscar splashed by together, arm in arm, making her feel uneasy. Oscar's face was turned away while Ben winked, maliciously. Her childhood bedroom loomed up from the depths next, with its flowery wallpaper border. Lauren was floating above the bed making notes in a book. When she saw Bella looking, she peeled back the covers and passed the book to Maggie Thatcher, who was lying stiff as a corpse beneath the sheets.

She woke up with a start. How long had she been there? Nothing seemed to have changed but it was hard to sense time passing in the humid gloom. Marvin should have been back by now. Taking care not to make any sudden movements to jolt her head or the throbbing cut in her hand, she reached into her rucksack for her phone. Dead. She hadn't remembered to put it on charge before going to bed. And she wasn't wearing a watch.

Clinging to the tree trunk, she hauled herself to her feet. If Marvin had sprained his ankle or toppled into a swamp, there might be no help coming. If she set off down the path at least she'd be nearer civilisation when they finally came looking.

Her progress was slow. She cursed team-building activities. She cursed alcohol. She cursed oak-leaf-shaped tropical islands. None of it made the trek any easier. At least there was just the one path, heading inexorably downwards. If she kept descending, she had to clear the jungle at some point. After about ten minutes she hit a fork in the path. Both ways looked identical. What Others Might Think of Her slid out from behind an enormous fern and bared its teeth, delighted. This would, no doubt, be what would be reported in the press when her body was found. How, at the critical point, when any normal person would have used her sense of direction to choose the correct path, Bella Black had gone the wrong way. She hesitated, then at random took the right-hand path. For a while it continued downwards then, almost imperceptibly, it began to ascend. Oh God. What now? Go back to the fork? Carry on? Sit down on the floor and cry? She decided to go for the third option, followed, a few minutes later, by the second.

Another fifteen minutes' walk and the jungle seemed to be thinning ahead. She increased her speed. Yes, the trees were undoubtedly getting sparser. And then the jungle was behind her and she was holding herself back from dropping to her knees and kissing the earth. There, at the foot of a steep slope, was what looked very much like the outskirts of the main OAK compound.

❧ ❧

As she approached the nearest hut, she allowed herself to acknowledge how awful she felt, like her knees might buckle at any moment. She tried the door; it was locked. Peering into the window on tiptoe she saw a large, empty training room. There was a more substantial-looking building across the way, perhaps she'd have more luck there. The door was unlocked and she went inside.

Utter silence. There were two rows of desks and chairs but no sign of any people. A door at the far side of the room opened on to a corridor, also deserted. She tried a door to her left and found herself in a miniature version of an observatory back home. The screens were all dead and Bella started to feel a little spooked. It reminded her of a horror film about a post-apocalyptic world where to all appearances humanity had been wiped out – until mutant survivors started popping up from dark corners. She tried to pull herself together. These were just empty buildings and there would no doubt be a reasonable explanation as to why no one was here.

Of course! As she closed the observatory door behind her, she realised. There must have been a satellite alert. She needed to find the entrance to the bunker from this building. After a few false turns, she found herself in a stairwell. Her walking boots clanged on the steel steps as she went down two flights. At the bottom was a small lobby and, facing her, a door. Forcing the heavy handle up she swung the door open.

Instead of the vast space she'd been expecting, there was a small cell-like room, lit by strip lighting. To the left was a narrow bed, clamped to the wall, beside it was a steel unit with taps and a basin. Over against the back wall was a table with tubular metal legs and a wooden top, one chair drawn up to it. She couldn't see much to the right as the door blocked her view, plus she was finding it hard to drag her eyes away from the body which lay motionless in the middle of the floor.

And the perfect oval of glossy red blood that ballooned from beneath its neck like a misplaced speech bubble.

As her knees gave way and the edges of her vision shimmered, a name popped into her head. The round body, round head and round 'o' of a mouth – she'd seen them before. The man on the floor was Teddy Thatcher.

She heard herself scream. The world was turning dark but in the last moment of consciousness, she realised there was someone else in the room. In the slash of light between the door and its frame was an eye, watching her. In the same moment she saw or rather sensed something else, something familiar – and then everything went blank.

Chapter Twelve

'Bella! Bella, are you okay?' Ben's voice was close to her ear, his hand brushing her hair off her face, fingers on her throat checking her pulse.

She reached up to push him away, her movements feeble. Her hand fell back to her side and the touch of the cold concrete reminded her where she was and what she'd just seen.

'Not yet. Take it easy.' Ben restrained her as she tried to get up. He spoke into a walkie-talkie, giving their location. 'They're bringing a stretcher.'

'I don't need a stretcher. He's hurt, who's looking after him?'

'Who?'

Ignoring his insistence that she lie still, Bella pushed herself up onto her elbows. Through the doorway, the pool of blood was smeared now, its perfect oval broken. There was no sign of Teddy Thatcher.

'You need to find him! He was dead – or dying. He needs help.' She pressed her palm to Ben's chest, pushing hard. 'It was Teddy Thatcher. The man who went missing. And I think I saw someone else in there with him but I can't be sure.'

Ben stood up and took an involuntary step back as if he'd been shoved, his wide eyes fixed on her face. They heard the metal steps reverberate as the paramedics approached.

'Stay there, let the medics take care of you.'

He went over to the cell door, peered around it and then stepped inside. The door closed behind him. After a few moments, he reappeared and, seeing that Bella was being tended to, hurried back upstairs.

The paramedics, once they were sure she wasn't suffering from any serious injuries, helped Bella to her feet. At the foot of the stairs, she turned back.

'I think I left something, hang on.' Before they could stop her, she was at the door of the cell, pushing it open. What she saw made her grab the door frame for support.

The blood had been wiped away; no trace remained.

Ben caught up to them as they were about to get in the ambulance, taking Bella's arm and pulling her to one side.

'One second, guys,' he called to the medics. Lowering his voice, he said to Bella, 'There was nothing there, no sign of anyone.'

'No sign because you made sure there wouldn't be?' Exhaustion and emotion were making her rash. Maggie had asked her to help and all she'd done was faint at the sight of poor Teddy bleeding on the ground. And now he'd disappeared again. 'How come you were there when I woke up, Ben? What were you doing in that building?'

What looked like genuine confusion passed across his face. 'What do you mean? I came looking for you. Marvin sent out search parties and as I passed by, I heard you scream.'

'Why did you clear up the blood?'

There were two beats of utter silence as they stared at each other.

'I had to.' His voice was urgent and he grabbed her hand, stepping closer towards her. 'Bella, you have to trust me. You mustn't tell anyone about Teddy.'

'Why the hell not?'

'Because wherever he is, if he's still alive he's in danger.'

'And keeping it a secret is going to help? What the fuck, Ben!'

'Yes,' he hissed, his face inches from hers. 'Because there are people here who want to find him and we can't let them. You *have* to trust me, Bella. If you don't, Teddy is dead.'

❦ ❦

If you don't, Teddy is dead.

Those words buzzed round and round in her brain as she leant her head against the cool surround of the aeroplane window, looking out through the layers of toughened glass to the smooth, dense rolls of cloud below. They'd been haunting her all day, ever since Ben had hissed them in her ear, flickering across the back of her mind like a faulty projection as she packed her case and boarded the overnight flight home with the rest of the team. Her actions – or to be more accurate, her lack of action – could be helping Teddy as Ben insisted. Or she could have left a man to bleed to death.

Poor Teddy, unconscious and bleeding on the floor of a cell on a tropical island far from home. What on earth was he doing there? The last that had been seen of him was when he set out to work in his little yellow kit car in rural England a few months before. What, or who, had brought him there, and who had tried to kill him? Who had she seen through the crack in the door? The Librarian? She couldn't even be sure if it had been a man or a woman.

And then there was Ben. What part was he playing in all this? Why, if you knew there'd been an attempted murder, would you want to keep it a secret? Who was he keeping it a secret from?

She wished she had someone to confide in. Oscar might have been that person, if she hadn't been such an idiot.

She rolled her head to the other side of the headrest in a vain attempt to get comfortable. If there was one thing that could elbow the looming anxiety and guilt about Teddy out of the way for a moment, it was the lesser anxiety and guilt about her drunken – and still, as yet unspecified – shenanigans with Oscar. He was a good friend, the person she'd most clicked with since she moved to her new job, and she didn't want to have lost that friend through a moment's stupidity. *Should have thought about that before you kissed him, you bloody idiot.*

All around her the films on people's screens paused and an announcement came over the PA.

'Ladies and gentlemen, this is the captain speaking. Can I have your attention, please. I have an important announcement. I'd appreciate it if you would wake any of your fellow passengers who are sleeping.' After a short pause, she continued. 'We have just received word from OAK headquarters that Isadora Faye has been kidnapped. I repeat, Isadora Faye has been kidnapped. Emergency protocols will be activated on landing.'

Uproar. All around her people were calling out questions, craning round to see what others were doing, some of them even scrambling out of their seats. Across the aisle, Lauren unbuckled her seat belt and slipped out into the gangway.

'Lauren!'

She paused with one hand on the headrest of Bella's seat, her whole body conveying her impatience to be elsewhere.

121

'Yes?'

'What's going on? What are the emergency protocols?'

'They don't apply to us,' Lauren said. 'The directors will go into OAK when we land for an emergency meeting.' She had already released her grip on the headrest and set off down the aisle, calling over her shoulder through the hubbub, 'I don't know anything else but I'll let you know if I find out more.'

Bella stayed in her seat and in time the cacophony died down to a hum. With no Wi-Fi onboard, there wasn't much people could do other than speculate on what had happened, debate the probable next steps and resign themselves to several more hours of inactivity. In spite of everything, after the meal had been served Bella found herself dropping off to sleep. As her thoughts started to lose coherence, fragments of old newsreels – real and imaginary – tumbled and merged in her tired brain: women screaming, a halted cavalcade, sniffer dogs straining at their leads in dripping woods. And then, in high definition, just before she lost consciousness, a newspaper headline above a picture of Isadora's face: 'Kidnapped!'

❧ ❧

The sky over Bella's head was the exact shade you would expect to find labelled 'Sky Blue' in a paint catalogue. The colour faded towards the horizon as if the painter had run out of steam after one coat on that section. A solitary white oval cloud drifted past like the ghost of a zeppelin. She let her eyelids droop, exhaustion and the pleasant warmth of the sun conspiring to weigh them down. An unexpected voice in her ear pinged them back open.

'I can't believe this!' Angela was holding out her phone which displayed the BBC news article about Isadora's kidnapping. The sound of her approach through the communal gardens had been covered by the rushing of the river through the weir.

Bella held up her own phone to show the same article. 'Snap.'

Angela sat down beside her on the bank, rolling up her jeans and dangling her feet in the water. 'What have they told you?'

'Not much yet. They made an announcement on the plane when we were flying back this morning.'

'Really?' Angela's eyes widened as she brushed a trailing strand of wiry grey hair out of her face. 'And what do they think happened?'

There had been no further updates on the plane after the initial announcement. When they'd taxied in there'd been a helicopter waiting alongside the runway. Ben, Catherine and another director who'd been on the trip had been hurried across to it by a group of forbidding-looking men and women. Lauren had whispered that they were cupuli, members of Isadora's personal guard. Bella had managed to catch Ben's eye as he passed her and he had mouthed what she thought was, 'Teddy's okay,' at her. The rest of the staff had been shepherded into their various OAK cars and told to report for work the following morning as usual. Lauren had managed to glean a bit more information which she'd shared with Bella but details were sparse.

Bella had been surprised to see the headline pop up on the BBC website: 'CEO of UK-based multinational kidnapped'. A publicity shot of Isadora, in her trademark Chanel suit and pearls, was followed by a couple of short paragraphs and a promise of more updates to follow. Given Acorn Consulting's ability to keep secrets, the media coverage must have been deliberate, perhaps to help in the search for Isadora.

'I don't know any more than what's been in the news, Angela, to be honest. She didn't turn up for a meeting on Saturday morning and when they went to look for her, they found one of her...' She was about to say bodyguards but stopped herself in time, reasoning that it would sound a little odd for a CEO of a consultancy to have bodyguards. 'One of her team unconscious outside her office. When they went in, there was no sign of Isadora.'

'Have they said how much they want? Or when they'll get in touch?'

Bella shook her head. 'Not as far as I know.'

'It makes that other business seem more sinister, doesn't it?' Angela gave her a meaningful look.

'You mean...?'

'Teddy Thatcher.'

A memory of a pudgy hand with neatly trimmed nails splayed on a concrete floor and, inches away, a glossy pool of blood.

'Yes. I suppose it does.'

'Poor Maggie. This'll bring it all back up to the surface.'

Angela's cat, Siberia brushed past Bella's bare arm and she jumped. 'Gosh, you gave me a fright!' The cat rubbed his cheek against her hand and accepted a tickle under the chin, tilting his head to give her better access.

Angela reached over and gave him a couple of vigorous strokes. 'Naughty old thing.'

Later on, they walked back to the main cluster of houses together. Something white flapped against the trunk of a tree on the drive, another on a telegraph pole. As they drew closer, they saw Maggie attaching a poster to the lamp post by the entrance gate. She heard them approaching and swung around, eyes red, cheeks mottled and damp. Angela raised a hand in greeting but Maggie was already scurrying away.

The poster was a blown-up screenshot of the BBC article, but in place of Isadora a badly cut-out picture of Teddy Thatcher had been pasted under the headline, his mouth a little round 'o' and Maggie's disembodied arm at his side.

Bella had fielded various calls from friends and family during the evening, including Zoe who had asked if she would get a personal bodyguard and gone on to sing Whitney Houston's 'I Will Always Love You' at the top of her voice until Bella hung up.

She was on the phone to her mum, who was advising her to move back to London as it was safer there, when the doorbell went.

'Hang on, Mum,' she said, trotting downstairs in her sheepskin slippers. 'There's someone at the door, let me find out who it is.'

In the doorway stood Maggie. They looked at each other, Bella still holding the phone to her ear. Maggie looked even worse than she had earlier on, a strand of damp hair stuck to one cheek and clear liquid running, unchecked, from her nose.

Bella opened her mouth to speak, but before she could, Maggie had pushed a brown paper bag into her hands. She stood close; eyes boring into Bella's as if trying to see her soul. And then she was gone.

Bella ended the call with her mum, having assured her that if anything else worrying happened she would, of course, consider leaving the perils of Wiltshire behind for the safer environs of the metropolis, and took the paper bag into the living room to open it.

Setting it down on the dining table she extricated a cellophane packet with the tips of her fingers. It contained a pair of white cotton knickers with a pale pink trim. They were folded into an oblong to display the design on the front: a picture of a strawberry and the word 'Tuesday'.

Chapter Thirteen

Right from the moment she walked into the entrance hall on Monday morning, things were different. Kelly wasn't smiling for a start. Bella hadn't been aware that Kelly was capable of any facial expressions other than a smile before today. In their office, there was no sign of Ben and the others were serious and subdued. Even Oscar didn't have his usual witticism to throw at her – although that could also be due to recent events.

'Briefing at ten,' Lauren said, before looking back at her screen.

At five to ten, they all filed downstairs to the huge OAK auditorium. Bella made sure to get a seat next to Oscar, intending to nip the lingering awkwardness in the bud. All around them people were taking their places. In the row in front, she saw a woman with her arm around another colleague's shoulders. Somewhere behind her, she could hear muffled sobs.

A man strode onto the stage whose face seemed familiar but she couldn't place him.

'Who's he?' she whispered to Oscar, leaning in so he could hear.

He started, seeming surprised at her closeness. 'Arran Finn. Head cupule.'

Of course, that was it. That first day when Isadora had shown her round OAK, Finn had been waiting outside the door of the library to escort them to the briefing. Bella hadn't paid him much attention; she did now, and wondered how she'd failed to take notice of him before. He was tall: at least six foot five, perhaps taller. His closely-cropped hair

127

allied to his tight black T-shirt and cargo trousers gave him a military air. He stood with the wide, relaxed stance of a man in control.

When he opened his mouth to speak the room fell silent.

'Our leader, Isadora Faye, was abducted from this building on Saturday morning, following an assault on members of her personal protection team. Extensive searches were initiated but to date, we have been unable to locate Miss Faye or her abductors.'

Finn paused, staring out into the darkened auditorium. His face was being projected on the big screen behind him, his blue eyes bloodshot but unblinking.

'We will find Miss Faye. I give you my personal commitment on that. Our investigations lead us to believe this was an inside job. Someone within OAK – someone within these four walls – is responsible.' There were gasps and mutterings from around the room, people looking around them as if the culprit were about to leap up and announce themselves. 'Our most valuable resource is you. Anything unusual you hear, anything unusual you see, report it to a cupule. With your help, we will find the perpetrators and bring Miss Faye safely home.'

Bella was reminded of school assemblies when the headmaster would urge whoever had committed the latest piece of mischief to own up. It had never been Bella, goody-goody that she was, but each time sweat would break out on her brow and she would feel as guilty as if she were responsible. It was the same thing going through airport security. Despite ensuring she had not so much as a stray mascara in her hand luggage, she knew her shifty eyes suggested that, at the very least, she had a couple of endangered species stuffed down her pants. She risked a glance at Oscar. He was looking as guilty as she felt. But then, the thought struck her, maybe he had something to be guilty about. Anyone in this room could be involved. Then she reminded herself that Oscar had been on Le Chêne at the time and told herself not to be so ridiculous. Plus, he was Oscar. Oscar! A less plausible master-criminal she couldn't imagine. This was what happened when you were asked to be an organisation's eyes and ears and to look out for unusual things. You started suspecting everyone.

Finn hadn't finished, it seemed.

'We will be relying on you to help us, both by relaying your suspicions to us, and just as importantly, by continuing your day-to-day work here at OAK. In that way, our kindnesses will continue and when Miss Faye returns, she will find an organisation as strong and effective as it was when she was snatched away from it. Thank you.'

And then he was gone from the light, as if he had dropped through a trapdoor. The crowded auditorium emptied out in a babble of concerned and animated voices as people discussed what they'd heard. Oscar and the others headed back towards the office but Bella let them get ahead of her and slipped down a side passage. There was something she needed to do first.

❧ ❧

Having regained the main atrium, she turned left down a corridor, passed a series of doors on her right and proceeded to the far end.

'Open.'

The door slid aside, she entered, and it closed behind her. She was in silence, surrounded by rows of identical books.

The library. She hadn't been back here since her first day at OAK. Few people came here, there was little reason to. Padding between the shelves she arrived at The Librarian's desk on which stood a half-full decanter and empty glass alongside a book; but of the man himself, there was no sign. The book, predictably, was bound in fawn leather, indistinguishable from all the others in the room. She reached out a hand to examine it.

'Don't. Touch. It,' hissed a voice.

The Librarian was lying flat on his back on the floor, squeezed underneath one of the bookshelves. His arms were by his sides, his head turned towards her. When he saw that she'd spotted him, he said, as if there were nothing unusual about their relative situations, 'No one touches the books without permission. No one except Isadora Faye.'

'What are you doing?'

'*What are you doing,*' he mimicked her voice, using a whiny tone. 'I'm waiting.'

'Waiting... for what?'

He looked her up and down, his expression that of a scientist who has just uncovered a new strain of stupidity. 'For Isadora to come back, of course.'

'Were you... were you here at OAK when she was taken?'

'Where else would I be?'

'Oh! I don't know. On holiday, maybe.'

He smiled a humourless smile that showed his incisors. Then without warning, he rolled at speed out from under the shelf, forcing Bella to jump out of the way. Hauling himself up with the aid of a chair he staggered across to the desk and took his usual seat. He took the top off the decanter with a clink of glass and poured himself some whisky, dribbling at least a shot's worth onto the desk.

'My job,' he said, when he'd taken a swig, 'is to protect the collection. How do you suppose I could do that if I went on holiday?'

Bella appeared to consider this. 'You might have holiday cover.'

He swung the glass and knocked it against the centre of his chest, splashing whisky down his filthy waistcoat. '*I* am The Librarian. *I* am. No one else.' He got up, rounded the desk and approached her, so close she could feel the fumes singeing her eyeballs. 'I haven't left OAK since 1973.'

'But…'

'Since 1973.'

She nodded. 'I see. Thank you. I'll leave you to your… work.'

He shrugged his shoulders as if it were a matter of utter indifference to him what she did. Then he replaced the empty glass on the desk and rolled back under the bookshelf.

Bella was aware of the presence of cupuli in the building. Before they'd been elusive, now she seemed to see a grim-faced, black-clad figure wherever she turned. There were other faces she didn't recognise too, field agents who'd been called in to help in the search for Isadora. One of the smaller observatories had been turned over to the search, observe and deploy staff had been seconded to the team not to facilitate kindnesses anymore, but to follow up leads and direct agents to check out reported sightings of Isadora. The police came in to talk to Ben and some of the other directors in the afternoon. When Bella saw them leave, trotting self-importantly down the front steps, she wondered how they would feel if they realised to what extent their search operation was being dwarfed by OAK's. All information on police computers had already been hacked and followed up by agents almost before the police had started to process it. Despite Finn's injunction to staff to remain focused on their day jobs, conversations revolved around the latest rumours – where she'd been sighted, who'd set off on the trail, even that she'd been found dead.

They didn't see much of Ben for the rest of the day. Bella wanted to ask him about Teddy Thatcher but couldn't get to speak to him on his own. Finn's urging to be on the lookout for anything suspicious had made her uncomfortable too. Ben had been with her in Le Chêne when Isadora had gone missing, true, but if anything counted as suspicious behaviour it was Ben's. The secret meeting with James and Lauren in The Royal Oak. His insistence that she keep the attempt on Teddy's life to herself. She wrangled in her mind all afternoon about whether she should tell Finn her suspicions, but in the end, she decided to give Ben one last chance. She planned to follow him home that evening. Either he'd be going straight home and she could speak to him alone and try to get him to tell her what was going on or he might go somewhere else, which could open up a whole new avenue of investigation. He might go to the supermarket. He might go to an evening class in basket-weaving (unlikely, but you never knew). Or he might go to the place where he was holding Isadora hostage.

He seemed preoccupied as he got into his car, a beautiful Aston Martin in racing green, and drove out of the car park. Other people were leaving too and she let a couple of cars out ahead of her before setting off. At the bottom of the drive, Ben and the car behind him turned left. The next car turned right, and then it was Bella. She hesitated for a moment. The way home was right. What Others Might Think of Her was crouching in her lap, clinging with a painful grip around her waist. What was she doing? To be caught, trailing your boss, would be a remarkably stupid thing to do and one she would have trouble explaining away. She would look like an idiot playing at being a spy in the midst of a very serious situation.

The car behind her revved its engine. Glancing in her rear-view mirror she raised an apologetic hand then pressed 'record route' on her satnav. The last thing she wanted was for Ben to lead her to his kidnapper's lair and then her horrendous sense of direction to mean she couldn't tell the police where it was. She indicated left and pulled out onto the main road.

Their little procession of three cars motored along the A-road. As they approached a crossroads, Ben indicated right while the other car looked to be carrying straight on. There was nothing behind her so Bella pulled up for a minute at the turning to provide some distance between her car and the Aston. Setting off again she started to panic – she'd played it too cool. She'd turned onto the road Ben had taken but his car was nowhere in sight and of course, she reminded herself, he was driving a high-performance sports car while she was at the wheel of an Alfa Romeo with a hundred thousand miles on the clock. She put her foot down. The hedges flew past and she prayed there were no speed cameras as she approached a sharp right-hand corner. Around the bend she caught up with him at a temporary traffic light by some roadworks. An estate car was waiting to pull out from a nearby driveway, she waved it out and it pulled up between her and Ben. The lights turned green and they set off.

In front of her, the battered Volvo estate chuntered along at forty. Bella found herself edging closer and closer to its rusty bumper, expletives filling the air like fireworks. When it braked and indicated left, she didn't even wait for it to complete the turn before putting her foot down and swerving around it. She shot along at seventy miles per hour, slowing for a bend which brought Ben's Aston Martin into view in the distance, turning right down a dirt track.

She drove past the turning at a crawl. The track that Ben had taken led through fields to a group of farm buildings silhouetted against the horizon. The countryside was quiet, with no other properties in sight. She couldn't risk driving down the track behind him. Pulling into a layby where she could see the farm across the fields, she watched the Aston Martin disappear round the back of one of the buildings.

Oh God, what to do? What Others Might Think of Her grazed her face with its teeth. Imagine, it seemed to be whispering, imagine Ben discovering you've followed him. What will you say? What will he think of you? Much better to give it all up and go home.

But imagine, she thought to herself, if Isadora is being held hostage in one of those barns. It struck her that up until that point she'd only given semi-credence to her own suspicions. Ben turning up at this isolated spot put a whole new spin on things.

There was no movement by the buildings. She rolled down the window and listened. No noise from the Aston Martin's engine. She gripped the wheel as she tried to make up her mind.

Why would Ben want Isadora out of the way? An ambitious young director, maybe he wasn't willing to wait around for the death of an elderly woman for his moment of glory? He could have arranged to have Isadora kidnapped while he was on Le Chêne to give himself an alibi. Perhaps Ben was forcing her to hand over the reins, to give him whatever knowledge, codes, access to funds were necessary to run OAK and AC.

She shoved What Others Might Think of Her off her lap, wound up the window and got out. A weapon – she needed a weapon. Opening the door again, she looked blankly at the contents of the car. There was a pair of old clogs on the floor in the back, but even she couldn't imagine charging into the barn with a war cry on her lips and a clog in each outstretched hand. There was an umbrella, that would have to do. At the last moment, she grabbed a pen from the centre console and stuck it in her pocket.

'What are you going to do?' enquired What Others Might Think of Her. 'Write him to death?'

Ignoring this jibe she clambered over the gate into the field, wobbling a little on the top bar – in her head, planning how she might relate this adventure should she ever be called upon to do so, she 'vaulted' it – and set off at a jog towards the barns.

Overhead a couple of birds of prey were wheeling around, coasting on the air currents. She wished she had their vantage point. One barn was side on to her; another at right angles, to it, its closed door facing her. All she could distinguish of a third building, visible through the gap between the two nearest barns, was corrugated iron.

Her heart was hammering in her chest, her breathing ragged. At any moment, Ben might appear around the corner of one of the buildings and see her jogging towards him. Ben, or an accomplice with a gun. What would she do then? Throw her umbrella at him? Threaten to take down his particulars with her trusty pen?

When Bella reached the nearest barn, she flattened herself against it, catching her breath. She strained her ears. Outside the barn, she could hear the wind rustling the leaves in a nearby clump of trees, a distant train, a slight hum from electricity lines crossing the field. Inside the barn, nothing. She started to shuffle along the wall. When she'd progressed about five feet along the side of the building, her fingers touched the edge of a hole in the wooden planking, about the size of a tennis ball, at waist height. Bella bent down and peered in.

At first, all she could see was a thin door-shaped square of light on the opposite side. As her eye grew accustomed to the gloom, she could make out something bulky – hay bales? Yes, they definitely looked like hay bales. And then she found it didn't matter if they were hay bales or elephants because someone had grabbed her arm and she'd snapped upright, striking out hard with the umbrella. The grip on her arm loosened and she spun round to see Ben nursing his jaw.

'What the hell, Bella?' Shock and pain were written across his brow in furrowed lines.

Her heart was pumping like it was supercharged, rebounding off the walls of her chest. What Others Might Think of Her was bouncing up and down at her side, urging her to apologise and beg forgiveness.

'What are you doing here?' She tried to make her stance convey a confidence she didn't feel, feet planted firmly on the scrubby grass, umbrella outstretched.

The shock fell from his face like a crumpled sheet tugged straight, and he laughed.

'I love that. You trail me all the way from work, smack me round the face with an umbrella and then ask *me* what *I'm* doing here!'

Heat rose in Bella's face as anger flooded her body.

'Isadora's been abducted. Teddy Thatcher's been attacked. Arran Finn is telling us it's an inside job.' With each point, she jabbed her umbrella at him and took a step closer, until the final jab caught him in the chest. 'You leave OAK this evening and drive to this place, which – unless you're moonlighting as a farmer – seems suspicious. So yes, I want to know what you're doing here.'

He took hold of the wrist that held the umbrella and moved it aside. 'I'll tell you, but without your lethal weapon being involved if you don't mind. I'm here because I saw you shadowing me as soon as we pulled out of the OAK gates. I could think of two reasons for that. One, you're trying to keep tabs on me. Two, you want to speak to me alone. Either way, this seemed like a nice deserted place to end up.'

She could still hear the blood rushing in her ears. His hand still held her wrist, and now his other hand was resting on her upper arm, she could feel the warmth of his fingers through her shirt.

'I want to know what happened with Teddy Thatcher,' she said.

His gaze dropped from her eyes to her lips and back again. 'He's alive. I can't tell you more than that. I wish I could, believe me. But at the moment it's too dangerous.'

She stared into his eyes, trying to read him. There was sincerity in his tone, she felt convinced of it, but was that because she was willing it to be true?

'Is that it?' She frowned. 'That's all you're going to tell me? And I'm supposed to be okay with that?'

'I'm sorry I can't tell you more. It would be a hell of a lot easier for me too. But seeing as I can't, you're going to have to trust me. Ask yourself, based on everything you know about me, if you think I'm capable of kidnap and murder. What's the likelihood?'

She asked herself and her mental swingometer, right at that moment with his face inches from hers as she breathed in the familiar citrus scent, was thundering towards 'no'. He sounded truthful. Didn't he?

'I have to take a leap of faith, then, is that what you're saying? On the basis that you don't *seem* like a murderer?' Bella's tone still held some defiance, as if to overcompensate for her deteriorating resolve.

'Come on, Bella. Think about it. If I was a murderer, I could have got rid of you in that basement in Le Chêne. I wouldn't have risked letting you go so you could tell people about Teddy.'

Their faces were so close now that she could see his hazel eyes had a narrow circle of bright green around the iris.

'You could be planning on getting rid of me now, out here,' she said. His breath tickled her cheek, making the hairs on the back of her neck stand up.

'That's not what I'm planning at all,' he said, just before his mouth touched hers.

One part of Bella's brain was jumping up and down and screaming that this wasn't in the plan, but it was soon overpowered by the bit of her brain that was finding Ben's latest argument irresistibly convincing.

Chapter Fourteen

Driving home later that evening, she glanced in the rear-view mirror and plucked a piece of hay from her hair.

She reflected on her detective skills. Although she could vouch that the main barn contained nothing other than scratchy hay bales, she hadn't investigated either of the other buildings.

At this moment, Isadora could be tied up, mumbling hopelessly through her gag, at the sound of Bella's car disappearing off into the night. Miss Marple would never have let the trail go cold while she took a vigorous roll in the hay – but then Miss Marple had never met Ben.

She placed the palm of her hand on the back of her neck, recalling the warmth of his arm underneath it as they'd lain side by side.

'Do you trust me now?' he'd asked.

She snorted. 'Why would I trust you any more now?'

He propped himself up on one elbow and looked at her, mock-shocked. 'You mean you'd do this with someone you don't trust?'

'I'm planning on making a habit of it.'

She pulled him down with a hand on the back of his head and their mouths were smiling as they kissed.

After Ben had watched Bella's car disappear down the dusty track, squinting his eyes against the setting sun, he turned and re-entered the barn. A scrap of blue fabric caught his eye, sticking out at the foot of the stack of hay bales.

Bending down to retrieve it, he realised it was Bella's umbrella.

He shook his head as he picked it up. It was one of those extra light ones, even in the hands of a seasoned martial arts exponent it wouldn't be much of a threat. What had she been planning to do with it?

On the way back to his car, he popped his head into the other buildings to check all was well and that the little yellow kit car was still well camouflaged behind stacks of straw.

When Bella got home, she felt happy and reckless. She got out her phone and called Zoe.

'I've done something stupid,' she blurted out as soon as Zoe answered.

'Oh good, what?'

'It begins with a B. Or rather he does.'

There was silence and then, 'Ben! Hooray! Tell me all.'

Bella flopped down on the sofa and flicked the TV on with the remote. Her next words stuck in her throat as the picture came on.

'Bella?' Zoe prompted. 'Still there?'

'Sorry, Zoe, there's something weird going on, I'll call you back.'

The national news had finished and they'd switched to local broadcasts. The kidnapping story was big news for the region and had been the headline on all local TV and radio bulletins since Isadora had gone missing, despite the lack of any firm information. The coverage reminded Bella of when the Duchess of Cambridge had gone into labour with her first child – journalists interviewing other journalists about nothing in increasing desperation as they waited for the birth of a prince. Except in this instance, it felt very much like they were waiting for a death.

Tonight, they'd found something to vary the monotony.

'After crucial hours passing with no developments in the Isadora Faye kidnapping story, *West Country Tonight* has uncovered an important new angle. Local woman, Maggie Thatcher, claims that Miss Faye is not the only Acorn Consulting employee to have been abducted. We join our reporter, Shobha Sharma, for this exclusive report from Acorn Consulting in Halfway.'

Bella turned up the volume, eyes fixed on the screen. The reporter's bronze bob gleamed and the camera zoomed out to reveal Maggie standing beside her, looking off to one side.

An attempt had been made to smooth down Maggie's hair but one intransigent tuft stuck out above her right ear. Her pale green jumper had a dark stain on it and her glasses were askew. Behind them, the iron gates of Acorn Consulting stood open as usual.

The reporter turned to Maggie. 'Mrs Thatcher, can you tell us what happened to your husband?'

'They took him.' She jerked a thumb backwards, towards the gates and the driveway beyond.

The reporter nodded understandingly. 'And by "them" you mean Acorn Consulting?'

'Yes, I mean Acorns! Them!' She glared at the reporter.

'When did you last see your husband, Edward Thatcher?'

'I've told you this! It was Tuesday because I'd done Teddy his ham and cheese sandwiches. Not cheddar.' She paused and pointed an accusatory finger at the reporter, who shook her head as if to disassociate herself with any suspicions of cheddar. 'He never liked cheddar. Edam it was. And honey roast ham, on Kingsmill.' She stopped, pressing her lips together as if that was all she had to say on the subject.

'And when he had taken the last lunch you ever gave your husband, what did he do then?'

'He got in his car and came here. Poor beggar.'

'And did you ever see him again?'

Maggie gawped at the woman. 'He disappeared! That's what I've been telling you! They took him.'

The reporter turned back to the camera, seemingly unaffected by Maggie's combative style.

'Mr Thatcher disappeared around four months ago and the police have never been able to establish his whereabouts. Acorn Consulting claims that he didn't arrive at work on that fateful day—'

'That's a lie!' Maggie broke in. 'He went to work and they shut him up. And I can prove it.'

'How can you prove it, Mrs Thatcher?'

'Stuff he left. Stuff they didn't want to get out. He knew they wanted to keep him quiet so he left it at our house.'

The reporter leaned in eagerly. 'Why have you never mentioned this before?'

'I did! I told that useless shower at the police station but they weren't interested. And now it's gone and happened again!'

⊰⊱

Back at home, Ben almost choked on his spaghetti carbonara as he watched Maggie yelling and glaring down the camera. He pressed a contact on his phone.

'Have you seen it? Let's get over there.'

Grabbing his car keys, he ran for the door.

It took him ten minutes, racing down empty country lanes, to reach the village where Maggie – and Bella, he remembered – lived. He parked a street away and hurried to Maggie's house.

She lived on a road of 1930s semis with large front gardens. The neighbouring house had a neat lawn and borders, in contrast with Maggie's garden which was like a meadow, the only sign of care and cultivation a semi-mature tree planted dead centre. An oak, he realised. Even with every sense on the alert, he wondered about the significance of that. A coincidence, planted by previous occupants? Or by Teddy, as a tribute?

Maggie's house was in darkness. He strode up to the house next door, and made as if to ring the bell, glancing up and down the street as he did so. Most cars were parked on wide two-vehicle driveways. There was an estate car parked on the opposite side of the street, a few houses away. It was hard to tell in the dusk, but there didn't seem to be anyone in it. Further away was a grey van and across from that a four-by-four. He didn't like the look of that. As he looked, the four-by-four revved into life and began crawling down the street towards him.

This time he rang the bell in earnest. A few seconds later the door inched open revealing an elderly man in a bulky brown cardigan and thick glasses. He peered uncertainly at Ben.

'Good evening, sir.' Ben pulled an identity badge out of his pocket and flicked it under the man's eyes before putting it away. 'No need to be alarmed but I need to access your garden.'

Ben glanced along the road, the four-by-four was still fifty metres away, gaining pace.

The old man looked flustered. 'I don't... Who are you?'

Ben took a step forward, smiling, forcing the man back into the house. 'Nothing to worry about, sir, won't take a moment. If you could direct me to the door into the garden.' He pulled the front door shut behind him. The house smelled musty, like damp clothes.

'Well, it's...' The man waved a shaky hand towards a door on the right. 'But I don't know why...'

'We've had reports of intruders in the neighbouring property, sir. Nothing to worry about but I would advise you to lock the door behind me.'

Ben opened a door into a grubby kitchen with chipped white units. The back door was stiff but he forced it open and stepped outside. Behind him, there were fumblings as the door was relocked from the inside.

Ben sent up a silent prayer of thanks to the gods of garden planning on finding that only a low, scraggy hedge separated the two gardens. Feeling along it, pressing for resistance, he found a thinning patch and half pushed, half climbed through and over.

On the other side, he paused, listening. No sound from within Maggie's house. He crept across the moss-covered patio and tried sliding the French door across. It was unlocked but he winced as metal screeched against metal. If anyone was waiting for him, he had just given them an early warning signal.

He slid the door shut behind him, pulled his phone out of his pocket and switched on the torch, swinging its beam across the room. It was empty – and chaotic. A coffee table was overturned, china figurines smashed on the hearth tiles, pictures scattered across the floor, their backs torn off.

Ben knew Maggie was an eccentric, but he couldn't believe that even she would have a house this messy. A carriage clock, face-up on the sideboard, continued to tick despite its smashed case. Careful to avoid making a noise, he picked his way through the debris into the hall. A quick look in the other ground floor rooms revealed similar scenes of carnage. He came back into the hall in time to hear the sound of the French door squealing. Someone else was sneaking into the living room.

The intruder tiptoed into the hall – and into the arms of Ben. There was a struggle and then, as Ben pointed his torch at his captive's face: 'It *is* you. Sorry, wasn't sure.'

Lauren put a hand to her throat. 'Shit, Ben! You scared the life out of me.'

'I had to be sure.' They were both whispering. 'I haven't been upstairs yet; they could still be here.'

Their inspection of the three bedrooms and bathroom revealed nothing more than further disarray and what looked like an anti-Acorns shrine on the wall of the master bedroom, created from defaced newspaper articles and Isadora's face on a dartboard. They had to assume that Maggie wasn't very good at darts, as most of the holes peppered the surrounding wall.

'Do you think they found it?' Lauren asked.

Ben shrugged. 'Impossible to say.'

'What do you think they've done with her?'

'Again, impossible to say.'

Lauren looked at Ben's face, stern and thoughtful in the dim light. 'Shit.' She nudged him. 'We'd better go. Police could be here any minute.'

❦ ❦

On the dining table at the other end of the room, still in their cellophane wrapper, were the 'Tuesday' knickers Maggie had pressed into Bella's hand the previous day. Bella turned off the TV and set the remote down on the table next to them. Up until now, she'd assumed the knickers was another eccentricity of Maggie's, but could they be significant in some way? Was the word 'Tuesday' important? Touching the packet, she realised the centre of the tightly folded material was firmer than she would have expected. Positively hard, in fact.

Flipping it over she unsealed the flap. Drawing out the knickers, she unfolded the white fabric. There, hidden in the centre, was a plain black USB stick.

❦ ❦

The doorbell rang at the exact moment that she was lining the USB up with the port on the side of her laptop. *No, no, no!* To be interrupted when she could be seconds away from finding out what had happened to Teddy and who was holding Isadora was excruciating. Particularly as no doubt it would be Maggie herself, demanding her knickers back. All the lights were on so there was no chance of pretending she was out this time. She hurried to open the door.

'Ben!' She held the door open, blocking the way.

He produced an umbrella from behind his back. 'You forgot this.'

'Oh! You didn't need to come all this way; you could have given it to me in the office.'

'I know. But it was a good excuse.' He leant forward and planted a light kiss on her lips. 'Can I come in?'

No! No, you can't bloody come in!

'Sure,' Bella heard herself say, scrambling to come up with a way to get him straight back out again. 'Get yourself inside before the neighbours see you. There'll be outraged letters in the parish magazine. I can see the headlines now, "Local spinster in doorstep-kissing shocker!"' She was babbling, she knew, while her brain whirred frantically.

Leading him into the living room she swept the knickers off the tabletop onto a chair before he could spot them. Ben indicated her open laptop. 'Working late?'

This was her moment to decide. Could she risk telling him? If she thought he was trustworthy it would make sense to look at the USB together.

She smiled and flipped the lid down. *Come on, Bella, use your bloody brain, what were you doing on your laptop? Think of something to get rid of him!* 'I was on Skype with an old friend in Australia. She's splitting up with her husband. She's in a real state.'

Ben looked at his watch. 'Wow, it must be the crack of dawn there?'

'Mmm. She couldn't sleep. Anyway, I hung up to answer the door, but she's very upset. I should call her back.'

He didn't seem to be listening. Walking over to the mantelpiece he picked up a marble candlestick, weighing it in his hand.

'Did you see the local news tonight?' he asked. 'Teddy Thatcher's wife was on it.'

He replaced the candlestick. Bella realised she was holding her breath and slowly let it out, trying not to make a noise. Had he seen her with the USB via her webcam?

'Oh! No, I didn't see it.'

'According to Maggie, Teddy left some kind of evidence against AC behind.' He was close behind her now, trailing his fingers down her neck. Then, taking a strand of her hair, he wound it around his finger. It made her shiver.

'Evidence against AC? What do you mean, evidence of what?'

The hair wound tighter. 'I've no idea. Probably nothing. AC is completely above board, as you know. But if someone suspected something incendiary existed, and that it was hidden in Mrs Thatcher's house...'

'Shouldn't you check on her?' The strand of hair was released and he went back to stroking her neck.

'I did. I was too late.'

'Too late! What do you mean?'

'She wasn't there. But the house had been ransacked.'

'Oh God.' Bella covered her mouth.

'Can't tell if they found anything. Or where she is now. I don't even know what they were looking for.'

It was as if the USB next to the laptop were pulsing, glowing red, yelling, 'Look at me! Look at me!' He was talking again, she tried to concentrate on what he was saying.

'I've phoned into OAK, of course. They've got agents looking for her.'

She frowned. 'What will they do when they find her?'

There was a pause. 'Take her home, of course. Make sure she's alright. What else would they do?'

The stroking had stopped now, she realised. There was cold air where his hand had been.

'I don't know... I hadn't thought about it.' She turned around. 'Listen, I really should call my friend back. She'll wonder why it's taking me so long.'

She saw his gaze linger on the laptop for a moment and then he smiled, trailing a finger down her jawline. 'Of course. Don't stay up too late, you'll need to be in a fit state for work tomorrow. You wouldn't want to get in trouble with your boss.'

'No,' Bella agreed. 'He can be a right arsehole.'

❦ ❦

She watched Ben get into his car, holding her breath. The headlights swung past the window, the sound of the engine dropped out as he pulled up at the exit, then purred into life and away. She pulled the curtains tight. Was OAK watching her now? If Ben knew she had the USB, and that it was important, he wouldn't have left without it, would he? She had to take the risk and assume she wasn't being watched. Switching off the webcam and Wi-Fi on her laptop to be on the safe side, she took it into the windowless downstairs loo. Flipping down the seat she settled the laptop on her lap and stuck in the USB.

There were four files, two Excel, one email and one image file. She opened the image file entitled 'Screenshot 14122019' first. It showed an HTML file filled with lines and lines of code. She scrutinised it for a while, willing it to make sense, but it was gobbledygook apart from the name of a well-known corporate bank near the top of the screen.

150

Next, she opened the Excel file named 'Transfers'. Along the top row, the headers were Date, Transaction ID, Client, Amount, Recipient ID. There were fifty-six rows and the figures were in the millions for each transaction. She recognised some of the names in the Client column as customers of Acorn Consulting. The dates started in late November 2019 and ended on the fourteenth of December that year.

If these transactions were above board, why save them to a USB alongside a screenshot of what, even to her untrained eye, looked very much like the evidence of someone doing something dodgy to the backend of a corporate bank's website.

Could it be that someone in OAK had been stealing money in the millions – *or even billions*, she thought as her eye scanned the row of figures again. Nowhere did AC or OAK's name appear on the spreadsheet and the Recipient IDs were all different, which gave her pause for thought. But then, if someone was sophisticated enough to hack a bank and steal funds in those amounts, they wouldn't pop it straight into their current account, would they? Presumably, the Recipient IDs represented offshore accounts or subsidiary companies that the money was being passed through.

Money that had been stolen from their clients. By whom? And why did Teddy have access to the audit trail?

The fingers that gripped the side of the laptop had gone white, and when she went to open the second Excel file her hand was shaking. This file was called 'Expansion' and its contents were more obscure. Once more she was faced with rows and columns of information but this time the left-hand

151

column contained the names of towns, some of which she recognised as being in America, others she hadn't heard of. The top row contained various dates throughout 2019, and against each town percentage figures had been entered right across the row, alongside each individual date. She mulled this over. How were these percentages related to the money stolen in the other spreadsheet? The Transfers spreadsheet showed figures in pounds not dollars, and the dates didn't seem to match up other than in one or two instances. No matter how lateral she tried to make her thinking, she couldn't find a connection.

Not for the first time, she wished she'd paid more attention when a boyfriend at university had tried to teach her how to do cryptic crosswords. Not only would she have been able to dazzle fellow train passengers by ostentatiously dashing off a *Guardian* crossword in the time it took to get from, say, Reading to Paddington, it might have offered the marginally greater benefit of helping her solve what appeared to be one of the largest corporate frauds of her era.

She gave up and double-clicked on the last file. An email opened on the screen.

Subject: Meeting
From: Ben Elliott
To: Teddy Thatcher
Date: 14th December 2019
Teddy,
I've stumbled across something you'll wish I hadn't. Meet me in Room 172 tomorrow at 7pm. If I have to come and find you it'll be worse for you.
B

Bella read the three short lines over and over. They didn't make sense. Why was Ben threatening Teddy? With what?

A bang on the front door made her leap from her seat, whacking the laptop against the sink.

'Shit, shit, shit!' she whispered, flying out of the loo and down the corridor in search of somewhere to hide the USB. She opened kitchen cupboards at random, pulled out a bag of icing sugar and poked the little black stick down into it until it was submerged.

The banging was repeated, louder. She rinsed the powder from her fingers under the tap and raced down the corridor to open the door.

A sour-looking cupule stood on the doorstep. 'I'm taking you into OAK. Finn's orders.'

Chapter Fifteen

A few words exchanged with the cupule as she got in the car had reassured her that the situation wasn't as dire as it seemed. All HQ employees were being called in, not just her, with cars being sent to collect those in the immediate vicinity.

The car flew down the country lanes, both occupants silent. Bella was concentrating on behaving as a guiltless member of OAK would do in this situation. She had to hope they knew nothing about the USB and act accordingly. She'd asked the cupule – with an expression suggesting calm concern, she hoped – why they were being called in and whether she should bring anything with her. He had been uncommunicative in the extreme, repeating that she had to leave right now with an overnight bag, and she had given up trying to extract anything else after they set off. Which at least meant her mind was free to try to untangle everything she'd seen and heard that evening.

Maggie had asked her for help before she went to Le Chêne, and then had given her the USB either in the hope that she would know what do with it or at least would keep it safe. Bella felt a wave of pity for Maggie, dismissed by the police and her own neighbours as an unhinged eccentric with paranoid delusions. When all the while she'd been right. Something was very wrong at Acorn Consulting.

How had Teddy got hold of the evidence, was he involved in the fraud or had he stumbled across it? Somehow, he'd got to Le Chêne and been attacked there. A parade of potential suspects trooped across Bella's mind's eye. Any number of people could be involved in the ordering of his abduction and murder including Isadora, Ben, The Librarian, Catherine, Lauren, James, Finn... even Oscar? Oscar, she had to acknowledge, seemed the least likely of all of them.

The car turned into the AC gates, between the uplit stone acorns, and joined the stream of cars rumbling down the drive.

Did the fact of Isadora's disappearance preclude her from involvement in Teddy's kidnapping and the corporate fraud on the USB? Or was that a double-bluff, had Isadora gone into hiding to throw everyone off the scent? Her mind struggled to map out all the potential scenarios. If only she had access to one of those crime scene walls from detective programmes, where she could take the tangled mess of her thoughts and pin them down with photos, Post-its and interconnecting lines.

Another thing any good detective needed was a partner. She had to find someone she could trust to help her. Ben was too risky; she still couldn't be sure how he was involved. Lauren was somehow caught up in whatever Ben was up to, so that ruled her out. The one single name that popped up, the one single person she could risk trusting with what she knew, was Oscar.

The car pulled up at the front steps, she thanked the driver and got out. In the entrance hall, a gaunt-looking Kelly was directing new arrivals to go and wait in their own offices. 'You'll be called down to OAK for a briefing once everyone gets here.'

Bella found Oscar alone in their office, staring at his computer screen. He glanced up as she came in, eyes glazed, then looked back at his monitor.

'Are you okay?' She walked over to see what he was looking at. His screen was blank.

'System's gone down.'

Bella gaped at him. Never had there been the slightest IT blip at OAK. Not during her own time there nor, as far as she was aware, prior to her arrival. She wasn't even sure where the IT support department was.

With no access to its systems, OAK's powers were decimated.

❧ ❧

The call came through, and Bella and Oscar joined the stream of people heading towards the lifts down to OAK. The lights were dimmer than usual and flickered on and off.

'I don't like this,' Bella whispered to Oscar as they queued for the lift.

'No shit,' he shot back. 'Do you think everyone else is having the time of their lives?'

'No, I mean if Finn is right that someone at OAK is behind all this, then it feels dangerous everyone being called in here together.' They shuffled forward into the lift and Bella kept silent while it descended.

When they got out into the hubbub of the atrium and followed the flow of people towards the auditorium she added, 'Whoever's shutting down the systems and kidnapping people could have us right where they want us. We're like rats in a sack.'

❧ ❧

Where once efficiency and determination reigned, now the faces they passed displayed panic, confusion and, in some cases, fear. In the corridors, people pushed and barged past like headless chickens.

When Lauren appeared from a side corridor it was a relief to see a familiar and relatively calm face. 'Hi, you two.' Her smile was a little forced.

'What's happened to the systems, do you know?' Bella asked.

Before she could answer, a door further up the corridor opened and Finn appeared, looking even more forbidding than usual.

Lauren nodded her head in his direction. 'He's the man with all the answers.'

Bella noticed the swarming of people around her had grown more purposeful, with everyone heading down the corridor in Finn's wake. As they passed an observatory, she looked in and was shocked to see all the screens were blank.

She nudged Oscar. 'Even down here…'

He looked where she was pointing and nodded.

'I thought they'd have some kind of backup,' she said, 'special servers, a failover system.'

Lauren, walking in front of them, called over her shoulder, 'They do. They've gone down too.'

'Christ.'

They filed into the half-filled, dimly lit auditorium and found seats.

Bella turned to Lauren. 'If there are no working observatories and the systems are down, how are they organising the acts of kindness?' she whispered.

Lauren looked at her, eyebrows raised, waiting for her to work it out.

'They're not?' Bella said.

Lauren shrugged her shoulders. 'There's no Plan B for this. No way to mitigate against the whole of OAK shutting down – how could there be?'

Bella tried to picture the impact. Tiny in individual cases, perhaps, but as a feeling, a consciousness leaching across the land… She felt sick.

The noise intensified as every seat was filled, people packed in together on the stairs, standing in rows at the back of the room, peering in through doorways. Finn leapt up onto the stage, his face reproduced in close-up on the big screen behind him. The skin on his temples and cheekbones caught the light, shiny and tight. A blue vein stood out under his left eye.

Bella had a flashback to an incident in her previous job when a colleague had collapsed. The first-aider they'd called had struggled to retain his glee as he put the prone woman into the recovery position and called the ambulance – after years of doling out plasters and paracetamol his moment of glory had arrived. If there was never an emergency, he could never show how essential he was. Would someone like Finn go as far as orchestrating chaos in order to get a chance to take control? His unblinking eyes, staring out into the darkness as he prepared to speak, certainly looked fanatical enough.

'Isadora Faye is still missing and we have no information as to her whereabouts,' he said, his amplified voice rich and soft in the vastness of the space. 'Both OAK and Acorn Consulting technology has been sabotaged and can't be relied on. Potential evidence as to the whereabouts of Teddy Thatcher and Isadora Faye appears to have been stolen from

Teddy Thatcher's house, we believe by an OAK employee.' He paused, to let this information sink in. 'For this reason, I have taken the unprecedented step of calling in every one of our office-based staff. OAK is under attack and I intend to find out who is behind it. No one will leave this complex until I give permission.'

Consternation from around the room. Lauren seemed unperturbed but Oscar's jaw had dropped. Rats in a sack. Bella had a sudden urge to get out of that windowless room into the cool night air.

'We have ample resources here to cater for everyone. The cupuli will be organising you into teams to set up dormitories and—' Finn broke off as he was drowned out by shouted questions.

'What about my kids?'

'I need to get home to give my mum her medicine in the morning!'

'Can we at least phone our families?'

Finn raised a hand and waited for quiet. 'I understand your concerns. But I cannot risk the safety of anyone in OAK until we find the perpetrators. As you leave this room, you'll be given a pack. It will show you which group you're in and where your base is. A cupule will be there to meet you and they will answer your questions.'

At least she, Bella, didn't have anyone at home waiting for her to come back – not so much as a cat needing to be fed. A few weeks ago, that thought might have prompted self-pity but now she felt relieved. She needed to be able to concentrate on working out what had happened to Isadora and Teddy without any distractions.

Acts of Kindness

Finn called the board members up onto the stage to report on the state of systems and staff attendance from their various departments. One by one they made their reports. Ben alone didn't appear.

'Before you leave, I have a piece of unpleasant news to share. You'll notice that Ben Elliott is not present among his fellow board members this evening. Ben has not been seen for several hours. We are investigating two potential scenarios. One, that Ben is another kidnapping victim. Two, that he is himself one of the perpetrators.'

There were gasps of disbelief.

Finn raised a hand for quiet. 'We will not rest until we have hunted down and brought to justice the people who have attacked us in this way, no matter who they are. If you have any information on Ben Elliott's whereabouts this evening, make it known to myself or another cupule at once.'

160

Chapter Sixteen

Shobha Sharma scrolled through her list of contacts and pressed 'Jed, Head of News.'

He answered and Shobha could hear the sounds of the busy newsroom on the tinny speakers of the van. 'Yeah?'

'I want to go and talk to that Thatcher woman. See if I can butter her up and get her to hand over whatever this "evidence" is. It'd make a great scoop.'

'Do it,' Jed said and hung up.

'You guys wait here. I don't want to spook her with the lights and cameras,' she said to her crew. 'I'll call you in when she's settled.'

She walked up the path to Maggie's 30s semi feeling like she already knew what kind of stuff she'd find inside. Her top three bets were china shepherdesses, old copies of the *Daily Mail* and those small round white plastic things that you shoved tea towels into.

The doorbell chimed a loud and elaborate run of notes. No answer. She rang the bell again and tried the handle. It was unlocked. She eased it open and slipped through the gap.

'Mrs Thatcher? Hello, Mrs Thatcher?'

She felt about on the wall to her left until she found a light switch.

'Oh shit.'

She stepped back out of the house and ran to the van. 'You've got to get in there now. The house has been burgled.'

❧ ❧

To avoid any backlash from the police for disturbing a crime scene, the crew filmed through the open front door.

The camera panned over the drawer of the hall table which had been pulled out and was lying upside down on the carpet, surrounded by keys, pens, string and various other bits of detritus. A couple of pairs of shoes were strewn across the floor. Through the open door to the left the living room was in a similar state.

When the camera shut off, Shobha said, 'We haven't interviewed the neighbours yet. We might get something there.'

Ailsa, the camera operator, nodded her head. 'Okay, let's do it before the police arrive.'

❧ ❧

By this time on a normal evening, Wilfred Perdew would have been in bed with his current large-print biography, his magnifying glass on a chain and a cup of weak tea. His son, Paul, kept trying to persuade him to try audiobooks but they weren't the same as reading.

Tonight, though, he was still jittery after the incident with the young man at his door. He sat on the bay window seat, holding the curtains open a fraction, watching the activity around the Thatchers' house. Two women broke away from the knot of people gathered there and walked up the path to his front door. He heard the knocker go.

He hesitated, waiting to see if the knock would be repeated. Ordinarily, he wouldn't consider opening the door this late at night, but one of the women seemed familiar. The knock came again and he levered himself up from the window seat with difficulty. The woman with the shiny bob smiled warmly at him as he opened the door.

'I'm sorry to disturb you this late at night.' She held out a slim, gold-ring-laden hand. 'I'm Shobha Sharma, *West Country Tonight*, and this is my colleague, Ailsa.'

That was where he knew her from! The six o'clock news was an old friend to Wilfred, heralding as it did the end of the long day and the approach of teatime. The cast of characters was familiar, from the newsreaders and weather girl down to the newer reporters such as this one.

'Oh!' He smiled back at her. This would be something to tell the postman in the morning, and the man at the newsagent. 'Hello. Pleased to meet you.'

'Would you mind if we came in?'

Once they were settled in the shabby lounge, clutching cups of coffee, Shobha on a faded burgundy and cream striped armchair, and Wilfred and Ailsa on the settee, which he didn't usually like to sit on because it was hard to get out of – once they were settled, Shobha got to work.

'Wilfred. May I call you Wilfred?' She paused and raised the mug to her mouth. Her beautiful black-ringed eyes watched him over the rim, belying the casualness of her tone. 'I wondered if you'd noticed anything out of the ordinary going on in the street this evening? Or strange noises next door?'

Wilfred considered her question. 'I'm a bit hard of hearing so there might have been noises next door. I couldn't say for certain.'

Shobha nodded encouragingly.

'But,' Wilfred went on, wanting to please her, 'there was something.'

She leaned forward. 'Yes?'

'A man. Came round earlier. Wanted to get in the garden.'

'Could you describe this man?'

Wilfred gave her Ben's description, which wasn't much to go on: a youngish, tallish man in dark clothes with a nondescript accent. And a badge – but he didn't know what kind of badge. Shobha pressed him on what time it had happened, whether he'd come in a car or on foot, where he'd gone after he'd entered the garden.

'I watched him through the back window. He went over the hedge and then disappeared along the back of Mrs Thatcher's.'

Shobha cocked her head. 'Did it occur to you that this man might pose a threat to Mrs Thatcher?'

Wilfred sat back, a grin spreading across his face. 'More likely she'd be a threat to him. Mad as a box of frogs, she is.'

Shobha chuckled. 'Well, yes. I interviewed Mrs Thatcher earlier today. She was what we in the trade call a challenging interviewee.'

Wilfred clapped his hands on his knees. 'I saw it! Yes, I'd forgotten. I saw you and Mrs Thatcher, outside the – err, oh. That's funny.'

'What is?'

'That just reminded me. Acorns.'

'We were outside the Acorn Consulting gates, yes?' Shobha encouraged him.

'That was what was on the badge he showed me. A picture of an acorn.'

'Ready, Shob?' Ailsa asked.

Shobha nodded, letting her eyes get adjusted to the glare of the light behind the camera. Ailsa had positioned her so the carved acorn atop the gate post would be picked out in the circle of light.

Shobha saw Ailsa's fingers counting her down, and kept her face an expressionless mask until she got the thumbs up.

'Tonight, the mystery surrounding the kidnapping of Acorn Consulting's CEO has deepened. Earlier this evening we interviewed local woman Maggie Thatcher about the recent disappearance of her husband, Edward Thatcher, also known as "Teddy". Since that interview, Mrs Thatcher's house has been burgled. *West Country Tonight* has spoken to neighbour Wilfred Perdew, who revealed that a man, of medium height, with dark hair, in his mid to late thirties, called at Mr Perdew's house earlier this evening. This man gained access to Mrs Thatcher's house through Mr Perdew's garden.'

She paused. This was it, the golden moment. She'd practised it in her head over and over in the car on the way there. Her intonation, the exact pausing, her facial expression.

'What we can be sure of is the design on the badge which the intruder flashed at Mr Perdew before entering his house. He has revealed that the logo,' she paused for a fraction to add to the reveal, 'was that of an acorn.' She turned her head and the camera followed her gaze, tilting upwards towards the uplit stone acorn on the gatepost.

'Is someone at Acorn Consulting involved in the disappearance of Isadora Faye and Teddy Thatcher? We can't know for sure. What is certain is the mystery continues to deepen here in the village of Halfway. This is Shobha Sharma reporting for *West Country Tonight*.'

Chapter Seventeen

Rain pattered against the windows. The sound soothed Bella, proving as it did the continued existence of an outside world, where ordinary people were sleeping in their beds at home, not on the floor of the offices of a top-secret organisation in lockdown. She looked up at the clock above the whiteboard. Three am.

Lauren was asleep, her breathing not quite a snore but more than a wheeze.

Bella turned her head on the pillow. Oscar lay on his back on his sleeping mat, eyes open and fixed on the ceiling. She could just make out his profile in the grey light provided by the tiny blue LEDs on various pieces of equipment, and the strip of yellow seeping under the door from the corridor outside.

'I always think this is the saddest time of the day,' she whispered.

He looked at her out of the corner of his eye, then shifted round to lie on his side facing her. 'What time?'

'Three in the morning. It's something to do with body clocks. I read somewhere that most people die between three and four o'clock.'

They were silent, Bella picturing the lives being extinguished around the globe as they lay there in the semi-darkness. 'Plus, this time of the day, it's all about things ending, loneliness, you know,' she continued, keeping her voice low so as not to wake Lauren. 'It's the dregs of a party or it's being alone and awake when you should be asleep.'

'And now,' Oscar murmured, 'it's thinking this'll probably be the time of day I end up dying. Thank you for that.'

'You're welcome.'

Lauren shuffled around on her narrow mattress and sighed, before resuming her wheeze-snoring. Oscar dropped his voice even lower, forcing Bella to strain to hear him.

'You're feeling maudlin because you've not had enough sleep. It'll all look better in the morning, as my old ma always says.'

'She sounds like a sensible woman.'

'Hmm. Flamboyant and unpredictable are words I would use to describe my mother. Sensible, not so much.'

A phone vibrated.

Bella shoved herself up on one elbow. 'Where did that come from?'

'Search me, I thought all the phones had been confiscated.'

They both pushed down their sleeping bags and hunted around in the feeble light.

The alert came again and Bella reached over to Lauren's rucksack. Lauren herself slept on, dead to the world.

Bella fumbled around in the bag, located the phone and motioned for Oscar to follow her. Easing open the door she looked both ways down the corridor. Empty, although she could hear voices at one end. Turning away from the voices, noiseless on bare feet, she led Oscar past the kitchen to a small adjacent storeroom. Opening the door, she shooed him in, ignoring the perturbed look on his face. When the door closed, they were in darkness, standing very close between the racks of catering packs of food and cartons of UHT milk.

'What in Jesus Christ's name are you doing?' he said

'I wanted to know how come Lauren had managed to keep hold of her phone.' She depressed the central button of the phone and it lit up to display the text message:

Latest package safely collected.

She showed Oscar.

'Amazon?' he hazarded.

'Don't mess around, Oscar! It must be code, and it's from someone calling themselves Ivy. Clever – ivy can bring down an oak, get it? So, we've got a coded message on Lauren's phone, that she's somehow kept back from the cupuli. What does that say to you?'

'You think Lauren's involved in Isadora's disappearance? Just because of that message?' Oscar hissed at her, his voice sounding harsh, disembodied above her in the darkness.

'Well it's weird, isn't it? You've known her longer than me. Could she be involved? How about Ben? Or Catherine? Why don't you put forward an actual opinion and do something useful instead of snarking from the cheap seats with one-liners all the bloody time?'

Her hands were clenched, nails digging painfully into her palms, throat hoarse from shouting at 0.5 of a decibel. Oscar didn't say anything for a few seconds, until she couldn't take it anymore and swung the phone up towards his face, pressing the button to light it up. He was looking stunned. The light went out and they were left in darkness. She reached out and took his hand.

'I'm sorry. I didn't mean to lash out at you. But I need your help.'

'To do what?' He didn't withdraw his hand but neither did he return the pressure.

'First off, to get out of here.'

They went via their office to get shoes and coats and replace Lauren's phone. While Oscar kept an eye on Lauren, who shifted position but slept on, Bella inched open her desk drawer, taking care not to dislodge any of the contents. Nestled between a packet of oatcakes and a stapler was her old phone, untouched since she had placed it there on the day she'd passed her probation. Thank goodness she'd never got around to recycling it. Pocketing the mobile, she slid the drawer out a little further to reveal her old charger at the back. Extricating it with care, she nodded to Oscar who left his sentry post, opened the door and led the way down the corridor towards the main entrance.

When Bella thought they were going to end up in the main entrance hall, Oscar turned along a corridor to the right and through an inconspicuous door in the panelling. A set of steps led down to a concrete-floored corridor lit by strip lights. At the end, he pushed through a door marked 'Exit' and they were in an enormous underground car park. Rows of pale blue Jaguars stretched away under the fluorescent lights.

Oscar walked across to a kiosk near the row of roller garage doors at the end. Inside were some lockers, a table and chairs, and shelves holding bottles of screen wash and oil. Bella spotted a plug point near the floor and plugged her phone in.

'Okay, what's the plan? How do we get out?' she asked as he paced up and down.

He stopped and spun round to look her in the face. 'My plan was to do as I was told, hope Isadora and Ben get found and that we all go home in time for a slap-up breakfast. But apparently, you've got other ideas. So, let's hear it. What's so critical that you, Bella Black, have to leave OAK when everyone else is sitting tight? Left your hair straighteners on? Afraid you'll miss an episode of *Love Island*?'

He looked almost comical, messy tufts of hair sticking out in all directions, jogging bottoms tucked into a pair of lace-up boots and an indignant look on his face.

'I know something about what's happened. At least... I've got something that I think will help clear things up. I need to go home and get it.'

'What is it?'

Bella glanced around. 'I don't want to say. Just help me get out, Oscar, please, and I'll tell you everything.'

She looked down at her phone. Four per cent charged.

'Are you saying if I help you get out it'll help Isadora?'

'Isadora, and maybe Teddy Thatcher. And even Ben, I don't know.'

Oscar flopped down onto a chair. 'Fine! I'll help you if I can. But it's going to rely on a bit of luck.'

Her next question died on her lips as they heard the door to the garage open and someone enter. A walkie-talkie crackled.

They both ducked down below the windows of the kiosk.

Oscar whispered in her ear, 'We're in luck. When you hear the engine, we're going to run towards the exit.'

A man clumped past the kiosk in heavy boots. From their vantage point, all that was visible was a black jacket and baseball cap, the uniform of a cupule. They heard him speak into the walkie-talkie.

'Yes, sir. Asthma inhaler from the twenty-four-hour pharmacy in Hungerford. Understood. Over and out.'

They heard the beep-beep of a car unlocking and the clunk of the door as it opened and closed. The engine fired up.

'Now!' hissed Oscar.

Bella yanked her phone and charger out of the wall and they ran, half-crouching, out of the kiosk and along the wall, keeping low between the rows of cars. The garage door rolled upwards and the car drove through. They held back for a moment, and then as the door slid down, they pelted it across the concrete floor and through the narrowing gap.

Outside, Bella grabbed Oscar's arm and they set off across the grass through the drizzle as if their lives, or someone else's, depended on it.

Chapter Eighteen

Catherine loved being in the library. All the annals of OAK rising up around her, uniform and ordered. Everything recorded in straight lines on white pages, stacked in bookshelves which had been purpose-crafted to fit the handbound registers.

Noise was shut out here. Many a time Catherine had found herself in the library, alone but for the semi-comatose presence of The Librarian in his chair. Once she picked up a book and started reading, she was gone – only returning to the present when The Librarian's glass slipped out of his hand and hit the thick carpet with a muffled thud or the door opened to admit someone, usually Isadora. Few others came here.

Today she couldn't allow herself to slip away between the pages. As each long second passed, so Isadora's breath might be slipping from her body. Every turn of the page was the rush of blood through the atria of Isadora's heart; soon to be stilled if she, Catherine, could not save her.

Her usual haunt was near the entrance to the library, where the oldest volumes of kindnesses were filed. Either there or up on the mezzanine where the Institute's records were held, the statutes, the constitution, the regulations, the policies – the heart and soul of OAK. It fascinated her, from the first rules set out by Emma Faye, to the more recent decrees laid down in Isadora's regime.

But she was nearer The Librarian's lair now, searching through the most recent pre-digitisation kindness registers. The failure of the systems meant she couldn't search the latest files, but she could at least look through the last hard copy registers. She didn't know what she was looking for exactly, but she'd know it when she found it: a clue, something to confirm her suspicion, someone's name mentioned where it shouldn't be. Something, anything, pointing to an intention to perpetrate the horrors which had been committed.

She'd been through five books and was reaching for a sixth, on a high shelf, when she heard a discreet cough behind her. Her hand remained poised, the index finger resting on the top of the book's spine.

'I'm sorry to disturb you, Catherine,' said Finn.

'News?' Her voice was calm and steady.

'Nothing. We've searched his house, he's not there. No clues as to where he might be.'

'Ben's disappeared off the face of the earth?'

'No, of course not. We'll find him. We've got teams out; we're looking for his car—'

'Not good enough, Arran!' She pulled the book out with a jerk, knocking its neighbour onto the floor. 'If we find Ben, we'll find Isadora, I'm sure of it. Every second he's allowed to go free is a second longer that Isadora's in danger. We're letting her down, for God's sake!'

She looked like she was on the verge of tears, her face flushed and lip trembling. He reached out a hand and gripped her shoulder.

'I want to find him as much as you do. If the observatories weren't down...'

'OAK existed before technology did. We need to go back to old ways – boots on the ground. Get more of your people out there, Arran. Find him. For Isadora. For OAK.'

She laid his hand on the book as if he was taking an oath, placed her own hand on top and closed her eyes.

Together they murmured, 'A single act of kindness may change a day, a life, the world. Kindness is powerful. OAK is mighty.'

After their flight across the parkland and final scramble over the boundary wall, they'd had to pause for a few minutes to get their breath back, shoulders rising and dropping as they panted. Bella could taste bitterness in her throat and thought for a moment she was going to throw up.

They set off trudging down the road that ran alongside AC's wall, hoods up against the rain. A car approached and they hurled themselves into the undergrowth on the verge until it passed. They set off again, picking wet leaves and twigs off their clothes and Oscar spoke up, in tones of impeccable politeness.

'Are you going to tell me what the hell we're doing, by any chance?'

Bella nodded then realised he wouldn't be able to see her in the pre-dawn light, with his hood up. 'Yes. Believe me, I want to tell you, I've been dying to share it with someone. But I'm taking a huge risk. So, before I do, quid pro quo, can you tell me anything you know about who might have taken Isadora?'

'Why would I know anything?'

'I don't know. But you've been here a long time. You know a lot of people at OAK and how they usually behave. You might have seen something suspicious.'

She heard him let out a long breath. 'I don't know anything for sure but there's been something going on with

Ben and Lauren. At first, I thought they were... you know, having it off. I kept catching them looking at each other when they thought I couldn't see.'

'Looking at each other in what way?'

'I don't know, like they knew something the rest of us didn't. There was other stuff too, but in the end, I decided it wasn't an affair.'

'Why not?' She hoped her voice sounded as casual as she intended.

'Because,' he kicked a stone off the path and it bounced into the road, 'Ben was obviously more interested in you. When I realised it wasn't an office romance, I was even more intrigued as to what the secret could be. And why was Lauren in on it and not me? I've been here a good while, I'm a team player, blah blah blah.' He paused, seeming to consider a new idea. 'Maybe I don't seem like someone you can rely on in a crisis. Too much "snarking from the cheap seats".'

She touched his arm and he flinched. 'I didn't mean...'

He sidestepped out of reach and ploughed on. 'One day I saw Ben go over and say something to Lauren, but I couldn't hear what. They both left the office, I let them get ahead and then went after them. They got into Ben's car and set off down the drive. Ninety-nine times out of a hundred that would have been the end of my first foray into detective work, but it so happened I still had my jacket on because I'd been out for lunch, and my car keys were in the pocket. Anyway, to cut a long story short, they went to a little pub in a village twenty minutes away. And in the pub was a field cupule. A guy named—'

'James?'

He jerked his head round. 'If you know the story, why are you getting me to tell it?'

'I don't know it. It was a guess.'

'Well anyway, it seemed odd. I'd seen this James once or twice before at OAK meetings. He's a proper undercover field cupule so why would he risk being seen out in the real world with AC-ers? Plus, what were Ben and Lauren doing with a guy like that? These field guys don't mess around, they're trained to track and shut down any threats to Isadora or OAK. They don't get talked about much because they don't fit in with the warm and fuzzy OAK brand Isadora likes to portray, but I've heard stories.'

'What happened?'

'Nothing. I saw them through the window but I couldn't work out a way to hear what they were saying without them spotting me. Ben and Lauren came out of the pub about half an hour later, I followed them and they went straight back to AC. That's it. Your turn.'

The rain was easing and Bella pushed back her hood.

'We need to get to my house before anyone finds Maggie and makes her tell them where the evidence she mentioned on the local news is. Because,' even walking along a deserted road she found herself lowering her voice, 'it's on a USB stick in a box of icing sugar in my kitchen cupboard.'

Oscar stopped dead.

'What? What's on the USB?'

'I think it's records of hacking into some of our clients' bank accounts. With millions of pounds being stolen. I can't tell from the files who did it, but maybe the police will be able to. Or maybe Maggie knows.'

'And we're sauntering along by foot? It's going to take forever!'

'Have you got a better idea in the middle of the night, miles from anywhere?'

'Yes.' Oscar held out his hand. 'Give me your phone.'

They crouched behind a hedge, listening to the approaching rattle and growl of an elderly motor. Oscar cleared his throat.

'I should probably say Mum is…' he took a breath, frowning. 'Mum was older when she had me. Late forties.'

Bella nodded, wondering what was coming. 'Right?'

'She…' Again, he seemed to be having some kind of internal struggle, scratching the back of his neck awkwardly. Eventually, he said, 'She's great. You'll see, anyway. She's great.'

Right, thought Bella. *Nothing weird there then.* 'She must be, to come and pick you up at the drop of a hat like this. Your dad's – not around anymore?'

'Never was. I'm a bastard, I'm afraid.'

'Oh, don't say that. At the very worst you're a bit of a bellend.'

The noise of the engine was nearly level with them now and Oscar popped his head over the hedge, then sprang upright, waving. The car lurched to a halt.

Bella stood up and saw an old green and white Citroen 2CV. The driver's door opened and out stepped an old lady of perhaps eighty. She arranged one satin-gloved hand elegantly against the door frame and placed her feet, clad in kitten-heel mules, in what Bella believed to be ballet position three. She wore a red dressing gown trimmed with feathers at the neck. Her silver hair was teased into a stiff bouffant style which would have been the height of fashion sometime around 1963. That such an elderly lady could have such lustrous eyelashes appeared unlikely, leading Bella to the conclusion that they were false. The overall impression was of a grande-dame of the West End taking a break in her dressing-room at the interval. Bella was surprised to find she wasn't clutching a bouquet of white roses.

They hurried around from behind the hedge.

'I hope I didn't keep you both?' Drawn-on eyebrows rose even higher than their initial vertiginous position, a gracious smile on her lips as she glanced at Oscar and then let her eyes rest on Bella's face. 'I had to throw on my robe, but I hurried, I assure you, I hurried.'

Oscar bent down to kiss her powdery cheek, towering over her. Even Bella felt like a giant as she leaned across and shook her hand.

'Bella, this is my mum, Gladys,' Oscar said.

Gladys clasped Bella's hand in hers. 'Such beautiful hands! Are you a pianist, my dear?'

Bella felt strangely guilty as she confessed that no, she wasn't a pianist.

'A painter, then?'

Not a painter either, Bella confessed. Before any more of her shortcomings could be revealed – neither a potter, saxophonist, brain-surgeon or harpist, but merely someone with quite long fingers – Oscar stepped in.

'Listen, Mum, we need to get to Bella's house as soon as possible. We'd better get going.'

Gladys released Bella's hand and instead cupped Oscar's cheek for a moment. 'Say no more, my darling. We shall fly like the wind. My timing has always been impeccable. My

178

West End reviews always said that. "Miss Rose. Expression – exquisite. Timing – impeccable".'

They piled in and having narrowly avoided a ditch, Gladys manoeuvred the car around and they were on their way. Bella gave directions then sat back onto the hard vinyl-covered seat. Oscar twisted round in the front.

'Okay. So, you've got evidence of criminal activity hidden in your cake decorating cupboard, is there anything else I should know?'

Bella threw a meaningful glance at Gladys. 'That was a secret, Oscar!'

'Imagine I'm not here, my dears!' trilled Gladys over her shoulder. 'I shan't listen. I'll entertain myself with a few old favourites.' She began humming, 'Hey, Big Spender'.

Under cover of the musical accompaniment, Bella told Oscar what she knew of Lauren and Ben's connection to James – her neighbours' drinks party and the guilty looks in the back room of The Royal Oak.

'And then, there was what happened on Le Chêne,' she said, lowering her voice.

'I don't pop my cork for every man I see!' warbled Gladys, before relapsing back into humming.

'I was on my way back to the compound from the jungle.' Bella continued, 'I stumbled across Teddy Thatcher in one of the huts – he was passed out on the floor, blood everywhere. It was horrible. I must have fainted and when I woke up Ben was there and Teddy was gone. Ben swore he didn't know where Teddy was, but since we've been back in the UK, he's told me that Teddy's alive. Last night I tracked Ben to some farm buildings, he said he'd led me there on purpose because he knew I was following him. But now after what Finn said about him, I don't know if that's true or if Ben's hiding something – or some*one* – there.'

'So he, Lauren, and James could be working together? And they've kidnapped Isadora and Teddy?'

'It's starting to look that way. And someone ransacked Teddy's house looking for the memory stick that he'd copied some incriminating files on to, but luckily his wife Maggie had already dropped that off with me.'

They both realised that instead of cheerful humming, there was silence, and the car was slowing down. The 2CV came to a complete halt and Gladys heaved the handbrake on with some difficulty. With the help of the steering wheel, she pulled herself round in her seat to see them better.

'I'm sorry, my dears, but I couldn't help overhearing a little of what you said. It sounds dangerous. I'm not sure I should be taking you somewhere where these types of people might find you.'

Bella leaned forward and put a hand on Gladys's shoulder.

'Please don't worry, there's no reason to think anyone would be coming to my house. As far as they're concerned Oscar and I are tucked up in our makeshift beds at the office and the USB is... well, they don't know where that is. But they won't suspect me of having it.'

'We'll be in and out of there in a couple of minutes,' Oscar reassured her. 'We can grab the USB, get Bella's car and go straight to the police. Please, Mum.'

She sighed and shook her head. 'I never could say no to you, Oscar. On we go then and I shan't spare the horses!'

Oscar and Bella exchanged a look that said 'no more talk of OAK', Oscar switching on the radio as a further distraction.

The song faded out and a jazzy jingle indicated it was time for the news.

'Good morning. This is Gina Rayford with your local news and weather at four o'clock. Local woman Maggie Thatcher has been declared missing after police were called to a break-in at her house in Little Ayling. Mrs Thatcher was interviewed yesterday by *West Country Tonight* about the disappearance of her husband, Acorn Consulting employee Edward Thatcher, in late 2019, and the more recent abduction of CEO Isadora Faye. Police are keen to speak to a man who was seen in the area and who is believed to possess an Acorn Consulting ID badge. The man is described as white with short, dark hair, in his mid to late thirties, of medium build and around six feet tall. Anyone with information should call...'

Bella couldn't concentrate on the rest of the bulletin. If Ben had Maggie, he might have forced her to say where the USB was. He and James and God knows who else could be waiting for them at the house.

She rubbed her eyes. God, she was exhausted. She wanted to be curled up in bed, drifting off to sleep, with OAK, Isadora, Teddy, Ben and all of it smudging and jumbling and floating away to join the other figments of her imagination. Why hadn't she stayed in London where secret institutes remained secret, like they were meant to, instead of interfering in innocent people's lives?

She opened her eyes and found Oscar watching her, anxiety written across his face.

'Too risky?' he mouthed.

Bella thought of Teddy, bleeding on Le Chêne. Of Maggie, lonely and desperate. Of Isadora – of that look on her face when she'd told Bella that OAK was her life.

She shrugged and mouthed back at him, 'We have to try.'

Chapter Nineteen

Catherine woke with a start. Drool covered the back of her hand where she'd rested her cheek on it. A couple of strands of hair were stuck to her face – she peeled them off. Next to her on the desk, the books were stacked high. She couldn't remember closing her eyes, but for the last hour or so of reading she'd struggled. There was a noise behind her and she realised she'd been awoken by someone entering the library. Finn appeared around the end of the bookshelves.

'News?' she asked, sitting up and straightening her shirt. 'Isadora? Ben?'

'Not about them.' There were purple shadows under Finn's eyes. He needed a shave. 'Two people have escaped the lockdown.'

'Who?'

'Bella Black and Oscar Rose.'

Catherine was astonished. 'Bella and Oscar? They can't be involved.'

She and Finn looked at each other.

'How long have they been gone?' she asked.

'Could be anytime between midnight and five minutes ago. Lauren Murray's in their room, says she was asleep, didn't hear a thing. We found out they were missing when we did a patrol.'

'They could still be on-site then.'

'Correct. We've got search parties out.'

'Bella and Oscar...' Catherine's eyebrows were drawn together. 'Seems odd. But on the other hand, they are close to Ben. If you can't find them in the grounds send a couple of teams to check their home addresses.'

Finn stood up even straighter and gave a quick duck of his head in confirmation.

❦ ❦

Lauren pressed the contact saved as 'Ivy' in her phone and waited while it rang. She was in a small janitor's room. Cleaning products lined the walls and worktops. Mops and brushes leaned up in the corner by a stainless-steel sink and what looked like sacks of sand. Lauren was sure that even if OAK had managed to keep some of their monitoring systems alive, this was a room they wouldn't bother to bug.

The call connected.

'Hi. Everything okay?'

'No.' Lauren replied. 'Bella and Oscar have disappeared.'

There was silence for a moment on the other end of the phone. 'Bella and Oscar? Shit.'

'I was asleep. Must have been the early hours.'

'You need to get after them, Lauren. I've been having an interesting conversation with Maggie Thatcher. She says Bella's got the USB.'

'What the...?' Lauren pulled herself together. 'Okay, no worries. I know how to get out. I'm on my way.'

❦ ❦

'Thanks, Mum,' said Oscar, leaning across to give her a peck on the cheek. I'll call you later, please don't worry.'

It had been a hard battle persuading Gladys not to wait for them but in the end, by suggesting that such a glamorous equipage as her 2CV would be too conspicuous outside

Bella's house, they'd convinced her to drop them a little way down the lane and then make her way home to Hungerford.

'I'll be waiting by the phone to hear from you when I get back, Oscar. And Bella! If anything happens to my boy...' she broke off and started riffling around in the glove compartment, dislodging leopard-print gloves, a glasses case and a packet of jelly. Extracting a small notebook with a slim gold pen attached, she noted down her phone number, ripped out the page and passed it to Bella. 'You will call me, dear, won't you?'

Bella assured her that she would and they got out of the car, watched her reverse it with great care into a tree, turn and drive back towards the main road.

'Come on then,' said Bella, grabbing Oscar's arm and leading him down the lane at a brisk pace, as much to fire up her own courage as his.

Trees and hedges formed a tunnel, broken periodically by the gates leading to houses set back from the road. After they'd passed two gates, she squeezed his arm to indicate this was their turning. They crept into the courtyard, crossing it as quietly as they could, the sound of their footsteps masked by the rushing of the mill stream. The houses were in darkness, the single light source a hazy globe around the lamp post at the courtyard entrance. At her front door, Bella scrabbled at the keyhole, her trembling hands fumbling a couple of times before she managed to turn the key in the lock. Pushing Oscar in first, she pulled the door shut behind them and they both held their breath, straining to hear if there was any noise in the house. The fridge in the kitchen whirred and the hall clock ticked but otherwise, silence. Their eyes grew accustomed to the light and she nodded to him, leading the way down the corridor.

In the kitchen, she went straight to the cupboard below the kettle where she kept her baking ingredients. Delving her hand into the box of icing sugar she found the USB and pulled it out.

She could hear Oscar's breathing beside her, short and panicked.

'I've got it,' she whispered. 'It's okay, we can go. I'll get my car keys.'

They came back out into the hall and she grabbed her keys from hook. At the same moment there came the sound of glass smashing in the kitchen.

'Fuck! The back door!' Bella's mind blanked, panic spreading across it like fire consuming a sheet of paper.

Oscar leapt to the kitchen door, slammed it shut and held on to the handle. 'Run! I'll try and slow them down!'

Run! Where? She grasped wildly for a sensible idea in the blank vacuum of her mind. She couldn't go out the front door, they'd catch her. *Think, Bella,* she urged herself. And then, almost as if her muscles – despairing of her feeble brain – took over, she darted up the stairs.

Up to the first floor, heart banging against her ribs, breath rasping in her ears, and then all the way up to the loft.

In the loft room, she opened one of the eaves cupboards, shoved the empty cardboard boxes and rolls of parcel tape to one side and clambered inside, feet first. Once in, she realised she wouldn't be able to pull the door shut behind her: there was no handle on the inside. She closed it as much as she could with her fingernails, then began crawling along inside the eaves, pulling a few boxes behind her to cover her escape route. Squeezing through the narrow gap at the side of the water tank she flicked on the torch on her phone and found what she was looking for. A piece of MDF faced her, blocking her way. A little bit of jiggling and she was able to move it, as she had the first time she'd explored the house. She crawled through the gap, then turned and wedged the MDF back in place. A cursory glance in torchlit darkness wouldn't reveal anything odd, she had to hope that the fact of the eaves door being ajar didn't point them in her direction. She paused, trying to stifle the sounds of her jerky breathing. *Should have opened some of the other cupboard doors to make it less obvious*, she thought. *Too late now*.

She began to edge her way along the narrow gap, shifting cat baskets and overflowing boxes of Christmas decorations, until her hand touched plywood on her right instead of breezeblocks. She shoved, and the door opened into a loft room which in shape and proportion was very like that she had just left, except this one was set up as an artist's studio.

Large canvases leant in neat stacks, purples, oranges and pinks with a recurring theme of poppy-like flowers. An easel was set up beside one of the large dormer windows.

She pushed the cupboard door shut and let herself out of the room, tiptoeing down the stairs to the first-floor landing.

Someone was rattling the handle on the other side of the kitchen door. Oscar clung on, the curved metal jabbing into his palm.

'Open up!'

The voice was strained but sounded familiar. It was followed by a kick against the door. Oscar braced himself with his shoulder pressed to the wood.

'Bella? Oscar?' The voice came again, 'Open the door! It's me, Lauren.'

Lauren? What the hell is she doing here? Oscar loosened his grip in a moment of indecision and the door flew open, knocking him backwards.

Lauren stood in the doorway with a gun. Oscar's eyes widened.

'What the hell, Lauren?'

She lowered the gun. 'Sorry. I wasn't sure what I'd find. Where's Bella?'

Oscar thought fast. Lauren wasn't someone he'd ever suspected would attack OAK, not someone he could see caught up in a kidnapping. But she was an ally of Ben's, and by all accounts, Ben was in this up to his neck. And would an innocent person have a gun?

'She's not here,' he said, leaning one shoulder against the bannisters in what he hoped was a casual attitude.

'What do you mean? Where is she?' Lauren advanced into the hallway, flicking on a torch and directing the beam into the adjacent living room. Finding it empty, she searched the other rooms on the ground floor.

'We thought it was too dangerous,' Oscar called after her. 'We decided to split up.'

Lauren came back into the hall and switched off the torch.

'Oscar, this isn't a game. I need to find the USB stick. People's lives depend on it. If Bella's got it, she's in danger.'

How the hell does she know Bella's got the USB? he thought. Pressing his lips together and shrugging his shoulders, he said out loud, 'I wish I could help you. But like I say, she's not here.'

There was a crunching of boots on broken glass and they turned to see two cupuli, guns raised, in the kitchen doorway.

'We'll make sure of that ourselves, if you don't mind,' one of them said as he motioned to Lauren to lower her gun.

She dropped it and kicked it across the tiles toward him. He gestured for her and Oscar to go into the living room. 'You two wait in here with me while my colleague looks around.'

Oscar's heart was thumping as the other cupule, having searched the ground floor, made her way upstairs. Lauren's eyes darted around the room as if she was looking for a weapon or an escape route. The cupule guarding them gave her a light tap on the side of the head with his gun.

'Take it easy,' he said. 'We don't want anyone to get hurt.'

They heard the second cupule opening doors and pulling furniture about. Oscar had never had a panic attack before but he found himself wondering if that was what was happening to him now as his heart took great, angry thumps and he held on to the edge of the table to stop himself swaying. *Please don't find her, please don't find her*, he willed. Every time there was a muffled bang, he expected to hear Bella scream.

The footsteps came back downstairs and the cupule joined them in the living room, shaking her head at her colleague.

Oscar's heart, which had started to ease off on the aerobics, launched itself into an even more energetic workout as the male cupule left Lauren and poked the muzzle of his pistol into Oscar's shoulder. It wasn't often that people could look Oscar in the eye but this guy had a couple of inches on him height-wise, and if you'd stripped him of his uniform you could have fitted Oscar inside it several times over.

They were standing toe to toe as the cupule said, not raising his voice, 'You know where she is.'

'I don't,' said Oscar, truthfully.

'You left OAK together. Where did she go? We won't hurt her but we need to find her before anyone else does.'

Out of the corner of his eye, Oscar was aware of Lauren paying close attention to this exchange. Sharp metal ground against the bone in his shoulder.

'I think,' Oscar said, so quietly that the cupule had to tilt his head to hear, 'I think you'll find her if you look' – his voice dropped further, barely audible now, the cupule's face millimetres from his own – 'up your own arse.'

And then there was nothing.

❧ ❧

Bella had crept down the first set of stairs, testing each step before she put her full weight on it, knowing the creak of certain steps could be heard through the wall in her own house.

She paused on the landing of the first floor. Snoring suggested Angela was in the room to her right. She padded across the carpet and took a deep breath, one hand on the bannister ready to descend the final set of stairs. Through the wall, she heard a step creak. Someone was coming up. She froze. The slightest movement forward or back and the floorboards beneath Bella's feet would give her away. She kept her breathing shallow, in and out through her mouth as she strained to hear more. Was that voices she could hear downstairs? Now furniture was being flung around, doors slammed. In Angela's room, the snoring stopped. *Oh God, please don't wake up, Angela. Don't get out of bed.*

By the time the banging stopped, Bella was shaking. She'd released the bannister in case her trembling hand jerked a telltale noise out of the wood. Instead, she had eased herself down into a crouch on the carpet, hands braced on either side of her feet like a sprinter on the blocks, ready to launch herself down the stairs if she heard the door on the landing above open.

The door above remained closed and the creaking of the stairs through the wall told her the intruder was retreating. There were muffled voices downstairs. Angela gave one great snore and relapsed into silence. Then Bella heard the front door in her own house slam.

She shot downstairs and into Angela's living room, which looked out on to the courtyard. Giving a prayer of thanks that the curtains weren't closed, Bella pressed herself to the wall on one side of the window and peered around the edge of the thick green velvet.

In the weak dawn light, she saw Lauren walking away from the house, hands clasped in front of her. Behind her, being supported between two stocky black-clad figures, feet trailing along the ground, was Oscar.

When Oscar came to, it took a moment to orient himself. He was slumped against the window of a car, head lolling, seat belt cutting into his neck. The car was going at a cracking pace, hurtling around bends, trees and telegraph poles whipping by outside. He changed position and the pain in his head intensified. He closed his eyes against the throbbing, trying to remember what had happened. He'd told a large cupule to go and look up his own arse, and then there was a fragment of memory of his face, purple and furious, and a bright flash of pain. It seemed sensible to conclude the cupule had knocked him out.

Oscar opened his eyes at the touch of cool fingers on his wrist.

Lauren was sitting next to him on the passenger seat, looking pale but otherwise unharmed. His groggy brain noted something odd about the way she'd reached over to tap him and then saw that her wrists were bound together with a zip tie.

'Are you okay?' she murmured.

He pulled a non-committal face, the corners of his mouth dragged down. 'You?' he mouthed.

She nodded.

In the front, the two cupuli sat in silence. The woman was driving while the man tapped something into his phone.

'Excuse me,' Oscar said, his voice croaky. 'I think I'm going to be sick.'

The man didn't look up as he said, 'Try not to make a mess.'

Oscar's nausea subsided a little as a blast of cold air was propelled at his face, presumably courtesy of the driver although from where he sat, he couldn't see her adjusting the air con. The car turned onto a wider, straighter road and after a couple of minutes of deep breathing, he felt better. Nausea gave way to anger.

'We're members of OAK. We're entitled to better treatment than this,' he said, leaning forward in his seat and then regretting it as the pain in his right temple redoubled.

'You're not entitled to shit unless Finn says so,' snarled the driver.

Oscar looked over at Lauren who shrugged and turned towards the window.

At last, they pulled into the familiar Acorn Consulting gates. Lauren sat up a little straighter in her seat. Once in the underground car park, the cupuli opened the back-passenger doors and the woman helped Oscar out. The man leant across Lauren to undo her seat belt.

'I've got my eye on you. Don't try anything stupid.'

And that was when she clasped the back of his head in her bound hands and rammed it downwards, jerking her knee up into his face.

❦ ❦

'I think it would have been better,' Oscar ventured, 'if you hadn't broken his nose.'

Lauren's head turned in his direction and her eyes narrowed. Her lips, restricted by the duct tape, barely moved as a sound that sounded like 'mo fit' came out of her mouth. Something about her intonation and disdainful look suggested an approximate translation might be 'no shit'.

The cupuli had been very angry at the broken nose incident. *Very* angry. Lauren had received a punch in the head and been dragged out of the back seat by her wrists, landing awkwardly on the concrete floor. Oscar had gone quiet and tried to become invisible. With the male cupule holding one protective hand in front of his bleeding nose,

Oscar and Lauren had been marched through some unfamiliar corridors in OAK to this wing which Oscar had never seen before and which he assumed was cupuli headquarters.

They were sitting in metal chairs set side by side in what appeared to be a cell. Oscar hadn't been aware that OAK was set up to receive criminals, but if this small, windowless room, with its iron bunks and chairs wasn't a cell, he couldn't imagine what it was intended for. He was cuffed but otherwise able to move around, while Lauren was strapped into her chair.

When the door had first clanged shut on them Oscar had had the distinct impression that through the animated movements of her eyebrows and head, Lauren was encouraging him to use this relative freedom to some effect.

'Mmm-mmm-mmm,' she urged. 'MMMM-MMMM-MM-MMMM!'

'I'm sorry, Lauren, but I have no idea what you're saying.'

She threw her head back in exasperation. 'MMMMMMMMMM!'

Oscar held up his cuffed hands. 'Look, unless you're suggesting I call in the guards and distract them with my own interpretation of *Riverdance* while you make a break for it, I'm not sure what you think I can do?'

Lauren locked her eyes onto his, opened them to their fullest extent and then rolled them down until she was staring down her nose.

'Oh, I see! Sorry.' Oscar had just reached out a hand to remove the tape from her mouth when he heard the tramping of boots in the corridor and the door swung open.

Two new cupuli entered, released Lauren from the chair and shoved both her and Oscar out of the room ahead of them.

They filed along narrow corridors past closed doors, and the occasional open one revealing groups of cupuli gathered round maps or receiving briefings. One of their guards opened a set of double doors and pushed Oscar and Lauren inside.

Sitting on the other side of a large, square table was Catherine. Her skin was pale and unhealthy looking, grey-blue shadows under her eyes. She didn't look like she'd changed her clothes for some time. Standing behind her chair, also pale but alert, was the imposing figure of Arran Finn.

Catherine motioned to Oscar and Lauren to sit down. A cupule brought them bottles of water and ripped the tape from Lauren's face, making her flinch. Oscar opened his water and gulped some down. Glancing at Lauren he saw she was staring blankly at Catherine, her water untouched on the table.

'Hello, you two,' said Catherine. 'I'm glad we caught up with you. I need you to tell me how we can find Bella. You were overheard asking Oscar about the USB at the house, Lauren, so please don't feign ignorance. If Bella's got it, we can sort this whole sorry mess out and bring Isadora home.' She smiled at them, and her eyes shone with what looked like genuine warmth but Oscar was distracted by her hands. They were clasped together on the table and she was using one thumbnail to pick at the skin of the other thumb. The other thumb was bleeding.

Oscar's mind was racing. Did chief people officer include being chief prison officer? Finn should be running the show, shouldn't he, not Catherine?

'Catherine, I'm confused...' he started.

The smile dropped from her face. 'This is all going to be a lot easier if everyone stops fucking around.'

Oscar was stunned. Never had he heard a swear word come out of Catherine's mouth. He glanced over at Lauren. Her eyes were glazed as if she were steeling herself for an ordeal.

'We don't have time for you to be confused, Oscar,' Catherine continued. 'Or for you to clam up, Lauren. Isadora is missing. OAK is collapsing. I'll do anything – *anything* – to find our leader and bring her home. So please do me the courtesy of taking me seriously.'

Without turning her head, Catherine held out her hand, palm upward. Finn placed a gun into it.

'You,' she said, indicating Lauren, 'were in possession of this gun. Along with Oscar and Bella, you broke the lockdown and escaped to Bella's house to look for the USB. You're up to your neck in Isadora's disappearance.'

Her tone softened when she turned to Oscar.

'Oscar, I can easily imagine that you were tricked into going along with this.'

Oscar wasn't sure whether to be relieved or offended.

'You won't face any recriminations if you tell us everything you know,' she added. 'I'm sure you're as desperate as I am to bring Isadora home.'

Lauren's eyes bore into him.

Oscar looked from Catherine's face to his surroundings, taking in the grilles on the windows, the bare concrete walls, cameras, cupuli standing guard near the exit.

'I want to help, Catherine, but can I ask one question first? Why is our chief people officer leading a modern-day version of the Spanish Inquisition?'

Finn's meaty palms slammed down on the table.

'She'll ask the fuckin' questions! You better start answering them.'

Oscar's heart leapt up to his throat and tried to batter its way out of his body. He didn't blame it; he'd like to be somewhere else himself. He tried to ignore the lurch in his bowels as he returned Finn's furious gaze.

'What exactly was it you wanted to know, Catherine?' Oscar asked, looking back at her.

'Where is Bella?'

'Oh!' He looked relieved. 'Easy. No idea.'

Finn growled and stepped forward. Catherine motioned for him to stay where he was.

'I'm not going to lose my temper with you, Oscar,' Catherine said in a measured tone. 'Why don't you tell us what happened after you left OAK.' She put the gun down on the table, one hand resting on top of it.

'We climbed over the wall onto the main road and walked to Bella's house.'

'Why did you go to Bella's house?'

Oscar had had plenty of time to think about this as he waited in the cell. 'She'll be very embarrassed that I'm telling you this. She didn't bring any spare contact lenses with her and she's too vain to wear her glasses. We thought we could nip out and back before anyone missed us. But then we lost each other in the dark as we ran through the grounds. I couldn't find her anywhere but I thought if I carried on to her house, I'd catch up with her.'

Catherine looked at him with a slight shake of the head. 'You must take me for an absolute idiot, Oscar,' she spat.

'No, it's true,' Oscar continued, 'that's what happened. She'd told me where the front door key was so I let myself in.'

'And the USB?'

'The first I heard of any USB was when Lauren asked me about it after she'd broken in through the back door.' He knew he was throwing Lauren under the bus but his loyalty was to Bella, and Lauren could well be the one who was putting them all in danger.

Catherine was watching him, the expression of contempt replaced by something he couldn't quite define. For a moment all was quiet in the room.

Finn glanced from Oscar's face to Catherine's, waiting for a signal.

Catherine grabbed the gun, shoved her chair back – so hard Finn had to leap out of the way – and strode around the table to stand beside Oscar. Pointing the gun at his thigh, she said, 'Someone's going to tell me what they know before I count to three, or I'm going to shoot.'

Oscar tried to jump up but two cupuli were already on him, holding him down. Lauren looked white but her lips were pressed together.

Catherine sighed. 'One.'

198

'For fuck's sake, Catherine!' Oscar's voice was panicked. 'Have you lost your fucking mind?'

'Two.'

'I don't know where Bella is! Or Isadora! Lauren? If you know, tell her for God's sake!'

'Three.'

Chapter Twenty

Bella had watched Lauren and Oscar being pushed into the back of a black four-by-four and driven away. She stood frozen in place by the window long after the car had disappeared. The courtyard was quiet, the only noises audible from within the house were the rush of the mill stream and a blackbird leading the dawn chorus from somewhere within the clump of trees beside the entrance gate. The fronds of the willow were tousled by a gentle breeze but the rain had stopped. It looked like it was going to be a beautiful day.

Something touched the back of her leg and she jumped. Siberia, Angela's cat, had padded in across the carpet, perhaps hoping he was going to get an early breakfast.

Bella bent down and stroked him as she tried to rally her brain into some rational thought. Pulling her phone and charger out of her coat pocket, she plugged them into a wall socket by the sofa. The phone was dead, she would need to charge it for half an hour at least if the battery was to last. In a way that made her feel calmer, she had half an hour to clear her head and come up with a plan.

Sitting on the sofa and pulling a willing Siberia on to her lap, she gave him some firm strokes as she thought hard.

The USB in her pocket appeared to suggest that she was the person with the key to this mystery. Many people were relying on her making the right decision, including Oscar, who seemed to be unconscious when the cupuli bundled him into the back seat. Poor Oscar, if it hadn't been for Bella, he'd be tucked up in his sleeping bag at OAK right now, or maybe waking up with one of his trademark one-liners on his lips. Whereas instead he was hurt, who knew how badly.

Siberia gave a complaining miaow and Bella realised she was stroking a little too hard.

Thoughts whirled in her head. Ben's threatening email on the USB. Lauren – who they'd left dead to the world in the office – turning up next door with a couple of cupuli. Maggie Thatcher, who had been alive and well after the news recording when she came round to give Bella the knickers, but who had apparently never returned to her ransacked house or contacted the police.

The police. If ever there was something that annoyed Bella in action films it was when the hero or heroine tried to save a hostage, defuse a bomb or undertake any other unnecessary heroics on their own when they could have gone to the police. Who, after all, were the ones qualified to deal with this kind of thing. That's what she should do – take the USB, tell the police everything she knew and let them take it from there. Her allotted half-hour was up, she would unplug her phone, get her car and drive to the police station.

The phone rang.

She answered it on instinct, terrified the noise would wake Angela in the room above. The name on the screen was Catherine Knight.

'Catherine?' Bella said, keeping her voice down.

'Bella! Thank God. Where are you?'

'What's going on? How did you know to phone my old number?'

'I've been talking to Oscar. He didn't want to tell me but thank God he did. Bella, I'm on your side. You have to believe me.'

'Let me speak to him.'

201

'He's not here right now, he had to go to the medical centre. He'll be fine, don't worry.'

'I'm not telling you anything until I speak to him.'

'Listen to me, Bella, this is too important. Oscar told me about the farm buildings that you tracked Ben to. You have to tell me where they are. I think that's where Ben's holding Isadora and Teddy. And maybe Maggie too. I know you've got the USB. If we can take that to Ben, we can negotiate with him to get Isadora and the others back in exchange for the evidence against him.'

Catherine paused and Bella could hear her eager breathing on the other end of the line.

'Bella?' Catherine urged. 'Tell me where it is. I just want to save Isadora. There's no time to explain all the background, I don't know what he'll have done by now. Please!'

Bella's resolve weakened. At the risk of reliving every stupid mistake she'd scoffed at in those action films she was tempted to do as Catherine said. If she went to the police it would mean long explanations and she didn't know if they would be able to get Ben to hand over Isadora without bloodshed, whereas it sounded like Catherine knew exactly what to say. Because – it dawned now on Bella as these thoughts tumbled through her brain – she had to accept that it was Ben who was behind everything. The secret meetings with James and Lauren, covering up Teddy's attack on Le Chêne, driving to an isolated barn for no good reason and then that final incriminating email on the USB. She couldn't ignore the avalanche of signals any longer.

'I don't know the address of the barn,' she said, 'but I can get it. I'll bring it to you at OAK, with the USB.'

'Tell me where you are, we'll pick you up on the way.'

'No, I'll come in.' The memory of the way those cupuli had dragged Oscar across the gravel was still fresh. Bella preferred to avoid any more contact with Isadora's personal guard.

❦ ❦

Safely in the car and on the road to OAK, Bella felt a little better. Sometimes the period before making a difficult decision was worse than actually making it, she reflected. Once you'd made a choice a lot of the anxiety slipped away. And she was on her way to Oscar, to be able to reassure herself that he was okay.

Before she'd set off, she'd checked in the Alfa's satnav memory that the route from OAK to the barn was recorded. Catherine and the cupuli would be able to use that to find Ben.

The radio was on, the newsreader announcing that there were no further updates in the Acorn Consulting missing persons enquiries. Her phone rang again. Glancing over at it on the seat beside her she saw the name flash up: Ben.

She turned her attention back to the road ahead and hit 'accept' on the Bluetooth.

'Hello?'

'Bella! I tried this phone as last resort, I'm glad I did. Where are you?'

'Oh, come on, Ben. Like I'm going to tell you that! I was an idiot to trust you before, I know what's going on now.'

'Really? Who have you been talking to?'

'Catherine.'

'Catherine! Ha. Isadora's anointed successor. You're hardly going to get an honest account from her.'

'Isadora's... what?'

'Haven't you ever wondered what will happen when Isadora dies or can't run OAK anymore?'

Bella had a flashback to Le Chêne, the heat of a tropical evening and Oscar's non-committal answer when she'd asked who would take over from Isadora.

'Isadora has no children,' Ben was continuing. 'A few years ago, she set about identifying and grooming a worthy successor. She decided on Catherine almost as soon as she was recruited. I think she saw something of herself in her, the fanatical devotion to OAK above all else. The pathological drive to succeed—'

'This is all very interesting, Ben,' Bella said as she indicated right and waited for a gap in the traffic, 'but what's your point?'

'My point is that Isadora and Catherine are on the same side. The wrong side. I'm going to tell you something now and I need you to listen to me, Bella. It's critical that you understand what I'm saying so you'll be able to make an informed decision on what to do.

'It started at the back end of last year. There were some financial problems at OAK. Isadora wanted to expand more aggressively than the board could agree to – we were concerned we'd overreach ourselves. But she has the final veto on any decision and she pushed ahead. Offices were being built in several new US locations at once, new equipment was being bought, staff recruited – it was a huge undertaking. Isadora signed off a risky investment to fund some of the work. The investment failed. At the time, I didn't know about the loss of funds and neither did most of the board. But I'm jumping ahead of myself.

'Isadora carried on as if everything was fine. Told us all that cashflow had never been better and that OAK would exceed its annual growth targets within six months. But the reality was she needed money fast to fill the shortfall from that catastrophic investment. She turned to our friend Teddy Thatcher. What do you know about Teddy's job at OAK?'

'Almost nothing,' Bella replied. 'I know he'd worked there a long time, that's all.'

'He had, and he was a devout OAK believer. A devout Isadora believer, too, he worshipped her. But she used him.

'Teddy was OAK's best programmer. He built a lot of the technical systems from scratch; he was a genius when it came to anything to do with coding. She called him into her office one day soon after she'd lost the money and told him she had a special job for him.

'Some of our clients, she told him, had asked AC to test their systems. Cybersecurity penetration tests, checking their firewalls and threat detection systems were fit for purpose, that kind of thing. She gave him a list of tests to carry out, telling him the clients were prepared and it was all a dry run. One of the tasks on his list was to see if he could hack their accounts and steal large sums of money. They all happened to bank at the same place, I don't know if Isadora had some insider knowledge of a security issue at that particular bank but it seems possible.

'Anyway, Teddy – who, remember, had worked alongside and trusted this woman for over twenty years – took the list away to his little cubbyhole office and got started. She'd given him the project in November but told him to spread the hits out. She sent him a spreadsheet of which accounts to take money from and where to transfer it to.

'But you've already seen that spreadsheet so you know what I'm talking about.'

Concentrating on the road was getting harder and harder. Bella saw a layby up ahead, indicated, and pulled into it.

'I've seen *a* spreadsheet,' she said, warily, when she'd brought the car to a stop. 'It doesn't prove what you're saying or who's behind it.'

'No, okay. Well, I'll come on to that. In the meantime, I had some suspicions about Isadora. Her behaviour and that of some in her inner circle was verging on obsession, and it worried me. I knew enough about OAK's finances to be sceptical about her explanations of how we were funding the US expansion. So, I started doing some digging, and by pulling in a couple of favours I managed to access some very interesting files. And then I stumbled across what Teddy was doing.

'I assumed he was a willing accomplice at the start, it seemed pretty incriminating. I thought he'd be easier to influence than Isadora and I sent him a message telling him to meet me, in the hope that I could persuade him to stop doing what he was doing.

'For Teddy, that message was a wake-up call. He's not a stupid man, but he is gullible. By this time, though, even for him questions had started to come up in his mind about why there were so many transactions, why the money was being transferred to different accounts, why he hadn't yet been instructed to transfer it back. He couldn't believe Isadora could be knowingly stealing from her clients, but he began to suspect something very wrong was happening. He copied evidence of what he'd been doing on to a data stick that he left with Maggie on the day he was due to come in for the meeting with me.'

So far, so plausible, thought Bella. *But Ben's a clever man. Of course he's got a believable story ready. He knows I've seen the USB, he had to have something prepared that would match what's on there.*

'When I met Teddy that evening,' Ben continued, 'I expected to see a guilty man. But what I found was that as soon as I confirmed he'd actually been stealing money, rather than *pretending* to steal money, he was distraught. He couldn't believe that Isadora could do such a thing but after I'd talked him through the circumstances leading up to it, he came to realise it was true. It was quite a blow for someone like Teddy, who thinks everyone is as honest as he is. The next thing to convince him of was that he was in danger. From what he told me of the amounts stolen, the cashflow shortfall had already been covered several times over. Isadora had realised there was an easy supply of money, and why should she stop because she'd solved her short-term issue? This money could fund an even greater expansion plan for OAK.'

'You're trying to make me believe,' Bella said, 'that Isadora has no moral compass? That the woman at the head of an organisation aimed at making the world a better place is no more than a petty thief?'

'No. I'm trying to make you see that for Isadora, nothing is more important than OAK. What were those AC clients planning on doing with that money? Paying dividends to their shareholders? Investing it back into their mundane businesses? How much better could that money be used if it were diverted into OAK! That would be the way Isadora could reconcile herself to stealing it.'

Bella ran a hand through her hair. She was struggling to see the fastidious, upstanding little woman who led OAK ordering someone to hack into banks and steal money.

Ben carried on. 'I needed to convince Teddy that Isadora would keep on making him steal. And that if he refused, he would become very dangerous to her. Because here was someone who could send her to prison and bring down OAK if he chose to speak out. I knew she'd never allow that. We had to make a plan then and there to get him out, I needed to send him somewhere no one would look until we'd worked out how to remove Isadora from the reins of OAK without bringing down the whole operation. I enlisted the help of a friend, James. I think you've met him.'

'At his "parents"' drinks party, yes. Although I expect they're not his parents?'

'No,' Ben confirmed. 'David and Pauline are field agents. It was a convenient way for James and Lauren to meet up.'

'Oh yes, Lauren,' said Bella. 'I also saw you, James and Lauren together in The Royal Oak that time. How's Lauren involved in all this?'

She heard exasperation slip into his tone as he replied. 'I'll fill you in on all the details when we've more time, Bella. For now, I need to tell you enough about what happened that you'll know you can trust me.

'James and I persuaded Teddy we needed to hide him somewhere. He wasn't happy about it, he wanted to get a message to Maggie but we couldn't risk that. We didn't want to leave any trace for Isadora, Catherine or Finn to find. We staged a disappearance, hiding his car at the barns where you found me the other night and smuggling Teddy out to Le Chêne. Where he stayed hidden until our trip out there.'

Bella's phone beeped and she looked at the screen. Incoming call from Catherine. They must be wondering where she was.

'Is this going to take much longer?' she asked. 'Because I'm expected somewhere.'

'I'm going as fast as I can,' he said, coldly. 'I thought you might be interested in what happened to Teddy.'

'I'm interested in the truth,' she snapped back.

Ben pressed on. 'Somehow when we were on Le Chêne, Teddy was discovered. I think Catherine might have stumbled across him.'

Bella had a sudden flashback to Catherine in the bunker, the noise in the 'cupboard' they'd both dismissed. Only maybe Catherine hadn't dismissed it, maybe she'd gone investigating... No, it was too preposterous, surely?

'I don't know what happened next,' Ben was saying, 'but I think Catherine must have let Isadora know and they sent The Librarian out there. Perhaps to kill Teddy, perhaps to bring him back so Isadora could force him to continue the hacking.'

Bella remembered Teddy's unconscious form, the blood on the floor. 'It didn't look like he was being gently persuaded to return.'

'No, well, that could have been The Librarian being ham-fisted about the job, which wouldn't surprise me.'

Bella almost laughed. 'For God's sake, Ben! What are you trying to get me to believe here? I know Isadora, remember. And I know Catherine. They're good people. I've seen nothing in them to make me suspect otherwise. You, however... you're a different story.'

'Let me finish, Bella, and you'll understand what's really happening here,' he was getting angry now, she could hear it in his voice. He was fighting to keep calm, she was glad she was on the other end of a phone, not in the same room.

'I think you disturbed The Librarian on Le Chêne,' he continued. 'My guess is after you screamed, he heard me coming into the building and had to dump Teddy in a side room and escape. When you woke up and told me to go and look for Teddy, I found him on the floor of a bathroom on the first floor. He was coming round. I put pressure on his wound and called Theresa, who came straight away and took him to be treated by a doctor we could trust to keep it quiet.'

'Theresa!' Bella scoffed. 'You're trying to tell me she's on your side too, now?'

Ben ignored this. 'Although there was a lot of blood on the floor,' he continued, 'and The Librarian had knocked him out, the wound was superficial and Teddy recovered quickly. He was on the plane with all of us when we flew back from Le Chêne, hidden in one of the crew's sleeping areas. I got a message to James back home and told him to abduct Isadora.'

Finally. He was admitting the truth, that he was behind the kidnapping. That right at this moment he was holding her captive.

'Hang on,' Bella interjected. 'Are you trying to say the reason you took Isadora was to rescue Teddy? If I asked you, hand on heart, if you abducted her so you could get your hands on OAK and run it yourself, could you say no?'

Of course, he'll lie, she thought. And then he surprised her.

'No, I couldn't. But—'

She ended the call before he could finish his sentence. Scrolling through her recent call history she pressed Catherine's number.

The call was answered before she even heard it ring.

'Bella? Where are you?' Catherine sounded frantic.

'Sorry. Ben called to "explain" everything. It took a while.'

There was silence on the other end of the phone. And then, 'Bella, why did you give him a hearing? The man's a psychopath!'

'I wanted to hear how he would explain himself. But you were right. He's got Isadora. Of course he's blaming all the stuff on the USB on her, he's not stupid. But it's as thin as air, his story. He's desperate to find a way to get hold of that evidence, he's trying everything he can.' She released the handbrake. 'I called to tell you not to worry, I'm on my way.'

Chapter Twenty-One

If she put her foot down it would take less than five minutes to reach the AC gates. Almost as soon as she'd pulled out of the layby back onto the road her phone rang.

She groaned in annoyance. The screen showed an unknown number. Ordinarily, she'd ignore it on the assumption it was someone wanting to chat about an accident she might have been involved in that wasn't her fault. But as it was... She accepted the call.

'Bella.' Ben's voice. 'Don't hang up. I know you don't believe me, but there's someone here you might find more convincing.' There was some rustling around and then she heard a familiar voice in the background saying, 'What is it you want me to do? Who?' And then much more audibly as if the person had taken the phone and was speaking into the receiver, Bella heard Maggie's voice say, 'Hello, dear?'

A car beeped and Bella realised she'd veered over the middle line, dangerously close to oncoming traffic. She swerved back onto her side of the road and braked hard, earning herself another beep – from the car behind her this time – and pulled into the verge, putting her hazard lights on.

'Maggie?'

'Yes, dear.'

'Maggie, are you okay?'

'I've not had my bacon buttie, since you ask. I like to have a bacon buttie first thing in the morning.'

'Is he... Is Ben holding you hostage? Has he hurt you?'

There was a peal of laughter. Bella heard her say to someone away from the phone, 'She wants to know if Ben's holding us hostage!' A male voice could be heard laughing.

Maggie moved her mouth back to the receiver and said to Bella, 'I don't know what gave you that idea, sweetheart. Living in London all that time, I expect. Made you suspicious.'

'But, Maggie,' Bella insisted, 'I don't understand. Why are you with Ben?'

'Well it's safest, you see,' she explained. 'I wasn't keen at first. He found me walking home from your house through the village and wanted to pick me up in his car. I thought, I know your game, you're from Acorns, you're up to no good. But then he explained about my Teddy and everything and asked if I'd like to see him. So, of course I said yes. And here we are.'

'Here... you are? You and Teddy?'

'Yes, and,' her voice turning into a hiss, 'that woman from Acorns. But my Teddy and I don't speak to her.'

'And Teddy's okay?'

'He's not been eating well. No one knows how to make his sandwiches the way he likes them except me, you see. But he's not too bad, considering.'

Bella heard muffled talking in the background, then Maggie said, 'What I'm supposed to be telling you, Teddy says, is that you can trust Ben. He saved Teddy on that nasty island and brought him home. To me.'

Her voice was replaced by Ben's. 'We can tell you all about it in person, Bella. You need to come here. Don't go to OAK, don't give Catherine the USB. Where are you now?'

'About half a mile from AC, pulled up at the side of the road.'

'Lock your doors and get back on the road as soon as you can, they might be out looking for you. You need to come here to the farm; do you remember where it is?'

'I've got it in my satnav.'

'Okay. So, you'll come?'

Her brain was grappling with the screeching U-turn it was having to negotiate. But there didn't seem to be any doubt.

'Yes. I'll be there as soon as I can.'

Bella reached the dirt track to the barns without incident, glancing every minute in her rear-view mirror to check she wasn't being followed. Bumping down the rutted road, she remembered the last time she'd visited that isolated spot. Ben had been so convincing then that she hadn't even given a cursory glance into the other buildings. If she had, how differently would everything have panned out? Ben had tricked her that time, could it be that he was pulling the wool over her eyes again now?

The car hit a large pothole, jolting her head back against the headrest.

The difference was, Ben alone hadn't convinced her this time, it had been the reassurance provided by Maggie and the fact that Teddy was with her. That was a piece of evidence that should put her mind at rest.

The dirt track petered out by a large area of cracked concrete bordering the nearest barn. Bella pulled up onto it and switched off the engine. She sat with her hands on the steering wheel, all energy gone. How long was it since she'd last eaten? Or slept properly? Exhaustion was fuelling her paranoia about Ben and who to trust. Catherine had made so much sense on the phone, she was such an implausible criminal. She'd never seen Catherine so much as put a bit of rubbish in the wrong recycling bin. *Come on, Bella*, she chided herself. *Pull yourself together. There'll be time to collapse in a heap when Oscar's safe and this whole OAK mess has been sorted out.*

There was a thud against the passenger window and she leapt out of her seat, banging her head on her window as she threw herself in the opposite direction. For a second all she could see was glasses and a haystack of blonde hair, and then the door was yanked open and Maggie was crawling across the seat towards her, pulling her in for an awkward hug with one arm.

'There you are! Thank goodness Acorns didn't get you!' She was half-sitting on the passenger seat now, one knee pressed into the gearstick, pulling a stunned Bella towards her. 'I knew I was right to ask you to help when I came to your house. Thank you for saving my Teddy.'

'I didn't...' Bella tried to extricate herself, patting the other woman's arm and pulling away. 'I didn't save him.'

Maggie wagged a finger in her face. 'Don't be a silly billy. If you hadn't told Ben to find him, my Teddy might not be here today.'

A shadow fell across Bella's side of the car and she looked up to see Ben opening her door.

'I'm glad you're here, Bella. We need to move your car though, to make sure it can't be seen from the road.'

After they'd persuaded Maggie to get out and the Alfa had been re-parked under a lean-to next to Ben's Aston Martin, Bella got out and looked around her. The three large barns that she'd seen before seemed as unused and deserted as the last time she'd been there. Open fields stretched in every direction, dotted with the occasional tree. The early sun was sparkling in drops of dew in the grass at her feet.

'Come on,' Ben invited her. 'We should all get inside out of sight. OAK's eyes are everywhere, despite our best efforts with the systems.'

As he strode ahead, dragging open the door of one of the barns, she ran to catch up. When they were all inside Bella helped him push the heavy tractor-sized door closed.

'Listen,' she said, as he led the way between a tractor and pick-up truck to the back of the barn. 'Catherine's got Lauren and Oscar. Cupuli caught them at my house, and when she called me, Catherine said Oscar wasn't well. She wouldn't let me speak to him. If Catherine and Isadora are as fanatical as you say I'm worried about what'll happen to them.'

Ben was opening the front cover of a fuse box on the wall. The false front flipped open and behind it were concealed a couple of switches. He reached for the top one. 'You should be. We all should be.'

He motioned for her to step back and the area of floor where she'd been standing slid aside as he flicked the switch, revealing a concrete shaft which had a metal ladder screwed to its side. Maggie was surprisingly gung-ho; the sound of her brogues rang out against the rungs as she scampered down. Bella had one last moment of doubt before taking a deep breath and following her.

She stepped off the bottom rung onto the floor of a small square lobby lit by fluorescent lights, one solitary door facing the ladder. Ben joined them, pressed a button in the wall and the trapdoor slid shut. At the touch of another button the door opened.

Bella found herself in a large, well-lit bunker. To her right was a control panel with a bank of screens, over towards the far wall was an area with tables and chairs and an open door into what looked like a kitchenette, from what she could see of a worktop and sink through the gap. On the other side of a glass partition she could see a row of camp beds and to her left were several closed doors, one of which had a clear panel through which could be seen racks of guns.

Aside from the amount of equipment and the level of sophistication with which the space had been kitted out, the main thing that shocked Bella was the number of people in the room.

She recognised Field Cupule James, sitting at the control panel – he turned and gave her a brief nod as she came in. Beside him was a woman she didn't recognise, and there must have been ten or fifteen other people she didn't know sitting around tables, most of them American by the sound of their accents. One of them turned around and Bella recognised Theresa.

'Hey, Bella!' Theresa got up and came across to give her a hug. 'Glad you decided to join us.'

'Theresa! I wasn't expecting to see you. What is this place?'

'An old field cupule outpost,' Ben said. After a quick word with James, he'd come over to join them. 'Decommissioned years ago, but James knew about it and was able to get it up and running for us.'

Ben brought Theresa up to speed about Oscar and Lauren. Maggie, who had shot off as soon as they got inside, reappeared round the side of the glass partition leading a familiar-looking man whose checked shirt bulged around his pot belly.

'Say hello to Bella, Teddy,' Maggie instructed.

Teddy held out a plump hand. 'It's a pleasure to meet you. Conscious, that is,' he added, with a shy smile.

'Hello, Teddy. Lovely to see you recovered,' Bella said, squeezing his hand before she released it.

'Not recovered,' Maggie admonished, reaching a hand across to pat his belly. 'He's a shadow of himself. Needs feeding up.' She slipped her arm under his and pulled him closer to her side.

Ben and Theresa had gone across to confer with James and, excusing herself, Bella joined them. As she approached, her eye was caught by the banks of screens. Some of them showed shots of the outside of the farm, some were linked up to cameras in the AC grounds and OAK interiors; but there was one in particular that caught her eye. In a bare, cell-like room sat a neat little woman in a Chanel suit and pearls, hands folded in her lap. On the table next to her was a full glass of water and an untouched plate of food. Almost as if she sensed Bella's eyes on her, Isadora slowly raised her head and stared down the lens of the camera, her face expressionless. After a moment or two when Bella found she was rooted to the spot, holding her breath, Isadora's lip curled into the faintest sneer before her face again lost all expression and she dropped her gaze. Bella shivered.

'Bella?'

She realised Ben had been trying to get her attention.

'Sorry, I was distracted by your guest.' She motioned towards the image of Isadora on the screen. 'What did you say?'

'I was asking for your opinion. We all agree we need to get Oscar and Lauren out as soon as possible. If Catherine and Finn know Lauren's working with me, they'll do all they can to get information out of her.'

Bella nodded. 'And they already pressured Oscar to tell Catherine how to get in touch with me, and that I have the USB. Plus, he told them about these farm buildings – he doesn't know where they are, but I'd lay odds Finn has teams searching local farms as we speak.'

'We need to catch them off guard,' James said. Indicating the group of people at the far side of the room, he said, 'We've got more manpower now, thanks to Theresa. They won't be expecting us to turn up at OAK. We can get in there, get Oscar and Lauren and get out. I know where they'll be holding them.'

'It's too risky,' was Theresa's instant response. 'These guys aren't cupuli, James. They're agents, we trained them to be kind, not to storm buildings.'

'We have to act,' James urged, punching one fist into his other palm. 'Waiting here doing nothing is suicide.'

'How about calling the police?' suggested Bella.

As one, all three turned and stared at her, as if she'd suggested they all smear themselves in chocolate and dance the Macarena.

'We can't send the police into OAK,' Ben explained, as if to a small child.

'But...'

'It's not an option,' Theresa said with an air of finality. 'We can go into the whys and the wherefores later, but for now, we need a plan that doesn't involve the police. A sensible plan,' – looking at James – 'that won't endanger the lives of my staff.'

'Agreed,' said Ben. 'Catherine's not going to stop until she's got Isadora back, along with that incriminating evidence on the USB.'

They were silent for a moment, Theresa removing her gold-rimmed glasses and rubbing the bridge of her nose. Bella watched her then took a sharp intake of breath.

'I've got an idea,' she said.

Chapter Twenty-Two

Oscar couldn't remember a time when he'd felt this miserable. In his late teens, he'd broken his jaw in rugby practice and had to drink all his food blended through a straw for weeks. The memory of the pain of the initial collision and the subsequent operation, as well as the misery of not being able to open his mouth wider than the diameter of a straw for all that time, paled into insignificance in comparison with this mental anguish.

At the moment of Catherine yelling 'Three!' he'd looked in desperation at Lauren, seen her lips pressed firmly together and been convinced no help was coming from that direction. He'd thrown his hands up in surrender and screamed that he'd tell Catherine whatever she wanted to know.

His panicked mind had tried to sift through his bits and pieces of knowledge and work out what to feed her and what to hold back, but in the end, he'd told her how they'd escaped from the garage at OAK, the fact of Bella having her old phone with her, that she'd been at her house to get the USB but had escaped somehow, and the description of the farm buildings where she'd found Ben.

The one thing he'd kept back was the phone call to his mum to pick them up and take them to Bella's house. No one noticed a timing issue between them leaving the AC grounds and arriving at Bella's – he'd been careful to be vague about when they'd escaped. Telling them about Gladys was too much, he couldn't bear the thought of her answering the door to an intimidating cupule.

Now the immediate jeopardy had passed, he went back over the scene in his mind, forcing himself to relive the moment he'd let physical cowardice overcome any principles of loyalty or a sense of standing up for what was right.

He'd heard it said you find out who you really are in a crisis. He'd found out – and it wasn't an acquaintance he was relishing.

Shivering, from cold and exhaustion, he pulled the grey blanket closer around his shoulders, hugging his knees to his chest. He was hunched on a bunk at the side of the cell. Lauren sat with her head in her hands in a chair on the other side of the room.

They hadn't tied her up this time, but Catherine had warned her when the cupuli were taking her and Oscar away, that if Oscar's information didn't get them what they wanted, they'd be back to speak to Lauren. Oscar had had his head injury checked out in the medical centre and then had been put back into the cell.

'Lauren,' he whispered.

No sign that she'd heard him.

He tried again. 'Lauren.'

She sighed and raised her head. 'What?'

'I'm sorry. I should have realised you wouldn't be working against OAK. I've known you long enough. But it all seemed so odd – I saw you and Ben with that field cupule, and then it seemed like Ben was the one behind Isadora going missing…'

She jerked around, putting a finger to her lips and looking around the room as if to indicate cameras and bugs.

Oscar rubbed his shins to get the circulation going. 'I'm not saying anything they don't already know. I mean, fuck it,

I don't *know* anything they don't already know after spilling my guts back there.'

Lauren crossed the cell and sat down next to Oscar on the narrow bed. She put an arm around his shoulders.

'She was threatening to shoot you in the leg. If you hadn't said something I would have done.'

He pulled back a little and twisted around so he could see her face.

'I looked at you,' he said. 'I thought you'd been turned to stone.'

'I was trying to stay strong because I knew what a risk it was for so many people if I said anything. But I promise you, I'd taken a breath to speak as soon as I heard her say "three". At first, I'd thought she was bluffing, but then I saw the expression in her eyes change when she was steeling herself to do it. I couldn't sit there and let it happen.'

The noise of a bolt being drawn back made them both jump.

Finn stood in the doorway. There was something different about his bearing from the desperate man they'd seen earlier. He stood a little straighter. Something had been done to freshen up his clothes.

'Up, both of you,' he barked. 'We're going for a ride.'

❧ ❧

Twenty minutes later they were being bundled out of the back of a van, blinking in the early morning sunlight. They'd been cuffed again and Oscar stumbled as he jumped down, Finn reaching out a meaty hand to haul him upright.

From a field on the other side of the road came the plaintive bleating of lambs. A light breeze caressed his skin. Oscar couldn't open his mind to the charms of a fresh spring morning, because it was too crammed full of apprehension. Finn and the other cupuli guarding them had given no indication as to why they were leaving OAK or where they were going. In the back of the van, he and Lauren had exchanged murmured guesses but anything they could come up with seemed worse than being left undisturbed in a cell. And his first thought on seeing the acres of empty landscape around him was that they'd been taken there to be… disposed of. A second glance as they stepped away from the back of the van, however, revealed a group of large farm buildings in the distance, and Bella's description of the barns where she'd found Ben sprang to mind.

Lauren clambered out of the vehicle and stood beside him, shivering a little despite the sun's rays.

Behind them two more vehicles pulled up, Catherine emerging from the first. She strode towards Finn, her attitude suggesting to Oscar an undergraduate crossing the stage to receive her degree, her buoyant step a mixture of anticipation and jubilation.

'This look like the right place?' she queried.

'By the group of ash trees, with the barns due south-west of us,' Finn confirmed, as if he were reciting an instruction. 'Rawson says he thinks there used to be a field cupule post round here.'

They both looked across the field to the steel-framed wooden buildings in the distance. There was no sign of life. Catherine gripped her phone in her hand.

'They're due to call back at seven am,' she said, looking at the time on the screen. Catherine and Finn exchanged glances and then surveyed the fields and barns again. They reminded Oscar of figures from an old Soviet poster, drawn in profile, chins uplifted against a rising sun, ready to face innumerable hardships in order to protect the motherland.

They all waited. A couple of cupuli lit cigarettes and talked in low tones.

The phone rang and Catherine answered before the first tone had finished ringing out.

'Yes?'

She'd put it on speakerphone and held it in the palm of her hand so Finn could hear.

'Catherine?'

It was Bella's voice on the other end of the line and Oscar's stomach lurched.

'Yes,' Catherine confirmed. 'We're here, where you told us.'

'Okay, good. You need to follow my instructions to the letter. If anything varies from what we agreed, the deal's off.'

'I understand.'

'We'll give you Isadora and the USB in exchange for Oscar and Lauren, as agreed.'

Out of the corner of his eye, Oscar saw Lauren shake her head no. He reached out with his bound hands and squeezed her arm.

'This is how we're going to do it,' Bella continued, her voice ringing metallically out from the phone, which Catherine had turned up to full volume. 'You're going to release Oscar and Lauren from where you're standing and they'll cross the field to the buildings. They won't be handcuffed or restrained in any way. At the same time, we'll release Isadora and she'll cross the field to you. She'll be holding the USB, raised in her right hand so you can see it. No one else will enter the field. We won't take a step past the boundary point of the buildings and if we see any of you on the field, the deal is off. When Isadora reaches you, you take her and the USB back to OAK and you get on with your lives. Don't try to come after any of us, don't go to the police. Agreed?'

'Wait,' Catherine snapped, then pressed mute on the phone.

Finn was watching her face as she digested what she'd heard. 'Do you trust them?' he asked.

Catherine laughed. Oscar rarely heard her laugh and it wasn't a pleasant sound, it reminded him of the humourless, ack-ack of a chimpanzee.

'No, I don't trust them at all. But if we do what they say, we're both in the same boat. We can station our team with Oscar and Lauren in their sights the whole way across the field. They'll have Isadora covered in the same way. But I need to know she's safe first.'

She unmuted the phone. 'I want to speak to Isadora.'

There was some muffled noise through the speaker, what sounded like chair legs scraping along the floor. After a couple of seconds, a new voice came on the line.

'Catherine?'

Oscar was close enough to see Catherine's eyes fill with tears as she peered down at the phone cradled in her hands.

'Isadora!' she cried. 'Are you alright?'

Finn had stepped up behind her and they both gazed down at the phone as if contemplating their newborn baby.

'I'm very well, Catherine, thank you,' Isadora replied, her voice fainter than Bella's had been. 'How is OAK?'

Before Catherine could reply, Bella was back.

'We don't have time for that. Are you happy with the arrangements now?'

'No!' Catherine snapped. 'Put Isadora back on. I need to know she has the USB before I agree to anything.'

They heard Bella say to Isadora, 'She wants to know if you've got the files,' before Isadora could be heard speaking into the phone once more.

'I have them,' she said. 'They put the memory stick into a computer to show me the documents then ejected it and passed it to me.'

'In that case,' Catherine responded, the slightest of smiles lightening her expression, 'we'll see you very soon.'

There was more rustling on the phone line then,

'Okay, you agree to the terms?' Bella asked. 'You'll bring Oscar and Lauren to the edge of the field now?'

Catherine nodded to Finn who took out some wire cutters and snapped off the hard plastic binding Lauren's wrists, then did the same for Oscar. Gripping them both above the elbow, he walked them up to a barred gate set in the hedge.

'Good,' Bella said. 'Get him to open the gate and then step back. Oscar and Lauren have to come through on their own.'

Finn made a move but Catherine called out, 'Stop.' Then, into the phone, 'We need to see Isadora first.'

'Hold on.' They could hear muffled movement and footsteps on the other end of the line, then silence as if the phone had been muted. A couple of minutes passed, then a diminutive figure appeared, dark against the bright sky between two barns. The figure moved forward until it was standing at the point where the concrete apron of the barns met the green-brown of the scrubby pasture.

Bella's voice could be heard again through the speakerphone. 'Get him to open the gate and send them through.'

Finn threw a questioning look at Catherine who nodded. Oscar reached out and took Lauren's hand — whether to reassure her or himself he wasn't sure.

The field sloped gently down to the barns, coarse grass punctuated here and there by clumps of cowslips and daisies. Finn stepped back from the open gate and the two hostages passed through, hand in hand. He pushed the gate closed behind them.

At the same time, the small figure in the distance began to walk.

❧ ❧

Catherine ended the call and put the phone in her pocket, clinging to the top bar of the gate as she watched Isadora pick her way across the pasture. One hand was raised as Bella had promised it would be, but she was too far away to be able to see what Isadora was holding.

She was vaguely aware of Finn conferring with the cupuli behind her, putting them into position along the hedge with their guns trained on the tall figure of Oscar and shorter one of Lauren beside him as they crossed the field. Lauren stumbled and Oscar grabbed her arm, pausing for a second to speak to her, before they continued on.

It seemed to Catherine to take an age. 'Come on, come on!' she urged under her breath.

After all the tension of not knowing where Isadora was or if she would ever see her again, to have her so close but to be unable to go to her was agony. And to see her like this, in her neat clothes and pristine court shoes picking her way through ankle-length grass and weeds, one hand in the air — it was undignified! The leader of OAK should never be treated in this way. It was a monstrous lack of respect for both the woman and the office of CEO of OAK, the most important organisation in the world.

Rage built inside Catherine as she saw Isadora nearly lose her balance and fling out a hand to steady herself. Bella might have made her promise to leave them all to get on with their lives, but Catherine had no intention of honouring that promise. As soon as Isadora was safe, Bella and the others wouldn't know what had hit them. Finn and his troops would storm the buildings and capture everyone inside. She wasn't going to risk them going free, possibly with copies of the USB files to make public.

She became more aware of the men and women ranged on either side of her as one of them shifted position and she heard the sound of a mechanism engaging on a rifle.

'Be careful!' she snapped. 'Isadora Faye is on that field.'

'Fingers off triggers,' Finn called out. 'No one shoots unless I give the order.'

The three hostages were nearing each other now, Isadora still holding one hand in the air, and it seemed to Catherine that perhaps she could see something small and black gripped in her fingers. But it could be her tired eyes playing tricks. She blinked several times, trying to relieve the dryness.

Isadora kept her head forward, chin dropped, eyes on the ground watching where she trod as she laboured up the slope. Oscar and Lauren could be seen to turn their heads to look at her as they passed. Catherine couldn't tell if words had been exchanged but suddenly Oscar stumbled and seemed to be trying to turn and grab Isadora. Lauren held on to him, one arm around his shoulder. He struggled.

'Keep walking!' yelled Catherine, cupping her hands around her mouth to help the sound carry.

Lauren pulled his head down and spoke into his ear. His shoulders drooped and he allowed himself to be led onwards towards the barn.

Catherine's attention switched from Oscar back to Isadora. She looked terribly thin. Catherine felt the cold metal hard against her palm as she gripped the bar harder. How dare Bella and Ben do this to Isadora! How dare they betray OAK in the process! She took deep breaths, trying to keep calm. She felt the reassuring presence of Finn close beside her.

'She looks… broken down,' he murmured.

'She's exhausted!' Catherine snapped, not able to bear even Finn passing comment on Isadora. 'She's been pushed to the limit with anxiety about OAK and not eating properly, I expect.'

'She's got the USB,' Finn said.

They both looked at the little black stick, now visible but held ever lower minute by minute as the strain took its toll on Isadora's muscles.

Catherine glanced back at Oscar and Lauren. They were almost three-quarters of the way across the field. Isadora was making slower progress, head still down, taking care not to stumble. She glanced up for a moment and Catherine gasped, releasing her grip on the gate.

'Stop!' she screamed, her panicked tones reverberating around the landscape.

Immediately, they heard another voice, hidden somewhere in the group of trees and shrubs to their left call out, 'Down!'

In the distance, Lauren dropped to her knees, pulling Oscar down with her until they were both flat on their fronts. Isadora lowered herself to the ground with some difficulty. The row of cupuli tensed, awaiting an order, but Finn had spun round towards the voice and now stood rooted to the spot.

At first, Catherine couldn't take in what was happening or who these newcomers were, had some of the cupuli turned on her? But as the group advanced towards them and she scanned their faces, she recognised Ben Eliott, and by his side, a field cupule called James. Spreading out behind them to cover the full line of cupuli with their weapons were six or seven others, some of whom she didn't recognise and others whose faces were familiar. All of this flashed through her head in the fraction of a second as she cast around for an escape.

'Lower your weapons,' James warned the cupuli. 'Now!'

He was approaching Catherine but his eyes were on Finn and the gun in Finn's hand. She took advantage of his attention being elsewhere to dart out of reach. Finn put out a protective arm as James launched himself towards her, giving her a vital opportunity to take off, sprinting towards the parked vehicles. Before she could reach them, panting as the adrenalin pumped through her body, a shot rang out and she heard Ben's voice.

'Stop! It's over, Catherine. Give it up.'

Glancing over her shoulder she saw that Finn had lowered his gun and the cupuli had their hands in the air, their weapons at their feet. Ben's gun was pointing skywards but as she turned, he brought the muzzle down to point towards her.

'It's over,' he repeated, more quietly. A woman with blonde hair who Catherine recognised from the US office jogged across and took her by the elbow to lead her back over to the others. Catherine shook her off.

'Don't touch me!' she snapped. For the space of a couple of breaths, she stood where she was, taking in the scene as her heart pounded in her chest. She looked at Finn, desperate to see resistance in his eyes, a signal that he had a plan to get them out of this – but all she saw was humiliation before he dropped his gaze to the floor. One of Ben's team was walking along the row of cupuli, gathering up weapons.

Ben motioned her over with his gun. 'Come on, Catherine. This is pointless.'

The blonde woman reached out again and in one last act of defiance, Catherine elbowed her in the stomach, leaving the poor woman doubled over and gasping as Catherine stalked away towards Ben, head held high.

Ben waited to see her safely under guard before opening the gate and running over to the Chanel-suited figure who was now on her feet. She brushed the dirt from her skirt and patted her hair back into place, then turned a triumphant smile on Ben.

'That was one of my finest performances. I wish the critics had been here to see it.'

She dropped into a low curtsey, Ben gripping her elbow to keep her from toppling over. As she levered herself back up with his help, he leaned over and kissed her on the cheek.

'Gladys,' he said, 'you deserve an Oscar.'

'I've got one,' she twinkled back at him. 'And now I'd very much like to see him.'

Chapter Twenty-Three

'You shouldn't have done it, Mum!' Oscar was furious. 'It was too risky!'

'Tut, dear! All's well that ends well.' Gladys patted his arm.

They were sitting across from Bella at one of the tables in the bunker, Oscar's angry tone belied by the arm cradling his mother's shoulders. She was wrapped in a thick pink shawl and trembling through her repeated protestations that she was fine and they needn't worry about her. Around them, Lauren, Theresa and the others variously sat, stood or – in Ben's case – paced up and down. Teddy and Maggie had taken themselves off to the area behind the glass partition and were resting on camp beds.

'When I saw you...' Oscar's face blanched at the memory and he shook his head. 'When I realised you were out there on that field walking towards those lunatics with guns—'

'You nearly gave the game away,' his mother finished for him, stroking his cheek. 'I know. Luckily your friend here is made of sterner stuff.'

Lauren waved the compliment away. 'It wasn't my mum out there! Plus, I knew Ben wouldn't have sent you if he wasn't certain you would be safe.'

Ben paused in his pacing and looked over. 'As certain as I could be, but it was still very brave of Gladys. *Very* brave.' The pacing resumed, interspersed with glances at the monitors, one of which showed the group of captured cupuli sitting around in a cell, looking despondent. On another screen could be seen a different room in which Finn, Isadora and Catherine conferred in a huddled knot.

'How on earth did you get involved in all this, Mum?' Oscar asked, rearranging the shawl that had slipped from her shoulder.

'I'm sorry, Oscar,' Bella said from across the table where she was watching them with her chin in her hand. 'That was me. And I feel very guilty about it.'

'Nonsense!' cried Gladys, reaching out across the table and forcing Bella to take her hand. 'You did the right thing. In fact, I wouldn't have forgiven you if you hadn't called me, my lovely girl.'

'We were stumped,' Bella explained to Oscar. 'We needed a way to get you two out of OAK but we knew Catherine would never give you up without getting Isadora back. And then I remembered – Theresa used to be a make-up artist. She fixed my face on Le Chêne on karaoke night when I was looking a bit worse for wear.'

'A bit!' Theresa was heard to mutter under her breath.

'My first thought was she could disguise me as Isadora but almost as soon as I thought of it, I realised how ridiculous it was. No one would fall for it. There was no one else here who would be any more convincing. And then I remembered I knew someone almost the same build as Isadora and with the same colour hair... it was a massive risk but there was a chance we could make it work. I called Gladys, told her you were in trouble and she was here in a flash.'

'I couldn't sleep anyway, darling.' Gladys said in an aside to Oscar. 'I was wide awake, wondering what had happened and why I hadn't heard from you. Having the chance to do something to help – well, I leapt at it. And of course, when I learnt I wouldn't be a bit player in the dramatis personae, but the star! I couldn't resist, my boy.'

235

'Theresa was able to style Gladys's hair and do her make-up so she would pass as Isadora at a distance,' Bella explained. 'We knew it wouldn't hold up when she got closer, but by keeping her head down as she was crossing the field, she made it further than we expected, didn't you, Gladys?'

Before she could answer, Theresa cut in. 'Gladys was faultless, but we never doubted she would be. To my mind, the critical moment when something could have gone wrong was when we did the swap. Isadora had told Catherine on the phone that she had the USB. When we hung up Isadora was expecting us to lead her out to the field. When I told her to start undressing, she was confused at first and then, my god, she was mad with rage. It took four of us to get her out of those clothes so Gladys could put them on. And we had very little time to do it.'

Gladys grimaced at the memory. 'She was very cross. Even when I gave her my precious mink and gown in return.'

As one, they all turned to look at the monitor where Isadora could be seen, clad in a floor-length evening gown, fur coat and silver sandals.

'But now, my dears,' Gladys said, consulting an elegant gold watch on her fragile wrist, 'it's about the time I have my morning cup of tea. I wonder if such a thing as tea is to be found down here?'

Three or four people sprang up, but Bella was quickest. 'I'll do it! Who else wants one?'

Most people did apart from Ben who dismissed the suggestion with a shake of his head. He now stood right in front of the monitors watching the little group of Isadora et al intently.

'James should be back soon with our bargaining chip,' he murmured. 'Plenty of time after that for cups of tea.'

In the kitchenette, Bella filled two battered kettles with water and took a handful of dusty mugs down from the shelf. She heard a footstep and turned to find Oscar in the doorway.

'Can I help?' he asked.

'Sure. Tea's over there.'

He nodded but made no move to get it, instead covering his face with both hands and taking a great breath in. She stopped what she was doing and went across to him, leading him into the room and pushing the door to behind them.

'Are you okay?' She kept hold of his sleeve and after a moment or two he lowered his hands and the look on his face made her well up.

'I'm sorry, Bella.' He couldn't meet her eye. 'I told Catherine everything. They'd found us at your house – Lauren and me – and marched us into OAK. Catherine and Finn were there and Catherine... I've never seen her like that. It was like she was a whole other person. So cold and detached. She said she was going to shoot me in the leg if I didn't tell her everything I knew. She counted to three and...'

His voice trailed off and Bella hugged him, hard.

'Of course you bloody told her! She was going to shoot you, for God's sake. You're a human being, Oscar, not a character in a film.'

He muttered something so quietly she couldn't hear.

'What's that?' she asked.

'Ben wouldn't have told her,' he repeated.

'We don't know what Ben would have done. He wasn't the one being threatened with a gun.'

'I just,' he pushed her away, moved over to the other side of the room and leaned back against the worktop, 'I just feel like shit, you know. I told her everything – that you'd been at your house, that you had the USB, stuff you'd told me about the barns. Even though I knew it meant they'd probably catch you. I hate the fact I did that. I hate myself. I feel like I don't know who I am at all. Even my eighty-year-old mother is a braver person than me. She risked her life for me!'

'Oscar!' She wanted to go over and hug him but his face plainly said that he wasn't ready to be comforted. 'Don't beat yourself up about it! You did what any normal person would do when faced with a madwoman with a gun. And we're all okay, everyone's fine – you, me, your mum. There's no point in all this guilt.'

He heaved a great sigh, his shoulders rising and falling, then he looked directly at her for the first time.

'I didn't come in here for sympathy. I came to say I'm sorry I let you down.' He saw she was opening her mouth to protest and held up a hand. 'I did let you down, no matter what you say. And you're one of the last people on earth I'd ever want to do that to.' He turned with an air of finality towards the kettles and mugs. 'And now I really, really want a cup of tea.'

Together they busied themselves with teabags and milk in silence, until he exclaimed, 'How the hell did you get out of your house? It was like a magic trick.'

'There's a way through to Angela's house next door from the loft. I was there when they searched the house and I saw you being dragged to the car afterwards.'

238

'Ah yes.' Oscar's hand went to his temple and patted it gingerly. 'One of those bastards didn't appreciate me telling him to go and look for you up his own arse.'

Bella laughed. 'And you say you're not brave!'

❧ ❧

Back at the table, cradling a cup of tea in both hands, Bella called over to Ben.

'What's the next move, Ben? We have to call the police now, right?'

Ben threw one last glance at the monitors, then crossed the room and drew up a chair beside her.

'Yes, we need to involve the police. But in such a way that OAK is protected.'

Theresa joined them at the table. 'Ben, don't you think it's about time we told these people what's been going on? It would make things a whole lot more straightforward.'

Ben glanced at his watch and then nodded. 'You're right. Let's kill two birds with one stone and let these guys in on it,' he added, getting up and unlocking one of the doors that led off the main room, swinging it open to reveal the group of cupuli. Those who'd been sitting on the floor got up as quickly as they could, hampered by their bound wrists. Ben invited them out with a jerk of his head and they filed into the main room, aggression and defiance in every look. Several of Theresa's US staff stood by, tense, as the cupuli installed themselves at a table in response to an instruction from Ben.

'What is all this bullshit?' called out a stocky cupule with contrasting grey hair and black eyebrows. 'You can't keep us here forever!'

'We're not going to,' Ben said. 'But before we let you go, I want you to hear what's been going on at OAK and why things need to change.'

For a moment he was silent, gazing down at his clasped hands on the scuffed tabletop.

'Like OAK itself,' he said, 'this whole mess started with the best of intentions. It started because Isadora loves OAK like nothing else in the world. She made Teddy Thatcher hack into AC's client accounts and steal their money because it would help OAK. She sent her brother to Le Chêne to kill or kidnap Teddy because it would help OAK. And if I've calculated correctly, she's going to solve this whole mess for us...' he gave a weary smile, 'because it will help OAK.'

The atmosphere had turned menacing over at the table of cupuli. Mutterings rippled around the table and dark looks were exchanged. The guy with the eyebrows, who seemed to be the most senior, slammed his bound hands down on the table.

'We're not going to sit here and listen to these lies about Isadora! Fuck you,' he yelled, jumping up and sending his chair flying backwards into the wall. The others followed suit and a couple of Theresa's agents grabbed their guns.

Ben was about to respond when a timid voice spoke up. Teddy had shambled around the end of the glass partition.

'It's all true, lads. The Librarian attacked me on Le Chêne. Look,' he approached the table and showed them a vivid pink welt on his neck. 'That's where he cut me. I was hiding from Isadora so she wouldn't make me steal any more money. Ben and James took me out there to keep me safe. And Theresa and some of these nice people,' he gestured to the agents who still had their guns trained on the cupuli, 'looked after me and helped smuggle me onto the plane home. I wish it wasn't true. I'd never have believed it of Isadora if I hadn't seen it all with my own eyes.'

All the fight seemed to have gone out of the cupuli leader at the unexpected appearance of Teddy Thatcher.

Ben signalled to the others to lower their guns.

'As soon as I found Teddy on Le Chêne,' Ben said, going over to stand beside him and putting an arm around his shoulder, 'I knew the game was up. I had to act fast. I didn't know if Teddy had said anything to The Librarian before passing out. If he had, Isadora would be hunting down anyone who'd helped in Teddy's escape from OAK. Plus, Bella here had seen Teddy injured and I didn't know who she would tell. I got a message to James to kidnap Isadora because although I didn't have a clear idea what our next move would be, the one thing I was sure about was she shouldn't be running OAK.'

'No,' agreed Maggie, who'd emerged from her camp bed to stand on the other side of Teddy. 'She's a very nasty woman.' Taking Teddy's arm, she led him to a chair and pushed him down onto it, standing by his side like a guard dog spoiling for a fight.

Ben took another look at his watch. 'We don't have long and I want to finish what I've got to say. Please,' he indicated the chairs that the cupuli had vacated, 'will you sit down?'

They looked to their leader who took his seat, his face grey.

'Isadora's drive to expand OAK has tipped over into mania,' Ben continued, when everyone was settled again. 'I shared my concerns with James and Lauren a few months ago and for a while – until I found out about the hacking –

we monitored things, trying to decide what to do.' He turned to Bella. 'There was a file called "Expansions" on the memory stick that Teddy left with Maggie, remember? Teddy had found some data on a drive that had been encrypted and he was curious as to what it was. He accessed the file and discovered the spreadsheet you've seen. What that spreadsheet revealed was the world doesn't need OAK. In fact, the world is a worse place because OAK exists.'

There were gasps from around the room.

Ben held up his hands. 'So far we have evidence in small samples but I'm convinced the same statistics would hold true everywhere. Isadora commissioned research to be done into the towns in the US where OAK planned to open outposts. She wanted to monitor the numbers of kindnesses carried out per head of the population so when OAK launched, she would be able to demonstrate the positive impact it had. We'd never done that kind of study in the UK before; we took it for granted that kindness levels would be higher where OAK operated. But when Isadora saw the figures, she realised something earth-shattering. The kindnesses per head in those US cities were the same as we were registering here in the UK, where OAK operates.'

A hubbub broke out all around the room.

'How can that be?' Bella wanted to know. 'What are you saying?'

'I'm saying where OAK doesn't exist, ordinary people step in and fill the void. While OAK still operates – every time an agent steps in ahead of you to perform a kindness – you're robbed of the sense of well-being that comes from helping others. The bond small kindnesses form between people, a bond that forms the basis of communities, is weaker while OAK is in operation. Not fully denied, there are still plenty of opportunities to be kind, agents can't be everywhere. But what Teddy's evidence showed us was that people's natural inclination is towards kindness and without OAK, they would have more opportunities to be kind.'

Ben stopped and let the idea sink in. All around the room concern showed on people's faces as they digested what they'd heard. The organisation they'd dedicated their lives to – that they'd lied to their families about, lost sleep over, risked their lives for in the past few hours – was worthless. Worse than worthless, it was making the world a poorer place.

'Believe me,' Ben said, taking in their horrified looks, 'I was as distraught as you when I realised what the data meant. OAK in its present form isn't a force for good. That's not to say it can't be, and that it's not worth saving – but that's for another day.

'When I understood what the data was showing I realised something else staggering. Isadora had seen this information and she'd buried it. Not because she's an inherently bad person but because she couldn't allow herself to believe it. OAK is Isadora's life's work. It's what her ancestors dedicated all their energy and money to create. This data wouldn't compute so she pretended it didn't exist and pushed on with her expansion plans regardless.

'It's her overriding passion for OAK that I'm banking on now. Because yes, Bella,' he turned towards her, 'we have to involve the police – there has to be some retribution for what she and the others have done. But I think OAK can be saved in some form and Isadora will help us do that. I've got two aces up my sleeve. Her love of OAK, and the one other thing she truly cares about.' His eyes had flicked back to the monitors, this time towards the far screen which showed the inside of the barn above them. Two figures could be seen passing between the tractor and the pick-up truck. 'Right on cue.'

They all waited in silence as the figures disappeared into the shadow behind the tractor. After a moment, muffled sounds could be heard in the lobby, growing louder. Footsteps paused outside the door.

'Here's our bargaining chip,' Ben said, standing up and pressing the button to open the door.

Stumbling a little as James pushed him into the room, hands tied behind his back, was the dishevelled figure of The Librarian.

Chapter Twenty-Four

The expression on Isadora's face turned from shock to suspicion when she saw The Librarian.

Ben had unlocked the door to her cell and she had emerged tentatively, eyes flickering between the faces.

She looks like she's aged ten years, Bella thought. Catherine stepped up to Isadora's side protectively. Finn loomed on her other side, looking very much as though if his hands weren't tied, he'd be using them to rip Ben's head off.

Everyone instinctively got up from their seats – *like children standing when the headmistress enters the room*, reflected Bella. The exception was Gladys, who remained in her chair and gave a cordial wave when she caught sight of Isadora.

'You look gorgeous in that dress, dear,' she called. 'It could have been made for you. Parisian couture, you know.'

Isadora stiffened and something of her usual regal bearing seemed to return to her as she pointedly ignored the other woman.

'Why,' she asked Ben, in a voice of ice, 'have you brought The Librarian here? He never leaves OAK.'

'Except when he's trying to murder people on tropical islands,' retorted Ben. 'Please take a seat – Isadora, Catherine, Arran.' The newly released captives sat down at the table with a show of reluctance, eyeing the weapons in the hands of Theresa's agents.

Lauren pushed a bottle of water toward Catherine who sent it flying with a blow from her bound hands.

'What the hell are you all playing at? What are you trying to achieve, keeping us prisoners here?'

'It won't be for much longer,' Ben promised. 'But we need to come to an understanding before we can let you go.'

James had taken The Librarian by one dirty tweed-clad arm and dragged him across to sit with the others. Isadora regarded him with troubled eyes.

'The Librarian has nothing to do with this,' she insisted. 'I demand that he be taken back to OAK.'

Ben took no notice of her, turning to address the room.

'At this point, ladies and gentlemen, it's worth providing a bit of backstory. I'm sure you all know how Isadora came home to run OAK after her mother died. As well as running the Institute, she also had to take on the care of her younger brother, who couldn't cope with losing his mother so soon after their father's early death. He had a breakdown and over the following years became an alcoholic. She kept him close by, giving him a ceremonial title that allowed him a position of respect at OAK without any associated responsibility. Most of you won't be aware that The Librarian is Isadora's brother.'

Bella heard Oscar mutter, 'What the...?' under his breath. He looked at her, eyes wide. She goggled back at him. A couple of the cupuli shifted round in their seats, shooting questioning looks at each other. Bella looked at Isadora, sitting primly in her borrowed evening dress, face white, and tried to make out some resemblance between her and the raddled man in the tweed suit.

The cupule with the eyebrows called out, 'Come on! Why should we believe this shit?'

To Bella's surprise, it was Isadora who replied. 'It's true. It's not a secret, it's just not widely known.'

'Isadora didn't think people knowing who The Librarian was would be helpful to OAK, did you, Isadora?' Ben said, calmly. 'Because, everyone, what you have to remember is Isadora's motivations are always – *always* – what's best for OAK. In this instance, Isadora, The Librarian is at the heart of our problem and our potential solution.' Looking over at Theresa he added, 'Could you explain?'

Theresa nodded.

'Isadora,' she said. 'I think you sent The Librarian out to Le Chêne to kill Teddy Thatcher. But whether you sent him or not, what's undeniable is that he was there and he attacked Teddy. I have the CCTV footage to prove it.' Isadora's hands gripped the edge of the table. 'The evidence on that tape,' Theresa continued, 'would make for a convincing attempted murder charge. Particularly when you add it to the testimony of Bella, Ben, and Teddy himself.' She gestured to Teddy who appeared to be trying to sink right through the seat of his chair, the floor, and several thousand miles of earth to start a new life in Australia. Maggie laid a hand on his shoulder and snarled at Isadora.

Catherine and Finn exchanged glances. Isadora appeared to have fallen to pieces, her eyes glued on her brother with a look of desperation. The Librarian was paying no attention to what was being said, his eyes flitting feverishly around the room.

Wondering if anyone's got any whisky, Bella guessed.

'What do you want, Ben?' snapped Catherine. 'If you had evidence and wanted The Librarian convicted, you'd have gone to the police by now.'

'I want the same as you – to save OAK.'

She snorted.

'I want to remove the elements who have been corrupting it, namely the four of you,' Ben went on, looking at her, Finn, Isadora and The Librarian. 'I want you to agree to be taken into custody and charged by the police for kidnapping, with a story that we will agree together. I want you to help prevent any investigation into fraud by AC against its clients.'

Catherine's eyes twitched. 'So, you're happy to profit from fraud? Your anti-corruption principles don't stretch that far?'

'No,' Ben said. 'With Teddy's help, we'll transfer the money back in a way that it can't be traced to us, even if we have to do it over a period of time. But if AC gets investigated the risk is that OAK will go down too. And I'm sure none of us want that.'

'All I ever wanted was to protect OAK,' said Isadora in a quiet voice. They all looked around, surprised. She had regained her composure somewhat and was watching Ben. 'My intentions have only ever been for good.'

'Then you'll do this. For OAK,' replied Ben.

Bella and Oscar helped move bits and pieces of furniture from the bunker up into the barn. Some people were stationed at the bottom of the shaft to push camp beds, chairs, a gas stove, catering packs of food and other sundries up to others who dragged them out through the opening and arranged them by some hay bales in one corner of the barn. Bella and Oscar were in the latter party – Bella adding some artful extra touches in the form of crumpled piles of clothes and half-empty bottles of water. By the time they finished, she was sweating, flapping the neckline of her T-shirt to waft cooler air to her clammy skin.

Everyone who wasn't required for the piece of theatre that was about to be staged was told to return to the bunker. The camera in the barn had been angled to cover the little group in the corner. Isadora, Catherine and Finn sat in a semi-circle on hay bales. The Librarian lay on a camp bed, facing away from them. The hands of all four were tied with baling twine. Maggie and Teddy stood hand in hand by the tractor while Ben paced back and forth between the captives and the entrance to the barn, a phone held to his ear. Nearby a hunting rifle leaned against the wall.

'Turns out Ben was right then,' Bella whispered to Oscar. 'When it comes down to it, Isadora will sacrifice almost anything for OAK.'

The atmosphere in the bunker was tense, everyone speaking in hushed tones as if they could be heard upstairs. The cupuli had been released from their restraints and a couple of them were lying, exhausted, in the dormitory area but most were in the main room, glued to the monitors.

Gladys joined her son and Bella, resplendent in her reclaimed dress and mink coat. Diamonds – or at least something that did a good impression of diamonds – sparkled at her ears.

'It's nice to feel properly dressed again after that dowdy old outfit.' She followed Oscar's gaze. 'Could you explain what's going on, dear? I think I drifted off and missed the important bits. That nice handsome Ben isn't going to shoot them, is he?'

'Of course not, Mum! He's calling the police. And then when they're on the way he's going to alert the media. Isadora's fall from grace needs to be public so there's no chance of her trying to take back OAK in the future.'

As they watched Ben took the phone away from his ear and touched the screen to end the call. He typed something else into his phone then replaced it to his ear.

'What has he told the police?' Gladys asked.

'The bare minimum, I expect,' Bella said. 'He'll keep the details for when they get here. The plan was he would say he'd found Isadora, Teddy, and Maggie and give them the location then hang up.'

'When they get here, he'll tell them the story they've all agreed to stick to,' Oscar added. 'Which is that The Librarian got drunk—'

'So far, so plausible,' interrupted Bella.

'The Librarian got drunk,' Oscar repeated, 'and picked a fight with Teddy, in which Teddy got hurt quite badly. Isadora panicked, worried her vulnerable, alcoholic brother would go to prison. To avoid that, she kidnapped Teddy then went into hiding herself. Her accomplices Catherine and Finn put it about that she'd been abducted. They thought Teddy might have smuggled footage of the fight out to Maggie when they heard about the "evidence" on the news so they snatched her from her house that evening. Ben had gone to her house to check she was okay, saw her being bundled into a van and followed the van here. He went home, got his hunting rifle and came back to investigate. He crept in, took them all by surprise and after tying them up and getting them to confess all, called the police. That's the story they've come up with, Mum, wrapped in a little bow ready to gift to the police.'

A look of perplexity clouded Gladys's brow. 'But that's not true. Why would Isadora and the others say it is? When they get to the police station and Isadora's on her own, she can tell them that Ben kidnapped her.'

'But she won't, Mum. Because she doesn't want Ben and Theresa to give the police the footage of The Librarian attacking Teddy. When they get to the police station Teddy will say the fight got out of hand but that both he and The Librarian were equally to blame and he doesn't want to press charges. So, although Isadora's brother may be charged as an accomplice to kidnapping and perverting the course of justice, he won't get anything like the sentence attempted murder would carry. And Isadora doesn't want the police investigating the fraud because it would lead them to OAK and would mean both AC and OAK would get shut down.'

'And your charity OAK is terribly important because...?' Gladys enquired, head on one side like a glamorous sparrow. 'It's all rather hard to follow.'

'It's best if we don't talk about it, Mum,' Oscar said. 'Because if I told you what OAK does,' he looked at her with mock-solemn eyes, 'I'd have to kill you.'

'Oh, you silly boy!' Gladys squealed with delighted laughter and slapped him on the arm.

On the screens, they saw Ben turn his head and one or two of the others look up, as if in response to a sound which hadn't yet penetrated to the bunker. Moments later, even underground, they heard sirens approaching.

Two or three more minutes passed in suspense and then in the corner of the screen armed police could be seen swarming forward, crouching low between the farm machinery, guns raised. There was no audio in the bunker but they seemed to be shouting orders, in response to which Ben set his rifle down on the floor and raised his hands. All the prisoners did likewise – as well as they could with bound wrists – as did Teddy. Maggie stood with her hands on her hips squaring up to an approaching officer until Teddy took her hands and raised them himself.

In the bunker, everyone held their breath. The only sound was the rattling of Gladys's jewellery as she fidgeted with her bangles.

The police made everyone stand up, including a reluctant Librarian, and two officers patted them down. A plain-clothes officer appeared and led Ben a little away from the rest, nodding in response to what he was telling her. Once everyone had been searched and all areas of the barn had been inspected by the armed officers, they started to round up Isadora, Finn and the rest and escort them towards the main doors to the barn.

All was proceeding without incident until the officer nearest the front of the group pulled up short and raised a hand to halt those behind him. He appeared to have seen something out of sight of the camera in the barn.

The lead officer strode forward out of the barn and out of sight. Minutes passed. Finally, he came back, spoke to another officer and again the group continued its procession towards the exit and out of sight of the camera.

For a minute or so no one moved. Then Theresa stood up.

'Well,' she said, 'I reckon we made it. Looks like the press got here on time too from the way that officer reacted. It's all down to Ben, Isadora and the rest of those guys now, let's hope the police go for their story. We'll wait ten minutes to be sure they've left, then take the emergency exit out of here through the other barn.'

❦ ❦

'Okay, Shobs,' Ailsa said, as she held up three fingers behind the camera.

Shobha nodded, arranging her face into her preferred on-screen expression of mixed professionalism and concern. She could hear the lunchtime news anchor in her earpiece announcing they were passing over to Shobha Sharma for an exclusive report from Wiltshire, where there had been developments in the Acorn Consulting kidnappings story.

'Three, two, one,' mouthed Ailsa.

'That's right, Rob,' Shobha said, nodding. 'Early this morning, *West Country Tonight* received an anonymous tip-off that the kidnappers of Isadora Faye, and Edward and Margaret Thatcher, were about to be apprehended by police.'

All around the country viewers watched as the shot of Shobha Sharma's face cut to shaky footage of the exterior of a barn with several police vans and an ambulance parked outside. Shobha could be seen, left of shot, running across the field towards the barn with a microphone in her hand, the camera jolting all over the place as its operator tried to keep up with her. They both slowed as they reached the building and Shobha pulled up, panting, out of sight of the door.

'I can hear voices inside the barn,' she rasped into her microphone as she struggled to catch her breath. 'I'm going to get a bit closer to see what's going on.'

She pressed herself against the wooden planking of the barn's exterior wall and edged along it to the doorway, the camera close behind her shoulder. As they both swung round into the barn, the camera struggling to refocus as it switched from sunlight to the windowless gloom, a voice yelled out.

'Get that camera out of here! Stop filming! Police, stop filming!'

An angry face, neck and top of a bulletproof vest filled the screen before the view swung down to show hay-strewn concrete. Then the shot cut back to the live feed of Shobha Sharma standing groomed and poised in her pastel green trench coat.

'The police ordered my crew and I to leave the property, but we were able to get some footage of what happened next.'

Again, the barn was the focus of the shot but this time from a distance, with foliage at the bottom of the frame as if the camera operator was crouching behind a hedge. Figures emerged from the building surrounded by police and Shobha's voice could be heard in voiceover.

'We are unable to identify everyone in this shot, but what we can be sure of is that both Mr and Mrs Thatcher, who have been missing, appear to be safe and well. Isadora Faye, CEO of Acorn Consulting, looks to be in police custody.'

Handcuffs were visible on Isadora's wrists as a police officer helped her climb into the back of the van.

Shobha's concerned expression filled the screen once more and the shot pulled back to reveal the barns behind her as she finished her report. All but one of the police vans had left and police tape was set up around the perimeter of the building.

'Today we're one step closer to unravelling the mystery of the Acorn Consulting kidnappings. Stay tuned to *West Country Tonight* for more updates. This is Shobha Sharma reporting.'

Chapter Twenty-Five

Theresa, Bella and the others drove straight back to AC with the cupuli and called everyone into the OAK auditorium. Looking at the haggard faces around her Bella could see many people looked exhausted, their nerves on edge. Some were still relatively well-kempt, but the majority looked as though they'd spent several years being held hostage in a cave. Evidence of a new development had filled them with hope and anticipation. Had Isadora been found? Was she dead? Either way, would they be able to go home?

Theresa stepped onto the stage.

'Friends and colleagues. It grieves me to tell you that Isadora Faye is in police custody, along with Arran Finn, Catherine Knight and The Librarian. It grieves me further to tell you that I expect them all to be charged with serious offences. I don't want to say more until we've had confirmation from the police and from Ben Elliott who is managing the situation with the authorities.' She paused for a few moments to allow the initial burst of consternation to die down. 'On a more positive note,' she called, lifting a hand for silence and raising her voice, 'I'm delighted to tell you that our colleague Teddy Thatcher has been found safe and well, along with his wife Maggie.'

'Where were they?' shouted someone in the front row.

'They were at a farm a few miles from here.'

'What has Isadora done?' someone else wanted to know.

'I'm sorry, I can't say any more for the time being. I want you to know the board and I are beyond grateful for your patience while you were held here. I know you must be desperate to get home, which you are now free to do. I promise the board will be holding a detailed enquiry into what happened and you will be given a full account in the next few days. Please take the rest of today off and enjoy some time at home with your families. You've earned it!'

Bella could see from the puzzled looks and shaking of heads that her colleagues were frustrated with the lack of information, but the relief of being able to go home ultimately overcame everything else. The auditorium emptied in minutes and only she, Theresa, Oscar, Lauren and the others from the bunker remained. Theresa contemplated them from her vantage point on the main stage as they sat, scattered across the front rows of the auditorium like the exhausted stalwarts at an all-night charity improv marathon.

She smiled. 'Well, you guys all look like shit, if you don't mind me saying. I'm planning a hot bath and then a king-size sleep in a king-size bed. I recommend a similar itinerary for the rest of you. Ben's going to message me with any updates and I'll let you all know as soon as there's news. Now get outta here, I don't want to see your faces until tomorrow.'

Bella experienced the familiar little lift of pleasure as her Alfa crested the hill two weeks later and the sprawling stone mansion came into view. On a whim, she brought the car to a halt, letting the engine idle as her eyes roamed across the building in front of her. She'd always loved the elegance of its lines, but today it struck her that the symmetry of the many windows and chimneys of the AC house was a homage to that found in nature – the mathematical perfection of shells and flowers. Isadora's ancestors, and their architects, had tried to mimic the natural world in their man-made construction. Which was ironic, when you thought about it, given that OAK had tried to put a man-made spin on a natural occurrence.

She remembered the very first time she'd made this journey, all those months ago, and her gaze switched to the manicured lawns and parterres surrounding the house. If someone had stopped her here, on that first trip, and told her what lay hidden underneath them, would she have continued on her way to the interview?

Bella snorted. To be honest, she probably would have done. It would have sounded too outlandish to be true – only the most dyed-in-the-wool conspiracy theorist could believe that this bastion of English gentility hid beneath it a high-tech, top-secret organisation which had infiltrated two continents and impacted the oblivious public on a daily basis. Particularly as she saw it today, its pristine walls and mullioned windows gleaming bright among the green; a gaggle of geese on the lake mirroring the white flecks of clouds in the otherwise clear blue sky.

She put the car back into drive and set off down the hill, her heart beating a little faster as she remembered the part she had to play in today's event. The view before her was no longer centre stage as her thoughts turned inward, running through mental notes, practising certain phrases. Ben had wanted them all to be involved – her, Lauren, Oscar... all of them. He wanted them to have a role in sharing the new vision. Normally, preparing to speak in public would be the cue for What Others Might Think of Her to pounce, but that creature was absent, Bella was pleased to discover. In fact, its hateful form crept up on her less and less often these days, and even when it did materialise in her peripheral vision it sat placidly on its haunches, wearing a collar and lead.

Something about dealing with matters of life and death had put the spectre of possible social embarrassment in perspective, perhaps. Or maybe having her own instincts proved right had made her less concerned with the opinions of others. Or perhaps, at the most basic level, she'd learnt that looking stupid wouldn't kill her.

❦

After the arrest of Isadora and her accomplices, AC had continued to operate, but OAK had been mothballed for a couple of weeks to give Theresa, Ben and the board time to make new plans.

Walking back in through the main doors today Bella was aware of a buzz about the place. People congregated in little knots in the entrance hall, swapping notes on the various rumours of what was going to be revealed in the all-staff meeting that morning.

Oscar waved her over. They'd swapped the odd message in the past fortnight but hadn't seen each other out of work, nor had she seen much of Lauren or Ben. Bella had gone away at the weekend, spending time with her parents and Zoe. She'd needed to immerse herself in normality after the frenzy of the past few days and weeks.

'Ready for your big moment?' Oscar asked as she joined him and Lauren at the foot of the staircase. His tone was a little too casual, as if he'd rehearsed that line; getting in first with a jokey comment before she could say anything. She decided to play along.

'I've practised it all apart from the lift at the end, I was hoping you could help me with that. You've seen *Dirty Dancing*, right?' enquired Bella.

'Nobody puts Bella in the corner,' confirmed Oscar.

'I'm looking forward to seeing that, you
Lauren as she glanced at her watch. 'Speaking o
better be getting down there.'

❧ ❧

The auditorium was overflowing, every seat taken and
pressed together by the doors and sitting in the gang
Bella, from her chair on stage between Oscar and Lau
squinted against the glare of the footlights and tried not
think about how far the rows of seats stretched into th
darkness beyond; how many pairs of ears would be listening
to her in a few minutes' time.

She was aware of a ripple of noise around the room and
then applause broke out as Ben jogged up the steps onto the
stage.

'Good morning.' He waited for the applause to die away.
This was corporate Ben again. Not a well-cut hair out of
place, tailored suit showing off his athletic build to
perfection. Bella found herself thinking she preferred the
dishevelled Ben of the underground bunker. 'Good morning
and thanks for your patience over the past couple of weeks.
I'm sorry it's taken a while to call this meeting. We wanted to
be able to share full details of what we hope the OAK
Institute can evolve into with your help, and that took a little
time to prepare.'

He took a step to the side and indicated the row of
occupied chairs set at an angle across the stage. 'As you
know, the board have appointed me CEO, but the only way
I'll be able to lead this organisation into the future is through
a team effort, which is why I've asked some of your
colleagues to come and help me share the vision.' Two chairs
at the end of the row were empty and Ben walked across to

259

d behind them, a hand on the back of each. 'To kick us
, I'd like you to welcome two very special guests – Teddy
d Maggie Thatcher.'

A spotlight flicked on by one of the doorways,
lluminating an uncertain-looking Teddy and Maggie with her
hand to her eyes to shield them from the light. People started
clapping and cheering and within moments the whole
auditorium was on its feet as the pair stumbled across the
floor towards the stage. Ben bounded down the steps to help
them climb up.

'Teddy and Maggie, everyone,' he said, straining to be
heard above the roar. Leaving Teddy standing in the middle
of the stage he led a reluctant Maggie to her seat next to
Lauren.

'Teddy has been the catalyst for OAK's change in
direction,' Ben said, as he rejoined the terrified-looking man
in the middle of the stage, 'so I wanted him to be the one to
kick off proceedings.' Giving him a reassuring pat on the
back, he said, 'Teddy, we're all here to listen to your story.
Tell us about the expansion data you unearthed.'

Forty minutes later and the ordeal for those on stage was
almost over. Teddy had started hesitantly enough, facing the
crowd as if they were a firing squad, but with Ben's
encouragement, he'd stuttered his way through the revelation
of the US expansion data. Ben had brought the others in like
the conductor of an orchestra – now inviting Theresa to
share restructure plans, now handing over to James for an
overview of the new security operation. As Bella's turn drew
closer, her heartbeat reverberated through her chest, as if she
was leaning against an amplifier with the bass turned up. She

sipped from the bottle of water in her hand to try and relieve the dryness in her throat – until she started feeling like she might need the loo, and the thought of having to excuse herself and dart offstage at the crucial moment made her set the bottle down at her feet.

In the end, and despite all appearances to the contrary, she found herself enjoying the limelight. After a husky start, she recovered her voice and relayed their revamped OAK marketing strategy to the packed room. Her ten minutes were over just as she was getting into her stride.

'And that about brings you up to date,' Ben concluded, as Bella retook her seat. 'What you've heard here this morning is a lot to take in, I know. This organisation, which was launched and run with the best intentions, has been demonstrated as doing the opposite of what it was set up to achieve. People don't need a corporate organisation to do their kindnesses for them.'

He paused there, letting his words sink in. The pause lasted so long that low-level murmurs started to grow in volume, like the approaching hum of a swarm of insects.

'This doesn't mean,' he continued, his words stopping the hum dead, 'that we should close OAK down. We still believe in the power of kindness. We still believe in our motto.' He opened his arms towards them and as he said the first word the whole room joined in as one, the massed voices almost musical as they rolled around the great, darkened space. 'A single act of kindness may change a day, a life, the world. Kindness is powerful. OAK is mighty.'

Applause broke out – heartfelt and sustained. Tears welled in Bella's eyes and as she turned her head, she could see moisture glistening on Lauren's cheeks.

'OAK will live on, but we'll take a new direction. Yes, retraining will be required, yes, massive efforts will be needed in terms of adapting processes, systems, personnel and equipment. But I hope that all of you will come on this journey with me to build something that we can be proud of, and something which, for the first time, we don't have to keep secret!'

The room rose to its feet and Ben stood stock-still as they applauded him. 'We'll break here for lunch, and then at two o'clock I'd like to invite you to join me in the gardens for a press conference and the official launch party of the all-new Organised Acts of Kindness Institute!'

He gave a signal and gold and silver oak leaves fluttered down from the darkness above their heads, shimmering in the coloured lights that spun around the room. Around the auditorium, people cheered until their voices echoed off the ceiling.

Chapter Twenty-Six

'I'd like to say something,' announced Maggie to the banks of photographers, reporters and TV crews assembled in front of the long narrow table behind which she sat, alongside Ben and Teddy. Not getting an immediate response, she pulled one of the tabletop microphones towards her across the green felt cloth. 'Listen to me!' she yelled, her words half obliterated by an ear-splitting squeal of feedback. The sound technician rushed forward and fiddled with the microphone.

Bella's eyes flicked to Ben's face and saw something like horror pass across it, but the expression was gone almost before she registered it.

'Of course,' he agreed. 'Mrs Thatcher has been appointed a trustee of our new charitable organisation in recognition of her contributions. We'd be delighted if you would share a few thoughts on your appointment, Maggie, before we fill everyone in on our plans.' He smiled out at the reporters and, behind them, the ranks of Acorn Consulting employees on the lawns under the bunting and Chinese lanterns, champagne glasses in hand.

Beside her, Bella sensed Lauren stiffen and even the unflappable Theresa could be seen to tighten her grip on her plate of canapés.

'I've…' Maggie started, before being distracted by a waiter passing by with a tray of drinks. 'You there!' she bellowed through the microphone, causing the startled waiter to throw his tray into the air and catch it again minus several glasses. 'Dubonnet on the rocks!' Maggie turned back to the audience. 'I've got something to say about Acorns. Nasty place, it used to be. With that woman in charge, going round, telling lies and sucking people in.' Teddy placed a restraining hand on her arm. She patted it reassuringly. 'But it's different now. That's what I wanted to say. You can trust them now, that's what my Teddy says and I believe him.'

In the front row, a manicured hand with pillar-box red nails shot into the air.

Maggie nodded. 'Have you got a question, dear?'

'Shobha Sharma, *West Country Tonight*,' said the owner of the immaculate nails. 'What's happened to change your mind about Acorn Consulting, Mrs Thatcher? When we last spoke, before you disappeared, you were vocal in your criticism of this company and its employees.'

Maggie stared at her. 'She's gone, hasn't she, like I said? That manipulating old bitch-bag! She was the bad blood poisoning it all. Good riddance to bad rubbish, that's what I say!' concluded Maggie, sitting back and giving the microphone a shove that brought the technician running again.

'Thank you, Maggie,' said Ben. 'Was that everything?'

She shook her head and leaned towards the microphone. 'I'm still waiting for my Dubonnet!'

Polite laughter greeted this pronouncement and after beckoning a waiter over and muttering something in his ear, Ben turned back to the audience.

'Ladies and gentlemen of the press, friends from the local community, and Acorn Consulting employees – welcome. Acorn Consulting has gone through some turbulent times. Our previous CEO and three of our ex-colleagues are currently in police custody awaiting trial on serious charges.

As an organisation, we've been through a lot, but I'm here to say that it won't break us. Acorn Consulting's board has drawn up an action plan to take the business through this difficult period and on to a new course. I'm delighted to say that my peers have appointed me chief executive officer, which is a role I'm humbled and honoured to accept.

'One of my first tasks as CEO is to rebuild trust in AC and to demonstrate that we are an organisation that believes in having a positive impact on the world around us. That's why I'm delighted to announce that we are launching a charitable foundation, to be known as the Organised Acts of Kindness Institute – or OAK, for short.'

He paused and acknowledged the applause from the press and others gathered on the lawn in front of him.

'Our name in recent weeks has been associated with unkindness and deceit thanks to the actions of our ex-colleagues. OAK will counteract that. We commit to investing ten per cent of AC's profits each year into running the Institute, as well as carrying out other fundraising activities to add to its coffers.

'OAK will be a facilitator for kindness. I genuinely believe – no, more than that, I *know* – that most people are inherently kind. Set aside a few bad apples and most of us, left to our own devices, are motivated to help others. If you don't believe me, think about the last time you saw an old lady slip over in the street, say, or spotted a child in a shop looking for its lost parent. Was your impetus to help, or to walk away?'

His eyes ranged over the faces in front of him and Bella found herself looking around at people too as they considered his question. She wouldn't vouch for a hundred per cent of the hard-bitten reporters in the front row, but other than that she thought most people could probably relate.

'I believe people want to be kind, and OAK will help them to do that. People will be able to ask us for help in order to carry out their own small acts of kindness. That help could take the form of funding, support from our team here or other interventions. We're open to suggestions from the public about that and excited to see what they come up with.'

A forest of hands were waving at him from the reporters' benches. He picked out one.

'Yes?'

'Can you give us an example?' asked a large, red-faced man whose bald head was shining in the sun.

'Sure,' replied Ben. 'Someone might come to us because their neighbour's lost her job and can't afford Christmas presents for her children. We'd provide the money for the presents or the presents themselves. Any individual request will be eligible for up to a maximum of one thousand pounds in funding or the equivalent cost of our staff's time. OAK's aim is to facilitate small acts of kindness within communities, not to make large-scale donations for bigger projects.'

'How will you know people are who they say they are?' the shiny-headed reporter wanted to know. 'How will you know they're going to use the money for what they claim?'

Ben shrugged. 'There will be a certain amount of trust involved. As I said, we come from a position of believing that apart from a few bad apples, people are basically good. But we'll look for whatever proof we can get. In the example

I gave you, if several neighbours made the request to us as a group, they'd have a stronger case to receive funding.'

'What non-financial support could you provide?' asked Shobha Sharma.

'Again,' Ben responded, 'we're open to ideas. But it might be that someone has an idea for a community project they want to get off the ground and they need help with the business plan, website build, sourcing premises – we have a vast range of skills here as you'd expect from a management consultancy so we should be able to help.'

By now a waiter had deposited a clinking tumbler in front of Maggie and glasses of champagne in front of Ben and Teddy. Ben picked his up and pushed back his chair.

'We'll be sharing a press release with more details about how OAK will operate, and if you have any more questions please speak to our PR team. And now, please raise your glasses, ladies and gentlemen, to the brand-new Organised Acts of Kindness Institute!'

❦ ❦

In one of the marquees, music was pumping and people were streaming through the entrance.

Bella turned to look at Lauren and Oscar.

'Not being a spoilsport or anything but I'm not sure I'm up for that.' She jerked her head towards the dance floor where some of their colleagues – in particular those who had been getting stuck into the champagne – were throwing imaginative shapes. Maggie could be seen marching towards the tent, Dubonnet in one hand and Teddy in the other.

'Me neither.' Lauren grabbed a bottle of champagne in an ice-bucket and three glasses from the bar. 'Come on, let's go somewhere a bit quieter.'

As they pushed through the crowd, heading for the benches that looked out over the ha-ha, someone tapped Bella on the arm.

'Have you got a minute, Bella?' Ben had ditched the jacket and tie and was looking cool in his open-necked shirt, despite the afternoon heat.

'I'll catch you up,' she called after the others, trying to ignore the momentary look of hurt in Oscar's eyes when he saw Ben's hand on her arm. She followed Ben round the back of the marquee where coloured lights flicked red, blue and green circles on the cream canvas, over to a secluded area of garden on the other side of the reflecting pool. They sat down on a stone bench and for half a minute neither of them spoke.

'I wanted to speak to you alone, Bella. So much has happened since we... we've not had the chance to talk about anything and...'

Bella realised with surprise that he was tongue-tied, stumbling over his words. She'd never seen him anything less than composed. As she looked at him, eyes downcast, biting his bottom lip, she wasn't sure if he was about to declare his love, say he wished it had never happened, or something in between – but she knew for the first time how she felt and what she needed to say. She reached out across the space between them and took his hand.

'I like you, Ben. And I think you're going to make a brilliant CEO. And you're annoyingly good-looking, which I'm sure you know.'

He frowned and looked like he was about to attempt a denial but she pressed on.

'Which I'm sure you know, and it was a lot of fun, that time at the barn. The first time at the barn,' she clarified, 'I obviously don't mean the whole sending Gladys out onto the field and wondering if Oscar and Lauren were going to get shot.'

'Yes,' he smiled. 'I knew which time you meant. And yes, it was a lot of fun.' They were still holding hands and he started to pull her towards him. She pressed her other hand against his chest to maintain the distance between them.

'But I don't think it would be fun if we did it again. It wouldn't be a good idea.'

He kept up the pressure on her hand for a moment then released it and sat back.

'I expect you're right. I've tried to work out what's best but I keep coming back to the fact that I'm about to rebuild an organisation that came this close,' he held his finger and thumb millimetres apart, 'to collapsing, so I'm not sure I'd give anyone the attention they deserve right now. Even you, Bella.'

She leaned over and gave him a kiss on the cheek. 'You're a good man, Ben, and you're going to do great things with OAK, I'm sure of it.'

❦ ❦

She tracked Lauren and Oscar down to a bench overlooking the wildflower meadow and plonked herself down on the end next to Lauren.

'That was quick,' said Oscar, eyebrows raised.

Making no comment on this, Bella reached out a hand. 'Come on then, don't hog the champagne.'

He poured her a glass and handed it over. They all sipped in silence, looking out over the meadows with the distant beat of music and hubbub of partygoers behind them.

'So. So, so, so, so, so,' said Oscar. Then stopped, unconscious of the fact the others were waiting for him to continue as he stared out into the distance.

'So... what, Oscar?' Lauren prompted.

'So... what now? Where do we go from here?'

'Home, I expect. You're not planning on going clubbing, are you?'

'No, no.' He elbowed her in the ribs. 'Silly. I mean work-wise. OAK-wise. Acorn-wise.'

'Ah. Well. I've been thinking about that.' Lauren flushed a little when she realised they were both looking expectantly at her. 'I've decided to ask for a transfer to the US. Life's too short to waste it. I love James. We should be together,' she finished, getting more and more terse as she tried to finish.

Bella reached over and gave her a clumsy hug. 'Good for you. That's a great idea.'

'Okay.' Oscar nodded and ticked it off on his fingers. 'Lauren goes to America, gets hitched, has sprogs, develops dreadful mid-Atlantic twang. Next. Bella?' Despite the casual tone, Bella could see he was watching her carefully.

'I...' As she spoke, she realised a thought that had been floating around was materialising as a definite decision. 'I'm going to move back to London. I loved being here, but it always felt a bit unreal, and the countryside's great and everything but all my friends are in London. Plus, in a way I came here to escape, from the divorce and stuff, you know. I was so confused at the time; I needed a new direction.' She realised she was rambling but it seemed important to try to explain. 'I... I feel different now, after everything that's happened. I'm ready to face the real world again so I'm going to look for a job back there. I'm sure lots of my friends will go "told you so" because lots of them said I was making a mistake coming here. But one thing I've learnt while I've been here is if you worry about what others might think you'll never do what's right for you. Who says they know any better than me anyway?'

She took a deep breath and looked at Oscar. His expression was hard to read and after meeting her eyes he looked down at his glass.

'What about you?' she asked.

'Well. Funny thing. I'm going to London too. I managed to fit in the odd deep thought or two in between word searches and *Homes Under the Hammer* over the weekend. And I agree with you, Lauren – life *is* short. I'm going to chuck in my well-paid, secure job, move to one of the most expensive cities on earth and try to make people laugh for a living. I'm going to have a crack at being a stand-up comedian.' He looked at Bella. 'Mum couldn't be happier.'

Bella was stunned for a moment and then said, 'I bet she couldn't! You'll be brilliant, Oscar. Good for you.'

❧ ❧

Lauren had gone off to Skype James, leaving Bella and Oscar on the bench, with a Lauren-sized gap between them. Oscar reached over to top up her glass and Bella drank, savouring the sensation of the bubbles fizzing on her tongue. For a moment she was propelled back to a hotel terrace, cicadas and a little gold cup glowing in the citronella candlelight.

'Oscar?'

'Mmmm.'

'What actually happened, that night on Le Chêne?'

There was silence for a moment and then, 'Nothing. Nothing happened after the kiss. We got into bed and you conked out. I took the hint and went back to my room.'

'What, you didn't even try anything?'

'Erm, I may not be the most successful when it comes to women but I don't need to resort to feeling up sleeping colleagues, thank you!'

'No, I didn't mean that! I... anyway. Fair enough.' She hummed along to the song they could hear playing in the dance tent then said, 'It's cool that you're coming to London too.'

'Yep.'

'We can hang out.'

'Yep. I'll need a superfan.'

'Yeah, right, heckler more like.'

'Well. Plenty of time to decide what our... reciprocal roles might be.'

She smiled and shuffled across the bench, leaning companionably against him as they looked out across the meadows and woods spread before them in the sunlight.

'Exactly. Plenty of time.'

One Year Later

Bella took out her phone and snapped a photo of the poster on the wall outside the pub.

Clapham Comedy Night!
Your favourite London comedy venue hosts comedy circuit regulars
plus up-and-coming newcomers
Oscar Rose | Jen Shoreham | Sarah Ravencroft | Ash Patel |
Rhiannon Whyte
£10 on the door, £8 advance tickets

Opening WhatsApp she clicked on Oscar's name, added the photo and wrote, *You made it!!! Am outside in the queue, see you in a bit. Break a leg x*

Before she could replace her phone in her handbag a couple of other messages had pinged up on the screen. They were from colleagues – or rather ex-colleagues now, she reminded herself – wishing her luck in her new venture. She'd come straight from her leaving party. She could tell that some of her colleagues were a little jealous and some thought she was crazy, leaving a full-time marketing director job to set up her own agency.

The queue moved forward and Bella shuffled along with it, checking the time on her phone. She should be able to make it inside before Oscar came on stage, there were only a couple of people in front of her.

The words of her now ex-boss echoed around her mind. 'It's a very brave decision, Bella. You're certainly a risk-taker!'

That was how people saw it – brave, a risk. But for Bella, it was simply the right thing to do. She'd learnt enough from her previous jobs to know she was ready to go it alone. It was exciting, nerve-wracking – yes. But brave? Brave and risky defined what Oscar was about to do, she thought as she neared the front of the queue and riffled around in her bag for her ticket. She knew she had it somewhere. She raised one leg and balanced the oversized handbag on her knee as, in increasing desperation, she shoved purse, umbrella, make-up bag and tissues around in the bottom of the bag to try and locate the ticket that Oscar had given her.

'What's the hold up?' called someone further back in the queue.

By practically diving into the bag headfirst she finally located the ticket, pulled it out and waved it in the unimpressed bouncer's face.

Inside, she heaved a sigh of relief at the sight of the empty stage and headed to the bar. It was rammed, but with luck, she'd have time to get her order in before the show started.

Five minutes later she was able to give her order to a heavily-tattooed girl in a black vest top.

'G&T please.'

The girl poured the drink and demanded the usual extortionate London price. Bella rummaged in her bag for her purse. It wasn't there. In rising panic, she took everything out of her bag and piled it up on the bar. No, definitely no purse. She felt a tap on her shoulder.

'I think this is yours.' The smiling woman handing her the familiar leather purse seemed to be standing in a shaft of light and wearing a halo. Until Bella blinked and realised she was more prosaically standing in a silver mac and wearing a yellow headscarf.

'Oh my God, thank you! Where did you find it?'

'I saw you drop it when you were getting your ticket out. I was walking past and shouted to you but you didn't hear me. So I picked it up, got in the queue, bought a ticket and came in.'

Bella's brow was furrowed. 'You bought a ticket just to give me back my purse? That's incredibly kind of you! Here,' she opened the purse and pulled out a ten-pound note, 'let me pay you back for the ticket.'

The woman held up a hand. 'No need. Please. If you want to do something with that ten pounds, perhaps you'll consider a donation?'

She pressed something cold and hard into Bella's hand then turned and threaded her way out through the crowd.

Bella uncurled her fingers and there in the palm of her hand was a small, round pin badge. It had a picture of an oak leaf in the background and was printed with the phrase, 'I've been helped by the OAK Institute!' At the bottom of the badge, in small letters that curved around the edge of the perimeter, it said, 'Kindness is powerful.'

And then she couldn't examine it anymore because the house lights had gone down and out in the spotlight Oscar was stepping up to the microphone.

Dear Reader,

Thank you for reading *Acts of Kindness*. The inspiration for the book came from witnessing commuters helping a woman who'd fallen down the stairs at Paddington station, intermingled with wondering what was behind some grand stone gateposts that I used to drive past in Wiltshire. Those disparate things swirled around in the back of my mind and came out as the secret OAK Institute which is at the core of the book.

If you would like to get involved in a wider conversation about my books, please review *Acts of Kindness* on Amazon, GoodReads, Bookbub, on any other online bookseller, on your own blog and social media accounts, or talk about it with friends, family or reading groups! Sharing your thoughts helps other readers, and I always enjoy hearing about what people experience from my writing.

Thanks again for your interest in this novel. For news about all my books, please visit me at my website – www.heatherbarnettauthor.com or join me on Twitter @WritesHeather.

All the best,

Heather

Acknowledgements

There's an African saying that it takes a village to raise a child. I can't vouch for that, but I do know that it takes a group of patient, supportive and talented people to manhandle several hundred pages of ramblings into something resembling a finished book.

There are many people who've helped me along the way, including my family and friends who've offered encouragement and sustained their interest in the development of this book long after any normal person would have given up. There are a few people I'd like to call out in particular. Adele Barnett-Ward and Alix Hunt for ploughing through the first draft and providing constructive feedback. Anya Tobin for unwavering support and enthusiasm. Carol and Mei Trow for casting an expert editorial eye on an early version – and for suggesting the quote by Adam Lindsay Gordon at the beginning of this book.

My editors Billie Norton and Amanda from LetsGetBooked, and proofreader Abbie from Abbie-Editorial.

Serpentine Books for seeing something they thought was worth championing.

And David Hart, for believing in the book, and in me.

Also by Heather Barnett...

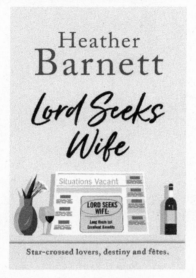

Heather
Barnett
Lord Seeks Wife

Situations Vacant

LORD SEEKS WIFE:
Long Hours but
Excellent Benefits

Star-crossed lovers, destiny and fêtes.

Take 1,000 women, add one earl and whip into a media frenzy.

Reclusive academic Lord Noblet de Beeble doesn't want to get married but his overbearing mother, Lady Caroline, is insisting he must. When he places an advert for a wife in the Situations Vacant section of his local newspaper, the national press pick up the story. A desperate Noblet calls on his handsome younger brother, Henry, to help him navigate the subsequent media frenzy.

Among the hordes of hopeful candidates to descend on the village of Gently Rising is the beautiful and mysterious Mia Wild, who befriends local primary school teacher, Alice Brand. Alice has been looking for something to spice up her life, but getting embroiled in a very public wife-hunt wasn't what she had in mind.

In a summer packed with suspicious exes, snobbery, social climbers and sausage rolls, Gently Rising will bear witness to a public courtship like no other. But who will come out on top?